In My House

IN MY HOUSE

Alex Hourston

FABER & FABER

For Neil, Archie and Martha, in no particular order.

First published in 2015
by Faber & Faber Ltd
Bloomsbury House
74–77 Great Russell Street
London WC1B 3DA

Typeset by Faber & Faber Ltd
Printed and bound by CPI Group (UK) Ltd, Croydon CR0 4YY

The right of Alex Hourston to be identified as author of this work
has been asserted in accordance with Section 77 of the Copyright,
Designs and Patents Act 1988

Lines from *Peepo!* by Janet & Allan Ahlberg (Kestrel, 1981)
© Janet and Allan Ahlberg, 1981

Lines from *Old Possum's Book of Practical Cats* by T. S. Eliot
(Faber & Faber, 1939)
© T. S. Eliot, 1939

A CIP record for this book
is available from the British Library

ISBN 978–0–571–31666–3

FSC
www.fsc.org
MIX
Paper from
responsible sources
FSC® C101712

2 4 6 8 10 9 7 5 3 1

First the plane was delayed; I could see that in the uniformed huddle at the gate. I went up and asked, and the way the woman reset her face as she turned to reply gave me the brief idea of slapping it. So yes, you could say I was in a bad mood. Plus something had gone in my back. Not conclusively, but in a number of sharp little suggestions.

It had happened the day before, halfway up a mountain in Spain. It was hot, I was the only native English speaker in the group and of just above median age. Pieter and Anna were mid-sixties, I'd estimate. Their calves matched; huge, hairless and tight but for the odd pop of vein. Efficient too, and a key feature of my landscape as they pulled away up yet another hill, and I do a lot of walking myself. It was those legs, plus the splat of pigment on their shoulders that put them five, maybe ten years ahead of me. They were nice people, considerate people. Dutch.

When I broke stride, Pieter was the first to reach me. He was walking ahead but must have heard something in the abruptness of my halt and was by my side before even Laura and Fab, who needed only to catch up. He crouched in imitation; laid a careful hand on my shoulder.

The pain was of the sort you'd expect in a tooth, bright and brief. I held my breath, stripped of belief in my spine's capacity to hold me, awaiting collapse in a ghastly suspense. Pieter saw in my face not to speak but then I had flapped my hand at him and he knew I was OK.

'Just a twinge,' I said.

He nodded and rejoined his wife at a small distance.

Carlos took over; did what he was paid for. Made me sit, take a drink, stand again carefully. He moved behind me and ran his thumbs either side of my spine, quite hard. It seemed incautious and my muscles felt braced, resistant. But it didn't hurt, and he continued to work, up and down. To soothe, per-haps, or merely to accompany the story that he had started to tell, over my head, about the time they'd had to carry a man back down the Tramuntana on a makeshift stretcher fash-ioned from bandages and foraged sticks. This person had been bitten by a snake. He was fat, his ankle swelling all the time. We listened; it was part of what we'd paid for.

I had seen straight away the incongruity of a young man touching an older woman, and imagined a range of plausible responses on my part. An uncomfortable awareness of the sweat on my shirt or the unseemly give of my flesh under his hands; a moment of unbidden arousal or emotion – tears even – which I'd seen a few times in yoga classes among the infrequently touched. Each scenario loaded with shame and I felt none of them. Instead I watched the others. The men and the German woman who travelled alone had looked away. In Anna, Pieter's wife, I saw pity; in Laura, who was beautiful, and still young, amuse-ment. Then the story was done, and so was the massage. Carlos clenched both my shoulders hard and peered round at me.

'You OK, Maggie?'

I said yes, and we continued. Susan asked me if I wanted to borrow her stick. She loved that stick. I told her no.

A pinch, next morning, as I got up fast, straight out of a dream, but I showered and dressed, and packed my case with no further problems. At breakfast it was not mentioned, we had our eggs and thin-sliced bacon and said our goodbyes. I was the first to leave. Nothing until I stepped from the cab at Palma and then a pain that made me shout out loud. The driver bore the brunt; took a glare, missed his tip. And then the delay, confirmed in Spanish and barely more comprehensible English.

The news got people moving but I stayed where I was, leant against a wall of huge textured plastic tiles. An hour more in the airport then forty minutes on the tarmac in a steadily warming plane. Finally in the air, and the cabin seemed noisy and fragile; that oppressive hum and the sudden plasticky clatter that sent a ribbon of panic through me. I picked up my book, read ten pages that failed to stick, and just sat, for a while; static, oblivious. Somewhere across the sky, I suppose, she sped towards me.

I like these walking breaks, they suit me well. I do two or three a year; one in the UK, perhaps, the Moors or Lakes; a Mediterranean island, and somewhere North African, or similar, at the season's end. I go at the popular times – that can't be helped, it is a question of weather – but book last minute, when the mood takes me, and as my job permits. My only mandate is progress. That you get somewhere. I can't bear those circular routes where you end up right where you started, exhausted and stiffening and facing last night's menu. So the holidays that I choose always move on, and include someone behind the scenes who drives your bags to the next destination. I like a guide, too, to tell me what I am seeing.

As for the other walkers, you take your chances, but it is less of an issue than you might think. There is a solidarity in walking that overrides all but the most strident differences. You start out as a snaggly crowd and very soon an order is established – a good guide knows to let this happen. Injury aside, I have never seen that initial order break, and in knowing your place most social difficulties fall away. There is a focus on the task of simply getting there, and no obligation beyond it.

This bunch was fairly typical. The German woman barely spoke a word; ate and drank what was offered, and read at the table at night. She used her eyebrows and shoulders to tell us that she didn't understand but I followed her once, on a break for postcards in Deia, and caught her speaking perfectly good English to a tourist who had stopped her for directions. She didn't see me, and I felt nothing but respect for her decision to stay silent. The other couple, Laura and Fabien, were in their late twenties. They talked at meals but leaked condescension and laughed at the rest of us in Spanish. Susan, my age, single, childless and robustly cheerful. This was the third time we had walked together and she pestered me by email in between. Then there was Anna, and Pieter, who loved to talk. He was the sort who would say that travel is really all about people, not places.

I enjoy the tone of these evenings, the loose easy companionship, the sour red wine, served chilled. Always lots of stories, though I myself prefer to listen. It's hard to find the equivalent in everyday life.

I began to feel a touch maudlin on the plane but recognised the feeling for what it was. Distance doing its bit; the whole thing assuming a value I hadn't felt in the living of it. The irritations smoothed away, the moments of boredom erased, or recast as 'down time' and the better parts buffed up – most often when the booze began to work. And just as certain was the episode's forgettability. Go back to it a few weeks on and the memory will be loose, benign. Maybe it's me, but I know it is not my age. I've always been like it. And never one for photos.

The flight went on, a long two hours. There was somebody famous a few rows back I should have recognised, but didn't. I bought a small bottle of white and a tube of Pringles and enjoyed them despite the hour. Chose a pack of sample-sized perfumes for the woman watching my dog and looked at all the places the airline flew to in the last pages of the magazine. I remembered my back and thought of the moment I'd have to stand.

Then we were there, and the descent into Gatwick was bumpy but so close to home that disaster seemed implausible. I looked down and noticed the same things as always: England cut up into tidy squares, the occasional blue of a Home Counties pool, the car parks that appeared about now, each vehicle a tab of blistering colour, curved and reflective like a beetle's back. I wondered if my own was down there; a Volvo, ten years old. More likely somewhere dodgier, tucked away on cheaper land. I'd left the mileage written on a strip of paper Sello-taped to the dash; a warning or deterrent against advantage not yet taken. A sense of aggravation took root, and I knew from experience that it would be hard to shift.

It was still there as I waited to get off. Aimed briefly at those people who stood too early and were left in a low squat above their chairs; nowhere to go. Then a thick slot of day at the end of the plane and we were moving. I started up the aisle but my case seemed suddenly too wide. It caught and tipped, forcing me to attend to it. My chest and neck were hot and the wool of my jumper itched where it met my skin. I was stomping, no doubt, by the time I hit the body of the airport, overtaking the more leisured passenger idling by on one of those stupid flat escalators. Slamming around in an inherited response that I hated but had never tried to change. I stood out, that's for sure, trying to put distance between me and something back there, most likely my earlier self.

I wondered, later, if it was then that she saw me. Assuming she had planned her move. She would have known that the whole thing hinged upon one person, a stranger. What a punt. And how best to choose? When I'd huffed into view, at odds, out of step, I might have looked like her best chance. But at this point I was headed for customs. That was no good.

I walked down the final ramp and saw the passport desks stretched out on my right. Already people were backed up before the three manned stations, the rest digitised; my own passport yet to be chipped. I took my place in the line and reached for my phone to let the car people know that I'd landed. Or the loo first? I looked up and down the stretch of queue, the very picture of indecision.

Maybe it was this gesture she read. Held her breath. Felt it as her first piece of luck in a long time. But I am overstating my role. I headed for the Ladies.

The sight of my face in a public-lavatory mirror is always a surprise, something I put down to the lighting, but a distraction nonetheless. There was a moment or two spent glancing at myself in each new panel as the line moved forwards. Still ten or so people ahead. I watched the other women look at themselves, pull special faces for their own reflections. Their lack of self-consciousness startled me, their absorption in the task. They couldn't all have someone meeting them off their planes. Some, surely, would merely return to whoever it was they'd left outside, an everyday person holding their spot. I wondered if the effort would be noticed, warrant a mention. I felt my own dislocation from that, and was fine with it.

Then my attention was free and almost instantly I had a sense of the person behind me. It was her breathing; short, hard and pulsed. She was panting almost, giving off an animal panic that I felt in an answering surge of adrenalin. My first thought was some kind of anxiety attack, and then that she'd done something bad. Left a bomb. I looked back to the mirror and found her there.

It was clear that she meant to tell me something. Her face was locked, its lack of response in breach of every protocol of civility. It was like standing in front of a painting knowing that there is meaning, hidden but suggested, if you only knew the language of the thing. A few seconds of this blank exchange and she turned, the girl, twisted her upper body round, deliberate eyes on me till the last, and whispered close and brief behind her. The woman she spoke to gave a flick of a nod. The girl left the line and walked past me, close enough that I smelt new sweat.

She went to a sink, bent deep at the waist and looked up at her face. She viewed herself differently from the previous women. Up close and frank, something brutal in it. She filled cupped hands with cold water and threw it at herself, darkening the roots of her hair, somehow shocking. Behind me the older woman watched.

The two were dressed the same. Clothes near to typical if you squinted – blue jeans, bright tops with zips and hoods – but look again and you could spot the differences. Colour and cut slightly off; I surprised myself with that acknowledgement. No branding or logos. Cheap. Not high-street cheap. Cheaper than that.

There was a similarity in their colouring. A thin milky paleness of skin. A shared ethnicity perhaps. Their hair was dyed a matching red. Family even? Surely not friends. Behind me the woman's phone pinged and the girl's eyes were back to mine. In that second they flared and I saw her fear, unmistakable.

The keys of the woman's mobile clicked and she hissed as she typed, the noise of air sucked hard through her teeth. She was still tapping when the phone rang in her hand and she answered in a language I didn't recognise. In the mirror, the girl mouthed: 'Help.'

She moved from the sink and slotted back in behind me and it took everything not to respond, to give her some sign that I had seen. There were three people to go; two, one, and the pressure to act grew huge and it was time to either take my turn or not, and I didn't; instead I said behind me: 'Sorry, I've just got to. Sorry. You go,' with a sort of smile.

I felt she knew I had understood. She stepped forward and shut the door behind her, eyes low. I left the queue, fumbled in my handbag, trying to explain away my actions with a show of fluster, but no one cared. For what seemed like ages, nothing happened and we all watched the front of the toilets.

There was a rustle of resentment up and down but at last a door opened, a good way along, and a mother and child came out. The other woman, the older woman, went inside.

9

Straight away I moved to the young girl's door. While I was waiting I'd been thinking of her age. Maybe eighteen? Early twenties? And that a best guess. I tapped gently with the pads of my fingers, tried to listen, and whispered: 'I'm here, be quick.'

The lock went and she was out, grabbed a handful of my jacket, and we were moving. She pushed open the first heavy door into a short corridor studded with vending machines selling condoms, tampons and toothbrushes in balls. We were alone, the exit sign was green ahead but she stopped and pushed me back against the wall. It wasn't rough, more intimate. She didn't speak, but looked that long look at me and I saw a change in the aspect of her face. The stress dropped out of it and I tried to do the same. She took my arm.

We walked back into the hall, and its noise and movement flipped my stomach. I started, unthinking, towards the desks, but she applied a gentle pressure and we banked smoothly.

We had got maybe six or ten paces and he was there. Slim and still, violence pouring off him. He stood in front of us and let his physical presence do its work. I simply started to scream. No, that sounds too defenceless. There was nothing womanly about it. Yell. Shout. I'm not sure what. Generic abuse that a woman can use against a man. And lunge at him too.

At first they thought it was me. The airport police, or who-ever, were there instantly; took the top of my arms, tried to move me away. But anger was pounding in my head and I couldn't claw back control enough to explain. The girl stood apart, like an onlooker, saying nothing. He started to back away, hands up in surrender, suggesting I was mad, I think. It seemed he was willing to let her go. But she began to move, stealthily; circling the rim of the drama. Then stepped in, and it was when she spoke that her story began to assume its true shape. I may have looked like a crumpled old crazy but there was authority in her words, although we couldn't understand them. She was cold and focused and undeniable as she spoke into his face. I was frightened by her, and at what it was he had done. We were all moved off into a room.

3

My name is Margaret Benson. I live in London and have done for over thirty years, always in the NWs. Queen's Park, if I'm asked, though I've heard it called Kensal Rise, Town and Green, West Kilburn and North Kensington. The house I'm in now was sold out of a Notting Hill estate agent's, but that seems like a push.

I've always liked the area for its relative understatement, without being a dump of course, although it has changed – hasn't everywhere? – and largely for the better. I have found that I'm as susceptible as the next woman to good things to eat and have come to prefer coffee with provenance, and organic this and that.

I'm closer to the park in this latest place. It has exerted some sort of pull across the years; each move has brought me closer. There is a permanence to it that I suppose is a quality of the land, and perhaps why people like it. I've seen several dogs grow old here, though the human families are more temporary. The pattern is the same; they appear in the early months, new mother and child, then she is gone, replaced by someone younger and accented, and one day they all vanish, off to bigger houses further out, I suppose. But the core of the walkers remain.

My house is a three-bedroom in the conservation area. Victorian I think, they must have told me once, though I don't recall; certainly it has those sort of features, sash windows, cornicing and so on, although I realise these can be installed later, to similar effect.

It was the best of the five I saw in terms of light and layout. I was the second person to view and put in a cash offer on the spot. That was seven years ago.

It is as large as can be expected for the money – I don't need to be near a Tube, which helps – and its best feature is the small garden which you can look out across while washing up and access through a set of white-painted French doors. I've surprised myself by coming to enjoy the gardening. A gin and tonic in a chair when the wisteria is out.

I got home from the airport late afternoon. The police had known the man. He was arrested and Anja – that was her name – taken somewhere safe. There were others, too, other girls. The thing seemed fleeting and exciting, and it felt empty at home without the dog. I walked down the road to buy the basics. Put on a wash. And moved around the house softly, unable to settle.

The kitchen is a rectangle with a doorway in from the hall bottom left, as I looked at it on the details. The units are a synthetic something in vivid blue that makes me think of Greece and which I have learnt, over time, to appreciate. One oddity – or feature, as I think it was described – is the small square of space growing out from the top right-hand corner; an extension, perhaps. An afterthought, certainly. It was sold to me as a diner, so I measured up and bought a fold-out table from IKEA. Once established, it blocked the route out to the garden. This now lives flat up against the wall. I tried a sofa – too cramped – and next a chair and a pouffe, but when I sat and tried to read there I felt observed. So I can't find the room a purpose. Its function remains oblique. And, to be frank, there is no sense of flow. Still I prefer the layout to the prevailing style of open plan. I feel marooned in those big spaces and also bored by them. Why live your life in one huge room?

The floorboards throughout are orangey yellow, too much so, like cheap pine. Once, long ago, I had plans to sand them, but that moment has passed.

There is a bedroom in the attic which I'd thought would be mine, but hadn't factored in the trip down to the loo in the dark. Now it is my office. Full of books and my desk and just the two Velux windows in the roof, so no distractions. I sleep in the second bedroom; the third is functionally furnished but barely used. The bathroom is white and was modern when I moved in.

I live here with the dog. A boy. My second. The first was killed by a car. His name is Buster and he is a chocolate Lab. A bit smelly but much loved. I like my house and never plan to leave.

I thought of ringing someone, but no one seemed quite right.

It is not that I don't have friends. There is Maureen, and Peter and Paul, who I walk with. Paul, I met that very first day out with the old dog, Ernie; right after his jabs. He approached us – that puppy was irresistible – and offered me the number of a socialisation class. I didn't use it, but things moved on from there. These are my favourite people. I would certainly tell them when I saw them, but to phone specifically? That would change the rules. Come across as self-aggrandising, even, and I wouldn't want that. We know when each of us walks and the routes that we take, so simply turn up and match stride. Paul and Maureen I see several times a week, most weeks.

We, as a group, are not at the centre of things. Our territory is the fringes; we are observers, commentators on others' excitements. This is what drew us together. A touch world-weary perhaps, wry even sometimes, but we don't judge. It is just our way, although there is no need to acknowledge it. Even when something really does happen – Peter and Paul were married, I was there, a London wedding in a register office and, after, a pub – we act like it is not much really.

There is also Nancy, who gets me my work. We have a wine sometimes when I go up to the agency, and I have two cousins who I could call if I had to, but haven't and couldn't imagine what kind of disaster would make that an idea.

I am not a restless person. My ability to absorb myself is acute. I like crosswords, books, the television and my work. They fill my time. I can do silence and the solitary. I have chosen these things. But that day, my environment felt changed. A sense of space as in emptiness, void, a thing to be filled. An unwelcome adjustment.

What happened earlier just bubbled away. It hung about me in a fashion that, I must admit, life rarely does. I felt a rattly annoyance and then gave up, gave in. I thought of her face, of Anja. That girl. That poor girl. And her plan. The nerve of it. And the fact that it worked. I felt exhilarated, and yes, if I'm honest, a bit of pride; a pleasure in my part.

I imagined her resting in a narrow bedroom, waking at a sound, drenched in dread, and remembering she was safe. A house of rescued girls with shining faces. I knew enough to recognise that as a dream.

I wondered what had made her break ranks? I had seen a documentary once about how a man like Goran keeps a woman in line – the psychology of subjugation. It is a delicate art. She must be made to feel worthless, dependent, but on no account tip into hopelessness. When there is nothing left to lose, she becomes dangerous. All she has to do is step out of line, speak up and the whole thing crumbles. In this sense, bizarrely, the trafficker is dependent on her. So what changed for Anja? I couldn't know.

And what would happen to her now? Would she go home to people who were worrying, or stay and make a new life? A sense of the chance to start again passed through me like a wish. I felt happy for her then.

One might suppose she had a bad past, but it is rarely that simple. Things go wrong for so many reasons. I myself had a good enough childhood, at times, maybe wonderful. A seaside childhood of wind and gulls and sugar. And women, my mother and aunties, doing women's things all day; things I took satisfaction in and thought I would turn back to, but haven't. My cooking's poor, I do not sew and am not fussed with keeping house.

The door went, and it was Carol and my dog. I bent as he wagged his whole length and scratched him at the necessary places – front armpits, the folds of his ears. He nosed me, and whined up and down a few octaves.

'I've given him a bath!' she said.

'You really didn't have to,' I replied, and meant it. He smelt of maiden aunt – dog shampoo is unreconstructed – but would be back to himself in a couple of walks' time. He sat back on his haunches and lifted alternate paws. When I wouldn't shake, he butted my thigh with his great domed head. I paid her and she left. Then I was truly home.

4

An odd day, the next one. A day that I could not have anticipated.

I woke slow-headed and with the loose sense that something had changed. I remembered the excitement of the previous afternoon; felt it again briefly, and it was gone.

The urgency to talk had drained and I started early with the dog so as not to see my friends. The sky was a promising blue and I left without a coat. No sign of autumn yet, though the children would soon return to school. Buster pulled, and I remembered my back, but a couple of roads and we were on to the grass. I loosened his lead, he dropped his nose to the ground and set off in frantic Zs.

There is a slice of time when the function of the park is changed. It is no longer a destination but a thoroughfare, a cut-through for people to get to where they are going. It is impossible to take a person seriously who is rushing when you yourself have no place to go. We daytimers tend to retreat, step off the path and let them pass, and I like the way it makes me feel about my choices. By half past eight it is finished and the life of the park resumes. Some of us even share a smile.

What does a woman think of as she walks alone? I find that the action can release things. The body is occupied, evenly, just enough. There is stimulus of a gentle kind; weather, whatever it may be, making itself felt against you. Sounds at a safe enough distance. And often I find that my attention hops and that is fine, although on occasion it is swamped; less good.

I completed two circuits of the main field and stopped for coffee and one of those Portuguese pastries. Eggy custard, blistered on top, flecks of vanilla like fine blown ash. Two mouthfuls maybe. Just the thing.

An old lady sat outside in a stiff high-collared coat despite the day's warmth. That, and the set of her shoulders, the clutch of her hands on the handle of her bag and the way her whole body was turned in on itself – don't look at me, don't bother me – made me think of my mother.

She had visited London three times to my knowledge but the idea of her here seemed impossible. It was in any literal sense – she had been dead six months – but, even so, for her to have made the trip this century, in my lifetime even, felt like a mistake. They didn't hurt, these thoughts, but they surprised me.

The woman seemed exposed, and I wondered why she wasn't inside. She was the only person without a dog or child, and dressed in something other than jeans. She looked as though she should be waiting at a station for an old-fashioned train. My coffee was done and the sun had gone in, but still she sat, the cross of her leather gloves contrived and inhuman. I made a friendly shape of my face at her and her eyes rested on me briefly and moved on. That pissed me off.

I flicked through an abandoned *Metro* but nothing caught my eye, and I got up to leave. But a wind caught at the upper pages and I saw that if it bust its seams, it would become my problem. I pinned the paper down with someone else's mug and reached to unhook Buster from my chair leg. A sharp gust lifted the flap of my coat and there was the noise of breaking china. I looked up to find the cup smashed and the paper flipped onto its back. The front page was yanked off the staples and gone in an instant. I tended lamely to the breakage and spotted the lost sheet wrapped dramatically around another walker's leg.

I felt ashamed on my way to the bin; eyes down, the shards wrapped loosely. Around my grip, I read fragments of page 4. A slim column, 'In Brief'. A stack of stories: a celebrity who planned to pen his tale, accompanied by a stamp-sized photo, blurred somehow in its production, the layers of colour just missing. Next: Pensioner Dies in Blazing Flat. I shifted the damp package in my hand. Police Charge Trafficking Suspect.

A 32-year-old Albanian man was arrested yesterday at Gatwick Airport and charged with Trafficking into the UK for Sexual Exploitation, after one of his alleged victims, Anja Maric, made a dash for freedom. It is believed that Maric, 19, also an Albanian national, was assisted by a stranger, Margaret Benson, 57, of Queen's Park. Ms Maric approached Ms Benson in the Ladies toilets and the two fled to safety.

It was the strangest thing to see my name in print, my actions described. It felt like a trick.

I read through again, more slowly this time.

It was definitely me. Name, yes. Benson is the name I was born with. Age. Fifty-seven. Correct. And I had been there, of course. Done these things. Yet I could not quite connect with the woman on the page. A separation had occurred, like Peter Pan and his shadow. I had the sense that the person that I read about could step up and away; do things on her own, or be made to do them. I felt the sudden pull of vertigo that is my stress response.

I held on to the top of the bin, the paper scrunched in my palm, fingers among the fag butts, and tried to breath.

Imagine you are driving on a motorway. One minute it is all about propulsion, your car moving hard in response to your foot. Now look at the lines on the road. Your perspective flips. They are streaming off behind you, backwards, and in that second of awareness there is a dizzying reversal; you feel that you must tip, be sucked under. That is the best way I can describe it. It is an intensely physical feeling, a shift in the properties of the universe. If an episode is particularly strong or unexpected, I can actually fall down.

Not today, though. I opened my eyes and the world reassembled.

I ripped off the page, grabbed the dog and walked.

There was a newsagent at the end of the road; I was there in ten minutes. I pushed open the door, the bell went ting, and the man looked up. We exchanged the usual good-mornings.

I moved straight to the rack and picked the top copy from each pile. I paid with a silly grin and the feeling that I was about to be recognised. ('Hey. Are you? You must be . . .') But there wasn't a picture in the *Metro*, and the people here who knew me knew me only as Maggie.

He made no comment, the man in the shop, as I handed him big armfuls of print and for this I was grateful. There were ten papers in total, which he packed for me into two striped bags whose handles narrowed to ribbon with the weight, and cut into my skin.

At home I went upstairs and laid them on the beige wool of the carpet. Three by three and one spare, though that didn't seem enough. I had arranged the broadsheets first, but saw that this was wrong and began at the end.

I leant forward onto hands and knees. Immediately my attention jumped, the layouts busy and incoherent. I steadied myself and worked through carefully, using a finger to track my progress. There was nothing in the *Mirror*, or the *Sun*. In the *Mail* I read, 'Police Nab Paedo', and my stomach dropped, but it was something else. Then I was finished and had the fleeting thought that I had dreamt the whole thing. I found the scrap in the bottom of my bag, one line of words already lost to a fold.

Margaret Benson. I stroked my name to ease out the pleats and the paper began to dissolve under my touch. I'd spoken it many times the day before; that was where each of them had started.

'Your name please, madam, if you wouldn't mind?'

The officer at the scene. Duly noted in his book.

An admin sort, later, 'for processing', she told me, and confirmed once more for the sake of the camera.

'Maggie. I mean Margaret,' I said, again and again, angry at myself for the repetition.

'Here. I've got my passport,' in the end, as if to prove it. It rested on the top of my bag, ready for customs. They took it from me briefly.

My name, proliferating in pads and files. It had sounded a bit old-fashioned in all those mouths. Unused. A little dusty. It didn't stand up.

How had it got to the papers? I couldn't know. Perhaps it sat, from the moment of my action, legitimate and visible, in some open-access place. Or travelled a murkier route? Offered in exchange for something. Notes in an envelope? A pint? Not these days, surely. Reciprocal information, or a future favour, shadowy for now, shapeless until someone else's need called it into being. I had no idea of its worth.

My name, out there, for all to see.

It made me itch, the very idea. Where was it? Still moving? Multiplying? That name is mine, I wanted it back.

I told myself it hardly mattered. That these things lay beyond my control. I told myself, but my pulse, if that is what it was – the beat throbbing hard in my temple – seemed not to listen.

Later, I took the page upstairs and flattened it between two books, which took me back to Rose as a girl, pressing flowers from the garden, and her scrapbooks, her love of all things stationery.

I found a clear wallet of the sort you clip into a lever-arch file. It was reluctant to separate and crackled with something like static. The article looked like a relic already, floating in the middle, raggedy-edged and finger-worn. Most of all, harmless.

I put it away; opened the bottom drawer of my desk and fed the sheet under an old pile of papers. It slid into place of its own volition, nothing of it now but a brief plastic tang. And I almost shut the drawer – I did – but uppermost lay a stiff-backed envelope. Inside were photos I knew by heart; still, I reached for them. What harm?

The first was of my mother, and I had been right, the coat that she was wearing was just like the woman's in the park, with the same close neck and structured drop. And there was Aunty Frannie and Aunt Bet and me too; the only child.

We were down the beach. We were always down the beach. We had taken the dog, a ratty thing, Jack. My father's idea, before he died. He barked at the wind, jumped and snapped, twisted at the middle and got my mother smiling.

Bet and Frannie, the double act, though Bet had a husband, a small man, who whenever I thought of him, was seated, very still, either reading or watching the radio. I couldn't recall a word he spoke.

Always together, Bet and Frannie, two years apart. Brighton born and bred and never left. My mother too.

The whole story in this photo. Mum at the front in that ludicrous coat on a fold-up chair, wobbly on the pebbles. Her hair set solid, her look that said 'I dare you'. Me, perhaps twelve, kneeling under her hand, chewing the insides of my cheeks, eyes wide – like a magazine would have told me. Wondering what I looked like, and who would notice and when. My eyes were miles from there.

Aunty Bet lay in front of us not even on a towel, like an Egyptian queen, head back, arm raised, a knee bent. Beckoning a servant, or pretending to feed herself a grape. It was the sort of thing she did. And Frannie, behind, the only one standing. Slim as a boy, well into middle age. And I could see that she was touching me gently, just to let me know she was there. All that showed of the dog was his tail.

That was us. My father already long dead. Bet's two boys elsewhere; I liked it better that way and used to think the others did too. A tight knot of women. Bound together for good or bad, and resigned to it.

Yet now of course we are long undone. Or rather (let's be accurate) I was cut free and in the act, the ties of the others loosened, though they held. No matter now, as they are all gone and traceless. There were other pictures in the pile but I left those. Saw to the dog.

5

Maureen called later, having missed us that morning. I told her, in the briefest terms, of my adventures at the airport. She responded predictably.

'Christ Almighty. We looked out for you at the park today. I wondered if something was up.'

'Oh, it's not anything. I just wasn't organised. After the holiday.'

'Blimey, Mags. Are you OK?'

'Yes, fine,' I said.

'Are you out again today?'

'Probably. After his tea.'

'Well, I look forward to hearing the whole thing. See you there.'

'OK.'

We start at Tiverton Green on Tuesdays, to give the dogs a run off the lead. Maureen and Paul were waiting for me and when I saw them I felt my face heat unaccountably.

I knew them first by their clothes and posture. Maureen, stamping from foot to foot, a heap in a raincoat – one of her daughter's from when she was pregnant – and Paul, his head neat as an otter rising above the turned-up collar of something navy and quilted. Then Paul shouted, 'Is there nothin' she cannae do?' in a stupid accent and made some kind of hand signal. It should have made it worse, but didn't. They were falling about when I reached them. It was what Super-gran used to say, Paul told me.

'Not that I'm suggesting you're old, Mags.'

It was the first thing he had thought of, he said, when Maureen came over and told him. She'd known the pro-gramme from her kids but Paul was vague, so they googled it on the laptop in the kitchen and downloaded an episode. It turned out Billy Connolly sung the theme tune. This was all as we stood there, fussing each other's dogs and rearranging our layers. I went to pick up after Buster.

We tended not to meet at each other's homes and I was sur-prised at the idea of Maureen there. I wondered when it had been organised, or if she popped in often. She was a gossip. There was that pinch of irritation that felt like dislike.

I tried to picture the scene. I recalled Peter's and Paul's kit-chen as white, with a lot of things out on display that in my home live in cupboards. It should have been a mess, but wasn't, being far too careful and perfectly expressive of them. A space that said something, about how they lived but also what they believed in, though I couldn't find the words for it myself. Then I thought of Maureen's great arse spilling off one of their arty stools, and her ratty cardigan and the South London shriek at the start of her laugh and that made me laugh too, and as I walked back over, they both asked, 'What?' and I said, 'Nothing.'

We moved off, the dogs looping around us. They wanted to know everything but it was over in a second.

'Hold on, back up,' said Paul. 'You're standing in the queue and next minute this girl is mouthing something at you in a mirror. How do you know it's for you? Or that she's not bonkers?'

No answer to that.

'So what is everyone else doing at this point, when you're getting dragged out of the toilet by a stranger? All the people in line?' he said.

I tried to go back, but I couldn't see their faces, only hers.

'Maybe it was them that got the police,' said Maureen, 'those other women.'

'I don't know. I really don't.'

'What did he say to you, the man, when he caught up with you?'

But the answer was nothing, of course, and when they asked me what I had said to him, I replied that it was all too fast.

'Where did she think you were gonna get to anyway? Surely he had her passport? You were in an airport, for god's sake. You can't just walk out of these places,' Paul said.

'Well, it may seem stupid to you, but it worked, didn't it? She got away.'

This was a new tone for them, a new Maggie, or rather a version of Maggie that had never been deployed against them.

'You're right, love. You're right of course.'

I saw Maureen in that moment as a mother, the mother she must have been to her daughters and her favourite, the boy, before they all left. Conciliatory. Happy to skip over the tricky bits.

Silence for a while, as we walked back to the park. We took the Woodland Walk and there was privacy there, away from the gaze of the main fields. The trees remained lush and close-coupled; oak, plane and ash in late-summer greens. The promise of nature too – animals advertised on boards along the path. Squirrels and toads that Buster spotted – I felt his tremors at my end of the lead – but I otherwise missed. There were no joggers for now and our route was shaded. It became easier to talk.

'There was something in the way she looked at me. She was desperate. You know it when you see it. That's all. Anyone would have done the same.'

'I'm not so sure. You can't know if you're going to read a situation. Not until it happens,' said Paul. 'Let alone act.'

Maureen nudged my arm with hers and I knew that she was thinking that a woman would, any woman who has lived a bit, though no doubt Paul has had his trials.

I felt agitated and tearful. Maureen saw and said, 'You did good, Mags. One less bastard out and about. I'll drink to that.'

'Me too,' said Paul.

We were at his turn-off now. He held my shoulders tight when he kissed me goodbye. Maureen stood there, raking her hair as she does, that glamorous hair, the only glamorous bit of her, thick salt and pepper that travelled up and off her forehead in one long curvy sweep like an old-fashioned movie star by way of Elsie Tanner.

So it was just the two of us, and she started on about Peter and Paul and the computer in the kitchen. They watch all their programmes that way and carry it around with them, all through the house, in the bathroom, up to bed. Hardly the same.

'Whatever next?' she said.

My house soon.

'Will you be out tomorrow?' Maureen asked.

'We'll see. Probably.'

'OK. See you. Nighty night.'

'Nunight, Mo.'

I was still in the hall when the phone rang, but it was not a number that I recognised.

I do not pick these up.

I heard my own voice, flat and gloomy, and a pause that stretched out after. I waited for someone to speak, but they did not and the dead tone sounded, though my answer machine showed up a message. Loan consolidation or accidents that earn you cash. And yet.

And yet I swear I heard a breath. My hand at my heart; a frightened old woman.

I went through, had a whisky. Took a look at what was on the TV.

6

I was at the paper shop when he opened. I'd been up for hours
– funny dreams, then couldn't get back off. The day was bright
enough to make you wince.

I heard him first, working through three or four locks and
then the churn of the security grille. He was revealed to me in
increments, bottom up. Soft, thin-soled shoes, grey trousers of
an office style but overwashed and loose. A sandy shirt that you
could see the dark of his body hair through and then it was too
late to step back, and there was his face, elegant, serious and,
above all, surprised at the proximity of mine.

We looked at each other and I felt an apology rise, and that
the can of Stella that had been resting against the metal curtain
and now leaked its last half-inch into his shop was somehow
my fault. A van pulled up and he went to it. I walked inside
and browsed the old-fashioned greetings cards at the far end
of the shop.

It was the newspapers, and I watched as he hauled the bundles inside and slit the cable ties with a small sharp knife. The
papers exhaled, and he took them to their shelves in slabs.
When he moved away, I approached. The titles lay side by side,
pressed and sweet-smelling, and I chose one of each. The man
said nothing at the till, except did I need a bag?

I was shaking when I got home and sped through them
clumsily, newsprint on my fingertips, still in my coat.

When I was finished, I knelt, a stiff tongue of denim cutting into the back of my knees, and stroked the dog, massaging the root of both ears till his eyes closed and his legs slid out from under him. I began to feel the crouch in all sorts of joints but didn't want to disappoint, so sat down, right there, and thought this is the first time in all my years I've sat on my own kitchen floor, and that the place could do with a sweep.

The dog stretched out and dropped his head onto my lap. Instantly he began to snore and I admired his opportunism and the detail of his design. The seams of his eyelids and the way they met perfectly, sealing him shut. The backward slant of tufty eyelash; a dense ridge of tiny hairs. And the odd crazy whisker that sprouted from his head, feeling its way out into the world. I flicked one and he twitched but he knew it was just me. And with my other hand I stroked him long and hard and felt the thick grease of his fur rise and coat my hand. He soothed me; he always did.

No mention of me today. Back in my hole, down low, hood raised, out of sight. I, Maggie, once held so high. Keeper of my mother's dreams, my aunties' too, Aunty Bet at least; it always worried Frannie.

Pushed out in front, a flesh-and-blood 'We'll see' to anyone who'd ever said the Bensons weren't up to much. Pretty from the cradle. A neat combed girl. A precocious reader, lovely singing voice, a hand-span waist. Gift of the gab as well. But it was none of that. It was something less material. A twinkle and a shine that you just couldn't learn and you certainly couldn't buy. A thing that got people saying, 'She'll go far', 'That's the one to watch', and 'The smart money's on Maggie'. A gift my mother thought was hers to polish and prime and walk up and down the promenade every Friday afternoon, her eyes snapping at anyone who would meet them, spitting, 'Ha.'

And I had felt her finger in my back but liked my place a few steps ahead, and my eyes snapped too and said, 'I'll show you. Just you wait.'

And each little advancement, each word of praise, each proof of preference, a look from the right type of man (scratch that, any man), further assured me of my spot.

And when it came to the big things, the visible things – when I got my job in town and married my pilot – each victory took me back to that walk and the weather on one cheek and the pinch in my shoe and the faces that approved as I passed, all looking forward to what would come next.

The habit was still there, of course, when things began to go wrong. I pictured myself setting out, but the faces were shut against me and the wind a shock that shoved me from my path; my mother gone altogether.

A couple more years saw all that forgotten. One day I stopped watching and simply got on.

It had been that way for a long time now. And my hands, resting on the pelt of my dog, were dry, the veins plump blue cords, the nails clipper-trimmed. My weight, a constant; probably less than during my heyday, which I would put at around twenty-eight. Late perhaps, and when I was as unhappy as I'd ever be. One last blast, looks-wise, approaching forty but no one around to notice it.

It would take half a day or so to make myself beautiful again, or at least bear relation to the woman I once was. My skin remains good; almost poreless. My eyes are still blue; the flesh around them yet to cave, as happens to so many women of my age. My hair merely in need of some attention. Yet I choose not to. The way I look is at once my essence and my best disguise. I resemble my mother, which was no one's plan, but perhaps my destiny all along.

Some of this reached the dog. He opened an eye, showing me the whites, but I shushed him and his teeth clinked like pennies as his chin met my leg once more.

And all of that is surface. What of character? The books I read are filled with people of character. Character and conviction. Explicable lives that follow a trajectory. Beset by challenge and hardship, of course – we all need drama. But still, they move forward. There is progress across time. A solid line.

Out here in the world, though, you find a different sort. Less fixed, more expedient. Less powerful. People who adapt. And I find that I exist among the latter. My younger self would despise me. You would have to plot my life on a Venn diagram, in distinct sets, with just the tiniest intersection. What you'd label that part – my essence, if you like; the person I truly am – I haven't the faintest idea.

7

I'd just made a coffee – the Argentinian blend – on the stove-top pot, next to a pan of milk. Stepped outside to drink it, was listening to next door's nanny smoke, and the planes and build-ers' radios, when the front door went. I hadn't ordered anything. Behind it stood a young girl, dressed as a policewoman.

'Mrs Benson?' she said.

'Yes,' said I.

'PC Keira Martin. Victim Liaison Officer.' One outstretched hand, the other holding eye-level ID. 'I'm here about the inci-dent you were involved in at Gatwick earlier this week.'

She smiled into the pause; it was probably there in the training.

'Yes. Yes. Hello. Do you want to come in? Nobody men-tioned this. You.'

'Oh right. Someone should of given you a victim-care card, Mrs Benson. Do you remember receiving one? Blue writing on it?'

She reached into a solid-looking bag resting on her hip and retrieved an example.

'One of these, Mrs Benson?'

'No.'

'Well, please accept my apologies for that. They should of. I'll make a note. Anyway it's purely routine, madam. Just to see how you're doing. May I come in?'

I opened the door wider and she took a couple of long steps in.

She hadn't noticed the rack of keys hammered into the wall and I saw the moment that she stood back and they jabbed her in the soft place at the top of her neck but there was no time to prevent it. She didn't make a fuss. A fairly comprehensive wince but no noise. I imagine she'd known worse in the houses of people she'd dropped in on unexpectedly.

I squeezed past her into the hall, and she followed me through.

My sitting room speaks of old woman, or worse, old woman and over-loved dog. Not the furniture, so much, which is bland and blank. More something in its arrangement.

The room is split in half by a long low set of open shelves; empty, save for a couple of vases and a terrible china horse, which I tell myself was a choice so as not to impede the passage of light, but is more likely due to a lack of interest in filling them.

The front part is the more comfortable, with the sofa in it – far too soft – and occupied currently by the dog, large, tail thumping at the sight of someone new.

In the back of the room, more formal, lives a ring of stiff chairs, each with its own little side table, gathered round an ottoman – an awful item embroidered in thick gold stitch that I bought on impulse in Kilburn. A replica of my mother's rooms, it struck me then. My mother and every other house-proud female of their age and class. A parlour, would you call it? A receiving room? God knows; I never sit there.

I indicated the sofa, which the woman fell back into. It is lower than most people expect.

I offered her tea, which I made in a cup in a hurry, wondering what she was looking at next door. She took it with both hands and said 'Ooh lovely' and 'So how are you feeling?' with her best serious face.

A resolute blonde in a stiff-looking uniform.

'Fine, thanks. Yes. How are you?'

Stupid, of course, but she ignored it.

I listened – I did my best – but it was hard to take seriously a grown woman wearing six kirby grips in her hair – the closest shade she could find, no doubt, to her own, but still plainly visible; prominent, even. Three each side, just above the ear, spaced so closely that the hair between was smoothed into greasy furrows. Noticing all this, I rallied.

'Well, I'm glad to hear it,' she said, 'and I wanted to let you know your crime number. I've written it down for you here, on this card, and there's a telephone number on there too, if you need to get in touch. This is me. My direct line.'

She opened her hand in front of me, the card already inside. She had written in bubbly biro characters. She seemed able and cheerful.

'Rest assured we will keep you fully up to speed with the investigation. If I don't hear from you, your next point of contact will be someone from the Witness Care Unit, who should get in touch in the next couple of weeks. And there's Victim Support if.'

'So I'm a victim? Or is it a witness?' I asked.

This didn't faze her. A welcome deviation, even. She moved her bag from lap to sofa and crossed her teeny legs. She looked about fifteen.

'Good question, Mrs Benson. We were talking about that actually before I came over. You fall between two stools really.

So you're sort of getting a combination of the victim and the witness follow-up.'

She sat back, delighted.

'We're just making sure we've covered all bases. So if there is anything you want to ask me? Or talk to me about? Any feelings that you'd like to discuss? It is quite usual to experience emotions such as anger, anxiety or even guilt.'

'No. Really. As I've said. I'm absolutely fine. And put me down as a witness, please. Really. I wasn't involved.'

'I understand, Mrs Benson, but my notes say that you experienced a verbal assault and these kind of incidents can be extremely traumatic for the individual. Perhaps even after a number of weeks you might experience a reaction.'

I stood at that and realised that if I walked towards the door she would follow. It worked; she pushed herself up from my sofa and acknowledged the dog hair trapped in the rough fabric of her trousers with a couple of loud slaps. Saw that she was doing it, and stopped.

'There's one other thing, Mrs Benson, that I wanted to talk to you about before I go. And this is your choice, there is no pressure at all for you to agree, but I have a request from Anja Maric, the girl.'

She stopped to gauge the impact of her words. I nodded, and she went on.

'Anja has asked if she can get in touch. She says she would like to say thank you. She could contact you, or you could take her details and call her yourself, if you'd prefer. You are in control of this situation, Mrs Benson, I do want to emphasise that. We would never pass on your number without consent. Or the meeting could be mediated. We have experts. Out of home, of course, that would certainly be our suggestion. If that.'

'No. No. That's fine. Tell her yes. I'll meet her. That's fine.'

'Well, I'm glad you said that because we often find that if we can bring together two parties who have shared some sort of.'

'It's fine. Tell her yes.'

8

Anja and I met in a cafe three days later. A neutral space, as recommended. I hadn't known where to suggest; spent an hour after the policewoman left, out with the dog, moving street by street beyond what I knew, till I found a suitable place.

When the morning came, and I was dressing carefully, looking out some old beads and a decent coat, I pulled myself up. I got there early, which made me think of the woman in the park, then sat there with one shoulder high and my own locked hands.

It seemed a bad choice, or perhaps that was my state of mind. Snatches of sound – children's yelps and barks, food hitting hot fat and blurts of ringtone that made me jump each time. Then she was there, a girl at the door on the dot of half past ten and I knew it was her without recognising a thing. Her hair was a fresh-looking red, pulled high off her face. Her jeans were tight and she wore a short bunched jacket with a rucksack slung over a shoulder. I thought how strong she looked, broad-shouldered and big-legged. A practical girl, an open child. I watched her look around and find me first time. I pushed my chair back as she approached, clumsy in outdoor things, and stood facing her, unsure.

'Mrs Benson? Margaret? I'm so pleased to meet you.'

She shook my hand, bent towards me in a brief show of

deference, and then her second hand joined us and my own was lost in her purple-mittened grip.

'Oh. Sorry,' she laughed and let me go.

She yanked off her gloves and appeared to toss them into the air before her, but when she lifted her arm, I saw one bob from a ratty string running up her sleeve. We faced one another.

'That's better,' she said. 'I'll go get a drink. Would you like something? Another perhaps?'

'Yes. Yes, please. A latte, thanks.'

I sat back down, hot and graceless, and tried to transfer the top of my coat to the back of my chair while still sitting on the bottom of it. Behind me, a woman swore second-hand, quoting a mate. Two terriers tied outside yapped a short and accurate volley.

I watched her weave around the packed-in tables. She got to the counter and switched into another language with the girl behind it. She brought two coffees back on a tray, hers short and black, and we started.

'Mrs Benson, I hope it is OK for us to meet. I wanted to say thank you, and also to know you a bit?'

'Yes. Well, don't worry. It's quite all right.'

'No. It was a frightening thing. You didn't have to help.'

A thick even layer of foundation covered her face, beige and moist. A naked look but bloodless too. Smoothed of edge and contour. Her eyebrows had been over-plucked, and then drawn back in, in thick black crumbling lines.

'You speak very good English. Anja.'

Her name came out like an apology.

'Oh and please call me Maggie. God. No one calls me Mrs Benson.'

'Thank you, Maggie. I like the name. I learnt the language on YouTube. I can only speak well. Reading and writing not so much.'

'Of course. I tried the CDs once. To teach myself Italian. The Michel Thomas Method. Was that? Did you?'

'Mainly the Internet. When I was growing up.'

Her attention on me was complete. Her eyes followed me unblinking, and she seemed forever on the edge of a smile. As a result, I babbled.

'So not. School. No, of course not. I don't suppose they taught you at school.'

'English? No! I did it myself. And now I am glad because I am here.'

Her face took on a look of posed wonder and she made a twirling gesture with a hand. It was exotic and at the same time naive. I wondered if she was joking.

'Oh. Yes. So you like it?'

'Of course. And they have lent me a bike. All day I ride around in the streets and the parks. It is wonderful. But my legs ache!'

'A bit wet though, lately? But you seem to have a decent coat!'

A bright and breezy statement, the like of which I never make.

'It's fine. So you have children yourself, I think?'

'Yes. Older though, of course. No one that needs fussing over.'

Two girls on an adjacent table watched and tried to work us out. She had drunk her coffee in a few swift sips, and I offered her another.

'No, thanks. It sucks, no?'

It did. This was a cafe of an earlier age, the all-day breakfast sort. Plate-glass window from the waist up, completely steamed. A child finger-painted Catherine wheels or lollipops or maybe snails in the condensation. There was a bell on the door, yanking my eyes to it every time it rang. But even Maureen wouldn't come in here. I didn't know what else to say.

'So where are you living now. Somewhere close?'

'Temporary accommodation. It's very nice. Fourteen beds.'

'And will you stay, do you think?' I asked.

She leant across towards me. Her eyes were dark and textureless.

'It is a long process. I am working with the police.'

'Oh goodness. That must be. Stressful.'

'But I will stay. You will see. And I have skills. I am good with the computer.'

'Ah yes. Me too. My work is typing.'

'But it's boring, no? In an office? I would prefer to clean. There is lots of work, I think? But either way, I will work hard.'

'Well, if there's anything I can do. To help. In fact. I've just had a thought. I have a dog, you see. He makes a mess. You could help me. Clean my house, if that's what you want. I mean. It's up to you, of course.'

'Maggie, you are kind. I am not supposed to work yet.'

'But they wouldn't know. Cash in hand. For coffee. Or savings. If you like. They pay twelve pounds an hour round here. In the big houses. A friend of mine said.'

My heart was racing and I took hold of her forearms. The wool wasn't wool, it was something thinner and scratchy but I felt the warmth of her beneath it.

'Think about it. If it helps. I don't want to get you into trouble. And please take the money for the coffee.'

I let go of her and scrabbled around in my purse. I had four fifty pences and pressed them into her hand.

'Maggie, you are so kind.'

Her face was broad, thick cheekboned, perfectly symmetrical. A strong face; the features of a woman who would endure.

She pulled her arms free and took my shoulders, bent in for what would have been a hug had there not been a table between us. Instead her head hung before me, her scalp dry and visible, sore from the dye. Some ghastly emotion travelled up my throat but I willed it back down. We stayed that way for what seemed like a while. God knows what we looked like.

9

We left, uncomfortable now; me at least. Outside was a relief. When she said she was taking the bus and pointed towards my stop, I said, 'OK. Bye,' and looked down into my bag.

She took her place in the line, close enough for one last acknowledgement. Our eyes met and she lifted a hand, then turned decisively. That helped, but still I stood, beached, pawing through my things. Hair blown horizontal, strands in my mouth. Unclear what to do next.

'Maggie? Maggie? Is that you?'

I felt a reprieve, and looked up with a smile straight away too familiar for its subject. The woman it landed on showed surprise.

'You recognise me!' she said. 'Most don't!'

I didn't. She was a woman about my age, sun-deprived and soft-looking, entirely unfamiliar until she did a thing with her eyes, opened them wide, just for a second, perfect circles of astonishment, and I saw that it was Sheila.

She'd been fat – obese – last time I'd seen her, years ago at Rose's leavers assembly. Her daughter was finishing too, though the girls were not friends. I had thought her shy. She arrived late with another woman, the pair of them clambering over cringing laps to the last free seats next to mine. I felt for her, and gave her my programme. She had started to cry as soon as she looked down at it and continued, through the skits and certificates and blown-up photos and finally the school song, her sobs punctuating a strong contralto that surprised me.

Now she looked entirely changed. Her clothes were novice, as if she had not yet learnt to dress her new shape, but she wore an assurance, a swagger, even. 'I've been ill. But I'm OK now,' she said, laying her shopping bag between her feet. Made over as a survivor.

'Good,' I said. 'You look well.'

'Oh, I am. Everyone says that!'

She smoothed down where her belly had once been.

'I'm fine. I feel great. Fancy seeing you though,' she said, and touched my arm briefly but quite hard, so it felt more like a poke.

'I'm not over this side much. I met a friend,' I said, and gestured backwards, but the queue had emptied into a bus.

'What a coincidence, though. And I've just been talking about you. With Annie. Remember her? Misha Reynold's mum? I think she did hockey with your Rosie?'

Rose had hated hockey. All sport.

'I'm not sure,' I said.

'So it is you?' she said next.

'Me? Of course.'

'No. In the paper, I mean. Hold on. I've got it here.'

She reached into her shopper and took out a huge purse.

'That's my Leila. Remember? And the grandkids.' She lifted up a flap and showed a photo behind plastic. A round-faced woman flanked by two similar boys. A proof from a cheap studio shoot.

'Oh yes. Lovely,' I said.

'Here we go.' The page was roughly folded but she opened

it carefully as if something was hidden inside. She'd drawn a wonky circle in a thick felt-tip around the piece.

'I took it to show Annie. See if she remembered,' she said. 'So. Is it you?'

'Well, yes,' I said. 'But it was nothing much.'

The paper flapped thinly between us. I thought of snatching it but she seemed to read this thought and plucked it back towards her, dropping it down into the deep of her bag.

'Knew it! Doesn't sound like nothing though! So what happened?'

She had more front than I remembered. And a brimming sort of energy that hadn't been there before.

'Just what they said.'

'Oh right.' She showed me her annoyance in the prolonged lift of her eyebrows.

'And we were wondering too,' she said, 'me and Annie, earlier, about your Rose. Did she get back all right? India or somewhere, wasn't it?'

'No,' I said. 'That wasn't her.'

There had been another girl, in trouble with drugs, who never came home.

'That was Stella,' I said. 'Not me. Not Rose. Oh look. My bus.'

I left her and ran for it unnecessarily. Took a seat, pavement side, laid my novel on my lap and waited for her to walk by, willing the bus to move. I remembered Stella. She had looked a bit like Rose. Outside the showy mainstream. And the mother. A single woman – there was that connection too. I saw her at the doctor's after it happened, her face blanked by the prescription she had come there to repeat.

They had thought that I was her.

45

Still the bus didn't go.

I looked around the head of the person in front and saw the hold-up was a wheelchair, the driver out of his seat, and just as I thought I would look – I couldn't help myself – Sheila walked by. She had forgotten me, the flesh-and-blood me; that much was clear. She was entirely oblivious, tapping into her phone with two agile thumbs and moving her lips as she did. Margaret Benson, spotted.

And so my story spread. And my unease, though there was no logic to it. What did it matter? The chat of a few London housewives. Their views had no traction and would not travel far. I would bob along the surface of their memories while they tried to join the dots between my action and what they knew of me, or thought they knew. She wouldn't correct her misinformation. I would remain, for her, the mother of a disappeared child. Odd, really, when it was I who had been hiding. I who once believed it possible to vanish.

Work called. Nancy, on her out-of-town number. She spoke like a singing teacher tutoring a child, her sentences bizarrely modulated and prone to leaps and drops of the scale. 'Hello, Maggie, how are you?' Falsetto till the last word, then a plummet. I imagined she thought it made her sound perky yet caring. It did, in fact. The good news was she had a backlog of transcriptions. As much work as I could do. A pinch of tension, barely there, disappeared. A woman needs to feed herself.

I am a medical transcriptionist – a virtual medical secretary, if you like, though the agencies like to position our role as supplementary. I type up doctors' notes, hundreds of them, thousands, across my working life. It's all online now, a voice speaking out of my computer, somehow more remote than the old way, with a dictaphone, though I can't say why.

The process has something of the race about it. A moment of poised wait in the space between my tap of the play button and the doctor's last inhale, and we're off. You can nearly always hear that final breath, technology as it is. Sometimes it's a sharp tug, others a longer thoughtful pull, and in that sound I form my first impressions. Male or female, most obviously, and in this, I'm nearly always right. And something of the speaker's temperament too. In playful mood I pause and let a picture take shape. Once I start though, I am pitted against that voice; to press stop, to fall behind, is, for me, to fail.

My method is as follows: I type the first draft exactly as I hear it, listen again and amend, just the once. Sometimes the doctor has made a mistake. He has not said what it is clear to me that he means. In these situations I write up my own interpretation. I have never had a transcript returned.

My role is, of course, invisible though occasionally I find myself acknowledged. If a doctor is over-prepared, or speaks as if reading from a script, I know he is thinking of me. It's a shame, and a waste of his time. Sometimes the pitch of voice will change midway and I am addressed directly, with some discomfort: 'And. If you wouldn't mind inserting the address of the hospital here, please. I'm sure it'll be online. Or something. Thanks.' Or: 'I'm not certain of the spelling of this name. He is a surgeon at City. Oncology. Perhaps you can . . .'

And I always can. Accuracy is key.

Over time I have come to recognise some of these doctors and hear in their tones that they are easier with me now. They ask for me personally, the agency has said, though they never know my name. But it works best when I am forgotten and I know that this has happened from the altered acoustics, an increase in sound effects, more slurps, sniffs and rustles.

How do you become such a thing? I can only describe my route, which had no map.

I once was a doctor's receptionist, back when school hours were an issue, I felt a value in getting out and about, and I could still smile on demand.

My qualifications: I was, and still am, an exemplary typist – I took a secretarial course in Brighton at seventeen and have only got faster and more accurate since.

I was single and had a child, and the doctor liked to appear generous.

The clincher: my obvious discretion, though he rephrased it later, saying that I had a way of viewing a thing outside its context that was rare in a woman. He joked that he would happily walk into war by my side. What he meant was that I could show a woman in for her cancer diagnosis with my same smooth smile, but also that my heart was hard and this would keep his safe.

I worked for him for ten years, and slept with him for five and he cried when I left. But by that point I was sick of the public, so the move to transcription was ideal. Nowadays you'd probably have to do a course.

I logged on to the website, keyed in my password and found the reassuring nest of files that Nancy had saved for me there. It took a couple of hours to complete; not a slip.

I checked my emails – nothing that mattered – and an old account that I had largely abandoned when it became overrun with spam. Still a problem, I found, but supplemented now with pages of Facebook requests. The work of Sue. On this last holiday she had suggested that we start a group, online. When I asked her why, I was laughed at, vigorously. To talk to one another, share tips, make plans, it seemed. I wasn't on Face-book, or any other site, and the idea made me anxious, which they couldn't understand. After wine I had let her borrow a laptop and set me up.

I offered the minimum of information. Where a picture should go, I left the default image – a silhouette of a young man, I think, with a silly tuft of hair. I gave this old email address, thinking myself clever, which she opened on an adjacent page. Immediately it filled with messages, ping upon ping. I accepted the advances of the people who sat before me and got rid of the rest. Still they came all evening, announced each time by that tinny little bell. The overtures and suggestions – so-and-so wants to be friends – the vernacular of a pushy child. I asked Sue to log out in the end, but still.

At home, I selected all and pressed delete. The intimacy of it gave me the shivers.

II

The police had said they would call – a follow-up, for feedback – and next day I found myself circling the telephone like a teenager; alert to it, reluctant to move beyond its reach. There was pleasure in waiting though, and I thought again of Anja. I wondered what she had wanted from our chat, and whether she got it. What, if anything, came next? Perhaps we are all done now. How would that make me feel?

The clothes were half out of the machine when the phone finally rang and by the time I got there, it had clicked onto message. I saw an 0207 number, and heard a bright head-girlsy voice.

'Hello there. I'm calling for Mrs Margaret Benson,' it said.

I grabbed for the handset, keen to know how I'd done. Expecting praise.

'Yes. Hello. Sorry. It's me. I was just – I've just come in,' I said.

'Oh brilliant. Well, if I could introduce myself. My name's Vicky Bernard and I'm calling about Anja Maric?'

'Yes. Yes. Of course.'

I took the phone through to the sitting room, sat down, and reached for the nearest part of the dog.

'Ah. You're expecting me?' she said.

'Well, yes,' I replied. I scratched hard at that place that made his leg kick out like a piston.

'Oh fantastic. I didn't get that message. All the better. Should we get together? So much nicer than the phone.'

'I suppose so, if that's necessary. They said it would just be a chat. To check everything went OK with Anja and me?'

I could hear traffic and her echoey steps.

'Oh. I see. I must be a bit behind. So you've spoken, have you, you and Anja?'

Suddenly she was louder and the background noise diminished. There was something under the surface of her voice, an appetite that I couldn't make sense of.

'I met with her yesterday. Out of home. As I was told,' I said.

'Oh brilliant. And how did that go?'

Her tone was wrong. Too chatty. A lack of care or format. Not the pitch of a public servant.

'Sorry. Who am I speaking to?' I asked.

'My apologies. Did I not say? It's Vicky. Vicky Bernard.'

'Yes, but who are you? Are you with the police?'

'The police? Oh no. Not at all. Nothing like that.'

As if this would be good news.

'What are you then, Vicky?' I asked, trying to blunt my tone.

'Well. I work for the *Daily Mail* and my area is really human-interest stories, you know, the nice ones. The sort that make people feel good –'

I held the phone away from me, fighting the urge to drop it. A volt of panic, my system reeling in its wake. When I brought the handset back to my face there was silence.

'Margaret? Can you hear me? Are you there?'

'Yes,' I said.

She tried a new approach.

'Has there been a mistake? Were you expecting someone else?'

'Yes.'

'My apologies for that. A call about Anja, was it though? I thought I heard you say?'

'Look. I don't really want to talk to the press. I don't think it's a good idea,' I said.

'I understand exactly what you're saying. I do. Thing is, there's a story here.'

'What do you mean?'

My big toe gouged a line in the tread of the carpet. A childhood habit. The nail was weak from it.

'Well, Margaret, our readers love a have-a-go hero, you know, the average citizen who steps up to help, and so on.'

'That's not how it was.'

'OK. Fine,' she answered as if I had agreed to something. 'Well, maybe you could tell me what did happen, in your own words?'

'It's not that. I don't want to be involved.'

'Yeah. It's a bit of a tricky one, that, to be honest, because it's out there now. I don't think you can stop it really. These stories take on a life of their own. Not all of them, but some. It's hard to predict which. Some just. Catch fire. So to speak.'

She stopped to let this idea settle.

'I mean the good thing is that you will come out of it really really well. What you did is amazing. That's what we want our readers to hear. An uplifting story among all the doom and gloom.'

I said nothing.

'Tell you what. Why don't you have a think? One thing I would say, though, is do expect others to call. It is a definite possibility. But I can help you manage all of that, if you like, so it doesn't get too hectic. If you and I choose to work together that is. It's up to you. Completely.'

She spoke again into the silence.

'Especially if there's a way to build on things, you know, grow the story. If you were to be meeting with Anja again, for example, and I could maybe be there? Or.'

'I'll think about it,' I said. 'Goodbye', and pressed end.

It rang again a second later as I stood in the hall. I heard my own dour recording, the beeps, and waited for her voice. But it wasn't a message, it was an SMS. She had texted me her number.

I googled her. Vicky Bernard. The right one first time. *Mail Online* – a page-worth of clicks. She was prolific, and something of a generalist. Nothing of interest or merit and never more than a paragraph or two. Either a junior or a failure.

I typed in 'have-a-go hero'. Predictable tales on local stages. Each with its quote from the ordinary citizen compelled to act – banal and fake-modest to a man. None had mushroomed beyond the initial telling.

And next my own name. The most searched Margaret Benson was a Victorian, an author and an amateur Egyptologist. Next came Steven Benson, who murdered his mother – a tobacco heiress – and brother, with a bomb under the car. Then an academic, a feminist and an archbishop's wife. Pages deep I found the *Metro* article. Nothing more.

I took a breath. Made a coffee. Stood out at the end of the garden and looked back at the blank face of my house. The dog dug a hole in the flowerbed, his paws rhythmed and mechanical, displacing the mud into two shallow slopes underneath him.

My heart, every now and again, gave a feeble *rat a tat tat* but I breathed into it, as I have learnt to do. This does not have to be a catastrophe. Nothing has changed.

I went inside and texted Vicky Bernard. Told her that I would not help. I have weathered worse.

Later though, at night, the telephone rang once more. I stood over it, electrified; snatched a table edge for balance, but there was nothing.

12

Anja came round. She had read my telephone number upside-down on her case notes and remembered it. A resourceful girl. Her text the purest surprise.

I bought lunch for us at the deli. I'd never been in there before; the place was like a gallery. All white with huge bowls of oil-slicked produce on staggered pedestals, the ingredients written on card, in ink, balanced up against each dish. One had suffered a spillage, its words obscured by a spreading orange stain.

I ladled what I wanted into white waxy boxes, taking turns with the other clientele. I chose squash, pancetta and sage, dressed with a hazelnut pesto. Bocconcini, zucchini, roasted chilli and mint. A puy lentil and spinach soup and a huge airy loaf with green olives and whole sea-salt crystals studding the top – it was all I could do not to grab a fist of it then and there. A bottle of white burgundy slippery from the fridge. I resisted the brownies and some immense meringues.

There was low-volume opera to be aware of, and a slim hand-some boy – an American, I think – in a shirt and clean waist apron who took the money. I paid him an amount that seemed fair at the time, and carried the food through the streets in two brown-paper bags; my secret, save for the discreetest stamp of a logo that you had to know to look for. My purchases made me happy and I longed to be home to see them again.

When I got in, I pulled out the table in the garden room, wished that I'd bought flowers – there was nothing outside to pick – and arranged everything in a fat wedge of chilly lunchtime sun.

She arrived with a hug and a box of fudge from the Tower of London.

'It's so kind of you to invite me into your home. I'm very glad to be here,' she said.

'I'm pleased to see you too,' I replied.

She pushed off her shoes, old white trainers, and set them together by the door. She took a pair of slippers from her bag.

'This is a lovely house,' she said, before she'd seen it. Buster came nosing along and she knelt and ran the back of her hands down the velvet of his ears.

'You like dogs?' I asked.

'Yes, of course. But I never had one. What's his name?'

'Buster.'

'Hello, Buster.' He sat and held up a paw. A stupid trick.

'Pleased to meet you, Buster. You trained him well!'

'Come through, come through,' I said.

Anja sighed when she saw the food and I wondered for a second if it was too much.

'So, how are things?' Innocent enough, I'd thought, until I heard myself say it.

'Good. Good. I have a friend now, Eleni, she shares my room and we have fun. She's from Albania also.'

She sat with a leg tucked under her, precise as a cat.

'Ah. Albania. I've never been there,' I said pointlessly.

'No,' she said. 'There are beautiful bits. And quite a lot of tourists now.'

'Yes, I'm sure. I've just never. Is there walking? I like to walk.'

'Of course! Have you heard of the Accursed Mountains?'

'No. I don't think so.'

'The tourists visit all the time! I can tell you how they got their name, if you like?'

'Yes please. I'd love to hear.'

'There were two brothers hunting and they found a fairy, a beautiful fairy.'

She told the story as if I were a child. Slow. Wide-eyed.

'They are both in love with her and they want her to choose. They ask who she prefers but she is clever and she says you, for being so brave and you, for being so handsome.'

She jabbed her finger at two imaginary men.

'Oh, right,' I said.

'But you know what happens next?' she asked.

'No,' I said, though I guessed it would not be good.

'Well, the brave one kills the handsome one and then takes the fairy home to meet his mother. But the mother is so angry that she curses the fairy and the mountains for ever. Right to this very day.'

She let out a hoot.

'Not such a happy ending, right?'

I cast around for a suitable response.

'No. I suppose not. I'll have to take a look next time I'm thinking about a holiday. Shall we eat?'

She peered carefully at her food, moving it around the plate with a fork.

'This is delicious. It's not British though, I think?'

'No. No. It's. I'm not sure actually. This one is sort of Mediterranean. In influence. And this. It's autumny. Pumpkin. You can grow it here, not that I do. And sage. There's a bush of that in the garden, though it's dead at the moment.'

'It doesn't matter. It's so good. Better than fish and chips!'

'It is. Have some more.'

She served herself.

'And are they being helpful? The people where you are staying?'

It wasn't that I meant to pry.

'Yes. Yes. There is a chance that I will be able to stay. Because of Goran. He is in trouble now, and it is my fault. It might be dangerous for me at home.'

'Of course. Yes. I hadn't thought of that.'

'At least I have no sisters.'

'Do you not? No. Well.'

'It is just me. And my parents. But I cannot worry for them. I have my own concerns. I can tell you my secret. I am pregnant.'

She touched her belly in the usual way.

'Oh. Wow.'

Her face took on a shuttered happiness.

'Congratulations. My goodness. Have you been able to tell your family?'

'No. But that is OK. I will not take my baby back. At this time they tell me not to worry. It is a period of. Recovery and reflection.'

She spoke these words as if I would recognise them. I indicated that I did.

'So this', she opened her hands above the table, 'will help me grow a nice healthy baby.'

She gave herself a blessing in her own language.

'Thank you, Maggie. But no more wine for me.'

She put her hand over her glass.

'Of course not, no. Here, have something else. There's one more spoonful. It'll only spoil.'

'Thank you but no more! I've had so much! Now I am ready to clean. Like we agreed.'

'What? No. Not if you're.'

'It's fine. I am strong. I must work and save money for our future. You understand?'

She gave off an elation that crept into me as I looked at her, shiny-eyed, almost hysterical.

'Yes, I do. Just take. Don't overdo it.'

'Of course. I'll start with this.'

She carried all the plates through to the kitchen in one go, balanced up an arm like she'd done it before. I followed behind with the half-done bottle.

'Let's see,' she said and crouched before the cupboard under the sink.

'We need more stuff, Maggie. And a box to carry it in.'

'Yes. Just tell me what. Write it down. I'll get it for next time. Or I could give you the money. If you think that's better.'

There was a tattoo, rather large, spread the width of her back, the top of it showing above her jeans. A circular symbol, with lines curving out to form wings. Popular, of the type I saw often in the streets of north-west London, and on girls of every sort, though the inking on Anja was not sharp; it had bled into her skin.

She seemed strong and capable, knees splayed above my floor in those tight cheap clothes; uncomfortable, surely, to clean in. She looked back.

'It's OK, Maggie. I'm fine. Do your thing.'

I drank down a glass of water and went for the dog.

It was an unusual time for me to be out, half past two, but I was glad for the solitude. There was the usual group of self-conscious young men, larking about and occupying too much space with their cartoon postures and exaggerated calls. No threat, to me at least. A couple of those ridiculous joggers with prams. Fewer children today. Some unfamiliar dogs. The wine was throbbing a beat in my head so I took off my hat. It wasn't cold yet, but the wind came in blusters and made my nose run. Buster tugged when he saw a squirrel, and ignored me when I pulled. I wondered how long Anja would be and when I should go back and felt briefly the stupidity of leaving an unknown and possibly desperate girl in my house.

Poor Anja, who has no one else to share the fact of her baby with. My own mother had guessed and told my aunts by the time I got to them. When I sat down, a cup balanced on my trembling legs, I saw straight away that they knew. Bouncing around with their silly looks and suppressed grins, as if it were they who had something for me.

'I was right!' she shrieked before I'd even finished. 'Your nose has changed! That's what gave you away! It'll be a girl, I'll bet.'

Her sisters congratulated her.

It was, of course.

They kept me close for those months and everyone else at arm's length. I felt a child again, fed by my mother with familiar dishes that she fetched up on the train. They made sure I was warm, too warm, with knitted blankets brought from home in those huge zip-up laundry bags, another layer pressed upon me. I slept a lot, and grew fat of course, but it didn't help. She came too early, by six weeks, though soon caught up.

And telling your man. Such a loaded, unpredictable moment. You throw a man's idea of you up in the air when you tell him you are pregnant, even if you planned it. You see how it has landed by the look on his face.

My husband was thrilled, genuinely. I think he thought it would make me more recognisable. Easier to know. We had the idea that the future came into view that day, though that kind of thinking is always mistaken.

But it can be done alone, if it has to. For Anja, motherhood had already begun. I believe that something starts between a woman and her child at the very moment that she finds she is expecting. Whatever there is inside you, it passes on. Your baby grows in it for months, some sort of pre-knowledge. She sees you before your eyes have met, and it is nothing that you can control.

Anja was working on her hands and knees at that moment, scrubbing my dirt clean for her unborn baby. Hers would be a lucky child.

13

Paul starts late on Mondays and picks up the trail around half past ten. Maureen is out every day, come rain or shine, and if she wants company, waits for him at Harvist Road, a spot before eleven. I found her there in sloping Uggs, her head under a beanie meant for someone younger and packed out with hair. Craggy, perhaps, but what I still knew as handsome. She raised a stumpy hand at me. Then the dogs saw Paul's, and off we went.

A pastel day, the sky blues and pinks with low woolly clouds obscuring the view and making it all feel old-fashioned. Real heat in the sun, the warmth pressing down on my skin; a sensation so acute it felt improper.

Peter's not good at the moment, Paul told us. Sad, he said, but not a heavy sad, more fearful. Always alert. They've been here before. This part can last for weeks, in ebb and flow. You wouldn't know it if you saw him. A collapse will come although it could be months away; that's the pattern, and then the slow road back.

'It's tiring,' he said. 'The dogs can feel it.'

He clicked his tongue and they were at his side, bristly and bouncy and hollow-boned. Ginger and white, one with a black splat on her chest. Sisters, which wasn't supposed to work, but in this case did. They each took a treat with careful teeth. Maureen put her arm through his.

'It's hard, love.'

'It is what it is,' Paul said.

I considered this alongside what I'd seen of the man. He had an indoors look, Peter, always covered up. A person who felt the cold. Long sleeves and trousers, a high-buttoned shirt or roll-neck. I had thought he had psoriasis, or a scar – something to hide – until I noticed a photo in their kitchen, a holiday snap on a foreign beach and saw that his body was blemish-free and strong; beautiful even. I was shocked, at my own suppositions and how far they'd taken me.

Peter is a watcher. He doesn't reveal as much as Paul, who simply speaks as he thinks, but we pause for Peter and his ideas. When he laughs, it is absolute and everyone is thrilled.

I thought of him as Paul spoke, and wished that he was here, though he only walked at the weekend. Neither man worked in an office (I refused to call them 'the boys', as Maureen did) but they had agreed to keep their 9-to-5 lives apart, save a shared lunch break, something home-made around the table. A decision made up front when Peter left his architecture practice, for the good of their relationship; their god, a thing of itself, to be cared for, like the dogs.

'It's the dread. The fear of it. But this is the third time now. It's part of our life. I honestly think that's better?'

The lift at the end of Paul's sentence that made everything sound like a question. Always seeking assurances, Paul.

'Now we can be prepared. Have a plan.'

'You'll get through it,' said Maureen.

'We will.'

We passed Pets' Corner, and Sammy, Maureen's dog – shaggy, huge, a terror to keep clean – raised her head at the squeaks, or perhaps the smells. A group of uniformed children waited at the entrance, their cries like birds. Clouds rushed us, and the wind picked up a handful of crisped leaves and threw them at the dogs. The beginnings of autumn, though we were not there yet.

Quiet is fine, as a rule, on our walks, but this time it began to feel like an issue. I waited for Maureen to speak, to offer up some misery of her own. She talked to us, now and again, about her daughters and her son. Long gone. Disappointments, all of them, but only because they hadn't come to need her enough. Nothing new or ongoing such as Paul could offer. Old hardships that had scabbed over, though she has the tendency to pick.

'I think it might be something like that for Rob's wife, you know. She can be very. Distant. I worry about him. Her.'

Maureen was off the mark with that one. I had met Robert's wife and she was a different sort entirely. A woman who was up, up and away, dragging her man behind her. A woman who didn't like to share, down in Chislehurst or wherever it was. A woman of nails and hair and teeth and a big white car that was always clean.

'Well, you can't make their choices for them, can you?' said Paul.

'No. That you can't, love.'

They huddled round their platitudes and I dropped back a bit, pretending to feel for something in my coat. Maureen turned her head and called to me.

'What about you, Mags? You heard anything from Rosie lately?'

Rosie. I wondered if that was a mistake, or where she'd heard it, though it could only have been from me. A name from a sweeter time when my child still submitted to my love. It was Rose now, had been for years. I spoke of her only when asked. One daughter, I had told them. We are not close.

'No. No. Nor do I expect to.'

I retracted the lead. Called for Buster harshly.

'Maggie. Come round here a minute.'

Paul stretched his free arm backwards. I could see the side of his face, one eyeball straining to find me. Young skin, a fore-shortened nose. There was nothing to do but catch up. We walked in a row of swollen coats and white-and-red faces.

'Ladies. I've got a crazy idea. It's twelve o'clock. Opening time, if I remember rightly. Why don't we go to the pub?'

We settled at the third one we tried, the only place to take dogs. A pub with the dimensions of a church and the longest bar I think I've ever seen. A huge flat telly was suspended from the ceiling with the racing on, volume down. Updates scrolled along its bottom and other people's messages. Texts, or maybe tweets: 'Go Highland Midnight!!!! love Tim and Tara xxxxx.'

The air felt warm and breathed as we pushed open the door. No one paid us any notice, and I felt a clutch of almost painful happiness. We paused a few steps in, uncertain of where to sit, and to buy time talked about what we might drink.

The room was filled with low round tables of maroon wood and matching stools; toy-town arrangements in the massive space. Long-legged chairs were tucked under the bar, and there were benches built beneath the windows. Once inside, as with all decent pubs, the outside world seemed some way away.

The place was pretty much empty. The few men at the bar were solitary and distant, possibly alcoholic. A couple with their necks craned up towards the sport had a scary-looking dog who it seemed best to avoid. So we settled at the edge of the room, on a window seat with an extra chair dragged over.

A huge glass arrived, three-quarters full and clouded from the dishwasher, but the wine inside was warm, rich and viscous, nourishing almost. I drank it, and went up for more.

We were together in a way we'd never been before, silly and scatty and trivial. We spread open bags of crisps unrecognisable as their flavours, and Paul showed us how to fold the empty packets into tight balls which we pinged across the table. We flicked beermats and snatched them from the air – I surprised myself by being rather good at it. Maureen suggested darts but that was a step too far.

In a while we found ourselves cheering with the telly each time the finish line approached, and when I went to the loo my face was puce and my lips stained red at the dry bits and I laughed at my own reflection.

We thought we'd better eat, and ordered three huge plates of fish, chips and peas, which came with batter an inch thick that burst to dust in our mouths, and fed handfuls to the dogs under the table, until we remembered that potatoes were bad for them.

They brought up Anja, and I told them of our lunch.

'That's amazing, Mags. She can do me as well. Twice a week if she likes,' said Paul.

Even Maureen, who would never countenance a cleaner, said she'd ask next door. We'd got to the stage by now that everything we said seemed fundamental.

'So did she tell you anything about what happened over there?'

That was Paul.

'No. No. And I wouldn't ask. Later perhaps.'

'Or maybe wait till she brings it up?' said Maureen.

'She was very. Together, I suppose.'

'Yeah, but people hide things,' said Paul.

'I know. I know. But I was surprised by her. She's got this sort of optimism. She's childlike. Well, she is a child, really, I suppose.'

Beliefs forming as I spoke them. My view of her changing by the moment.

'It might be some kind of coping mechanism. A response to trauma, or something. I don't know.'

Paul's face had changed.

'What?'

'Nothing. Nothing. But you know she might be. Damaged, Maggie.'

'What do you mean by that?' I asked.

I knew what he meant, that perhaps she was dangerous.

Maureen saw it too.

'Maybe she is. But who wouldn't be? Who isn't, in their own way?' she said. She coughed out her emotion. Paul looked sorry, and ashamed perhaps.

'I know. Look, I'm not saying. Anything really. I was just pointing it out. We'll help. I wouldn't. God.'

He looked at his phone, angry at the picture that Maureen had drawn of him. She took my hand in hers. It was freezing cold and damp from her cider.

'I wonder if she's got family or friends, or anything. Back where she comes from,' she said, trying to imagine her way into Anja's life.

'I don't know. But she doesn't feel like someone with no one, if you see what I mean.'

68

'Well. We'll do what we can. Tell her now, won't you?' she said.

Our mood had dipped; we divided the bill and Paul went to pay. He looked like a boy at the bar. I watched his left hand wander, to his pocket first, and then hang awkward by his side, fiddling with itself.

'D'you think he's really all right? What with Peter and everything?' Maureen said. 'I know he talks a good game, but.'

'Course he is. He's fine. The last thing he'll want is us fussing over him, that's for sure.'

Back home and it was darkening. The hall was dim but for the digital '1' that blinked on the panel of my phone. I pressed the forward arrow. There was emptiness and a click of disconnection. I crouched down, bent my ear close to the grid of the speaker and played it again.

This time I heard a sigh.

Not the deliberate type, the type to send a message, but an exhalation caught on the phone's trip back to its cradle.

A huff, more than anything; exasperation but also the smug comfort of expectations met.

I wondered, could it be Chris? My husband, or rather my ex. In not replacing him, he never came to be renamed.

14

Drinking with girlfriends, newly metropolitan, sure of my own appeal. Feeling the part under feathered hair and floppy hats, in clothes that swam behind me. Sleeping with a boy who looked like Joe Strummer and wondering what that might mean for my look. Working hard, head down, thrilled at my wage. And one day there was Christopher, cheek in his palm, cap parked beside him. Smooth and well pressed; amused, I had thought, at the picture he made.

We were giddy, me, Michelle and Julie, sat up against the bar in that funny old hotel Brian took us to each month on a Thursday, to thank us for all our hard work, whether we'd done any or not.

Brian Barclay, my first boss, a mentor of sorts.

I forget the name of the place, but can see the room, the residents' lounge, though of course we never stayed. Windowless and warm, the walls textured like carpet, a maroon lozenge pattern laid over mustard. No music and low chat; muffled, but strangely accommodating.

It must have looked odd, our arrangement. Three young girls and Brian; balding, fiftyish, suited, obscenely cheerful. Yet we were welcomed, each visit, with a solemnity that flattered us but we also wanted to push against, play young and wild, which we weren't. Not that there was anything dodgy in it. Brian was a man of an unusual sort – a lady's man in the rarest of senses. 'I simply love the female mind,' he said, and it seemed to be true.

He would buy us a cocktail each, listen as we talked – we put it on a bit, just to make him blush – then hop down and head back home to Hemel, to Marjorie and his twin daughters, once he had checked that we had money enough to get home. We scoffed at him when he left, silly old pet, and emptied our purses to see if we had cash for another.

I noticed Chris first. He was already settled when we arrived, by the wall at the far end of the bar. We came in with noise and bluster and gathered up stools that we reset in a messy half-circle. When we came to sit, I made sure I was facing him.

'Hellooo,' Michelle said at one point, waving at me, as I watched him over her shoulder. She looked.

'Oh, got it,' she said.

Brian grinned on benignly.

I remember the bones of his nose and cheeks and the blonde of his hair pushed back across his head. Polished black shoes, and the uniform too, of course. He seemed dropped in from another time, a permanence about him that made me feel flimsy. But he didn't look up. He seemed immune. Which didn't harm.

And when Brian had left, and we raked through our scattered coins, he called to us.

'Excuse me, ladies. Your. That man you were with. I think he left his brolly.'

He pointed at our portion of the bar and I leant right out onto one leg of my stool to see. He was right. It hung on a brass rail built into the underside.

We looked at the umbrella, we looked back at Chris; more time passed than seemed necessary.

'Oh well,' Julie said. 'Don't worry. We can give it back to him tomorrow. He's our boss.'

'Or I could?' Chris replied.

He stood up as if he meant to get it, but stopped just short of Michelle. To reach across her would mean coming closer than was appropriate. I saw that he was tall and broader across the shoulders than he appeared in profile. This was good. My experience so far had tended towards the slim. I recall that thought as some sort of precognition. We are still animals, after all.

'Oh, don't bother,' Julie said. 'It isn't raining,' though of course we couldn't know. Michelle snorted.

'Well, don't trouble yourselves, ladies,' Chris said, with a spot of tease in it. 'I'll take it, shall I?'

He held out an arm and I unhooked the umbrella and passed it to him. We shared the smallest of looks and he headed out. He was back in a minute or two, fat raindrops sitting unbroken on the shoulders of his jacket. He didn't look my way again.

And that was it, until six months later. I was on the train back to Brighton for a weekend at Mum's, bare legs on a scratchy seat and the bite of burnt rail in my throat. The train stopped just before East Croydon and when I pressed my temple against the window, I saw him waiting further down the platform. The train started up and I watched for a few stretched-out seconds as I was carried closer. There was the moment that we were to pass, my head sharp to the glass, and I saw his eyes blink me into focus. We stopped and I waited. Three people later he was there. He sat on the chair across from me which gave a punctured sound that we pretended not to hear.

'It's you, isn't it? The girl from the bar? I knew you straight away.'

72

He settled unselfconsciously; brushed down the lapels of his jacket with the back of his hand, crossed his legs. The train bounced and the toe of his shoe with its bird-beak shine gave a hop, and almost touched my knee.

'Really?' I said. 'How come?'

Braced for a compliment.

'I never forget a face,' he said. 'That's how come. It's one of my talents.'

'Do you not? I do. I'm hopeless,' I said, which wasn't true. Outside sped off behind us.

'You surprise me,' he said. 'You struck me last time as rather capable.'

'Compared to the others? That's not saying much.'

It was hot and the back of my dress felt sticky all the way down. My calves were flattened against the bottom of the seat and I tried to adjust my posture quietly. I slid my heels towards him then across and my skin peeled free.

He registered the movement; his eyes dropped, but he made a slick recovery. He raised his arm and pushed his nails through his hair and I saw that he wore a ring on his little finger, which meant nothing at the time, and when he dropped his hand to his lap, he eased it round tenderly, under cover of his palm.

'Some friend you are!' he said.

'They're just people from work,' I replied.

'Not friends then?'

'Somewhere in between, I suppose.'

'Oh yes. I know the sort.'

There was silence for a while and he was still, his gaze faintly ticklish on my cheek.

'Are you a pilot?' I said, in the end.

'No. I'm on the way to fancy dress.'

'God, I bet that line's had some use.'

'That's more like it,' he said and bent over his lap towards me. There was an old woman across the aisle, ogling without restraint.

'How about I take you out when I get back?' he said in a low close voice, his face beneath mine, his eyes the white blue of holiday sky.

And then: 'Oops.'

The train had lurched and he grasped my knee, each finger distinct, the faintest press of nail.

'Sorry about that,' Chris said, and sat back with a chuckle. 'What do you think?'

It took twenty minutes to Gatwick. His trip was long haul, four days, and he came back to me straight off the plane – same suit, same shoes. We met at another hotel, the Grosvenor in Victoria, a better place than I was used to.

Something old-fashioned happened. I knew it for what it was, which was surrender, but called it by its other names for a long time. In instant thrall to his authority. A man who took responsibility for hundreds of souls, crossed time zones daily, and returned, unaltered. He bought me my first glass of champagne and told me about Concorde. I went back to my flat and threw out my waistcoats.

His schedule kept me dizzy as if I were the one travelling. A life lived in anticipation and recollection. With another man I think the shape of it could have suited me. He wore a cologne, as he called it, that broadcast his return and had me pivoting in the street if I smelt it on another and yet never quite disguised a chemical undertow of dry cleaning or air-conditioning maybe, even after he showered. He carried the cabin around with him.

He said he wanted to know my family and so I took him to our home. My mother was thrilled, Bet goggle-eyed, Fran shy. I watched them change in his presence, wait for his cues, follow his lead. Felt their relief at having a man in the house, especially one of his calibre. How much easier it all became. It made me despise them, that visit, but love him more.

When it was time to head back to Town, as he called it, we left the three of them crammed into the doorway competing with their neat little waves, but I could see the grip that Mum had on Bettie's hand, and that it was triumph. No matter that he lived in Purley, which wasn't Town by anyone's standards, this felt like progress; to them, and to me too.

His family? The Kents were of a better class, that much was clear. A tidy home of lowered voices and good manners. The truth of things covered, for decency's sake; food decanted into serving bowls, toilet rolls dressed, tights whatever the weather, selected to appear like skin. When his mother appeared in a shift, wearing pearls, as I fed the baby in their kitchen one morning before dawn, I laughed at her – it was the tiredness – but when she asked me what was wrong, I didn't have the nerve to say.

Nothing shown plainly – my own mother's paradise – but she had her sisters to keep her straight.

There was Michael, of course, Chris's brother, the prodigal, but he was kept hidden for the first little while.

Chris showed me how to read the sky. A cirrus cloud – feathery, casts no shadow – means fair weather. Unless the day is already fine; then there will be change. Ripples of cloud – a mackerel sky – and it will be dry. When we were engaged, he taught me to drive and I would take him to the airport for the early runs. Brief journeys on empty roads. Chris peering into the sunrise. Brilliance was bad news. A fiery red meant rain. A muted shade boded well. His belief surprised me, and I read it as depth, a complexity in this most rational of men. An incorrect assumption, as it turned out. Later, when we were married, he got himself to work.

A pilot to his bones. The most clear-eyed man I ever met. Supreme self-knowledge. Instant in his grasp of a situation. Brutal in execution. And he was beautiful. I should mention that. There was always that, and it counted for something.

He told me he had wanted me from the very first time in the bar.

'I could see you were a woman with oomph. And you meet so very few of those.'

Who wouldn't have responded?

15

I was still buying the papers, switching every few days to avoid the shopkeeper's question or the question I thought I saw behind our ordinary interactions.

The dog was confused, but enjoying the change.

Once paid for, I found the newsprint in my bag wouldn't wait. I told myself it was too heavy to lug around, that I might hurt my back, but that was not the reason I went straight home every time.

I splashed the papers over the kitchen, hungry to get started. When it was over and there was just scrambled print, I felt ashamed, but knew that the next day, I would do it all again.

Later I went over them more carefully. I knew the titles well, their personalities crisp and distinct. I saw patterns too; the way stories overlapped, how they bent and changed. I came to spot in advance which would balloon and where, the equivalent space in each paper. The pages a landscape that I could read; made expert in their topography.

I was not resolutely old school – I searched the Internet as well – but there was no satisfaction in that. It made me afraid, the endlessness of it. I could search for ever and never be done. I felt that I could drown down there.

I told myself calm. That I understood the news cycle and logic declared my story dead. Just that one brief illumination. London only. A mere day's opportunity to read.

He would not have seen it. It was not Chris who called. There was nothing there.

Just my fright. My own neurosis. I am prone to compulsions, I know, but I always defeat them in the end.

16

A month on. I let myself in with a bag of corner-shop things I didn't need and heard her singing, competing with the Hoover – one of her favourites by a group of good-looking boys she had showed me in a magazine.

We had agreed that she should visit Tuesdays and Fridays, for two to three hours depending on need. I liked to go out and do my chores while she worked, knowing that I left life behind me in my home. I encouraged her to change the station from Radio 4 to something she preferred and enjoyed the blurt of music when I next came to listen. I recognised the songs over time, and began to hear them everywhere. Did I like them? Not exactly, but they did something pleasant to my mood.

I crept through the hall, so that she wouldn't stop, but she met me in the doorway to the kitchen, the smell of lemon, fake pine and bleach behind her.

'Hey,' she said. 'Shall I put the kettle on?'

'I've got no money, Anja. I'm sorry. I went, but the machine was broken.'

'No problem. Pay me next week? Or I can call in some other time?'

'I could drop it to you, if that's any easier?' I said.

'Next week is good. I wanna save it anyway.'

I went back through to the hall to take off my outdoor things. She followed me.

'Do you want a sugar? Is it OK if I have a cup too?'

'Of course, you don't have to ask. Yes, a sugar, please.' I add a spoon, sometimes two, if I have just come in.

She brought in the mugs and sat next to me on the sofa; dropped her slippers from her feet and crossed her legs beneath her, swift and limber. She pivoted, and I felt her gaze on the side of my head. I faced forwards, in the usual way, sipping the scalding tea from a thick-rimmed mug I'd never used.

'I'm done now. I took all the pictures down and cleaned them with the spray, you see?'

'Oh, great. That's a job needed doing. Thanks, Anja,' I said.

'That is a photo of your daughter over there? I think she has your chin.'

I looked to where she pointed, at an old 5"× 7" in an easel frame which no longer balanced. It had lived the past few years against the wall but Anja must have mended it, for now it was established at the lip of the shelf with its neighbours (a wooden box of matches, a collection of ghastly crystal animals, a china shepherdess and sheep, of all things) pushed behind. It was strange to see it there, prominent again.

'You found something then? In her and me? Not everybody can.'

'It's the same, for sure. Can I look?'

She went across and picked it up – a horrid item – a lattice-work of three over-polished woods. It came apart in her hand, split into its components: frame, glass, the photo and its thickened cardboard backing.

'Oops,' she said.

'Don't worry. The glue must have gone. I'll fix it.'

I reached to take the bits from her but she pretended not

to see. She looked down into Rose's face.

'How old is she here? Six?'

Thereabouts, in a stiff posed shot. An unmoulded face, but already that hair that lay in a solid chunk, her eyes a matching shade of dark that made her seem designed. She looked like a child plucked from the wild, an unguardedness she was just about to lose. I think that's why I'd liked the shot, though it hadn't captured much of her. I displayed it the same day it was developed, put aside as I rushed through the rest in that greedy way we used to, back when photographs came in waxy packets and each one was a surprise.

Anja stroked the picture with a mucky thumb. I moved behind her.

It was my chin all right. Short and sharpened, and it stayed with her as she grew. The rest was entirely her own, her features surfacing eerily year by year. A face that pre-empted personality; dreamy and melancholy. Everything too close to the surface. Purple under the eyes. Stars of red that outlived each knock. Little twitches. A sensitive child. She hardened into something different.

I sat back down.

'Are there more?' Anja asked, looking in extravagant sweeps around the room, though we both knew there were not.

'Upstairs somewhere. A couple of old albums. I'll show you sometime,' I said.

'What is her name?'

'Rose. Rose Frances Benson.'

'Rose! That's beautiful.'

She loved it too. I'd pick up a scrap to write a list and find that she'd got there first; inscribed herself across its surface with a brand new cursive every time. I know too little of children to say if they are all like this. I don't remember it myself – we used to try on the surnames of boys we liked, that I much I recall – but had no particular interest in ours, or rather our father's. Are names, after all, ever really our own?

'And Frances, after my aunt.'

I'd written to Frannie to tell her so and she sent back a nice letter that I still have somewhere. I've loved no one more, nor ever felt as wholly loved as by Aunty Fran. She could speak it all in a look or gesture, and make it seem our secret. But there was nothing of that in her note.

'She is your only aunt?' Anja asked.

'No. There's Bet as well.'

Bet, with her huge chest that I loved, laid my head on, couldn't drag my eyes from, forever kicking off her shoes and stretching out those naked feet that made me blush with their humps of bunion and thick peeling nails. A seaside habit; the sea ran through us all.

'Bet. Bettie. Yes. Very English! I am thinking of names for my baby. What was your mother called?'

'Helen,' I said.

Not as beautiful as the name demands, but as haughty. I got my tut from her.

'So, if she is a girl, I am thinking maybe Liljana. A flower, like your Rose. It has lots of meanings where I come from.'

The photo and fragments of frame lay on her lap. She shifted, and one part slipped off.

'That's lovely. I like it,' I said, which was true, though not the flower itself. Its perfume is too rich and the stamens stain your clothes and poison cats.

'So does she live close by? Rose?'

She moved off, running a finger along the surface of the shelf and checking it for dust.

'No. Not really. In London though. But not this side.'

'So that is not so bad. There is the Tube.'

'Yes. There is. Yes.'

'And she has children, now, too?'

'She does, a boy.' I had seen that child once, and almost had to beg for it.

'So you are a grandma! You can tell me what to do when my baby comes!'

Holding the child in my arms had not been as I expected. I felt frightened and unsure; had a sense of the world's instability. Nothing like when I first held my own daughter and she made me strong. I think Rose must have seen some of this for she quickly took him back.

'Oh. I'm not much of an expert. But of course. If you're. I'm happy to help.'

His smell though, of warm skin and milk.

'So what is she like, Rose? Is she like you?'

A question a mother always asks herself, less in arrogance, rather guilt. In search of inherited flaws, or damage done.

'She. In some ways. Now, perhaps. She didn't used to be so much. She knows her own mind.'

'This is good! If I have a daughter I hope that she will be strong.'

Anja stopped her circuits.

'Do you mind, Maggie? Can I ask you? You were alone some of the time with Rose? I wondered. I don't see a man around.'

She crouched before me and rested there, low, broad-legged.

'Yes, Anja. Most of the time.'

'And was it hard?'

'Easier than being with the father.'

She made a gesture of acknowledgement with her shoulders and her brows.

'And this is why only one child?' she said.

I didn't reply and she saw that she had gone too far. Traffic honked a few roads away and the letterbox went.

'And does Rose see him at all? Her father?'

'No. She doesn't.'

'And did this make problems?'

'It did. She wanted to see him. She couldn't understand.'

Anja was off again in her swift way of moving. She stopped at the bay windows. The top of someone's head passed the length of my hedge.

I wondered what she would tell her child about its own father. No doubt fall back on the standard script.

'He was not ready', or 'We could not be together'.

The kindest version, this, though none of it absolved the child.

'He was not a good person' – sinister, and alarming from the genetic point of view.

'I didn't even know him' tended not to endear.

There is 'He is dead', of course, though I found I myself couldn't take that step.

Unless she chose to tell the truth, but I assumed that would be unsayable.

'Look, Anja. You're a long way off that. You're doing every-thing you can. You can't do any more.'

She came towards me with a grown-up face.

'I was only there six months, you know. In Milan, where he took us. I am still strong.'

'You are, Anja. You are. I can see that. You got away. That in itself is quite a feat. And you will make a tremendous mother. I feel sure you will.'

'I can lie if I have to,' she said, twisting a lock of hair around her finger and snapping off dead ends.

'Yes. You'll do what it takes.'

She nodded.

'Thanks, Maggie. You are a great help to me.'

The old look was back, dreamy and removed.

'Oh. Well. I don't know about that. If I had my time again and so on.'

I didn't think she understood but she patted my arm, put her slippers in her bag. She left, the smell of her strong sweet perfume on my coat where hers had lain.

17

Dear Mum

I'm writing this because when I try and speak to you and you just close down, it makes me so angry that it is impossible for me to put my thoughts across. Yes, I want to know about my father, but this is about so much more than that now. When I see how completely you can withhold from me and sit there while I plead, my whole idea of you as my mother and a person is smashed up, Mum, to be honest. I am heartbroken and disbelieving that you would be so cold and stubborn towards me when it always felt like we were together in things, the two of us. I just don't know how to get past or over this.

Rosie

As soon as Anja left, I went up, the old stuff out before I had the time to think.

Fifteen here. Full of melodrama. Gone to the bother of using her writing set. Purple ink on matching paper, which I had bought, initially, for a birthday, and replenished from the stationers a bus ride away.

How grown up it seemed, when she first took it up – declared she'd write on nothing else. My signature style, she said, constructing her identity, block by block, in plain sight. I took pleasure in it, in having started something that took root.

I would have loved the idea too, as a girl, had I read it in a book; something so fine as a heroine who wrote only on paper thin enough to see through and with a real ink pen. The ritual of the cartridge change; ducking down the ball into its barrel of colour. My mother would have rolled her eyes.

Rose kept these things in the top drawer of a red-spotted box of coated cardboard bought for the job. Paper to be used for thank-you notes and daily letters to Alex (female) and Sarah, best friends from girlhood and still now, I imagine. Then Philip, her first, who emerged about that time, putting thoughts down on paper for him that were easier to write than speak. In the bottom went letters received – unguarded – Rosie safe in the surety that her privacy would never be breached.

And one day, she went to that drawer, pulled out a sheet in anger and distress to write to me, her mother, whom she could no longer find a way to reach.

I could have taken it from a page ripped from an exercise book, written with the pull and splat of a biro. It was the purple that made me cry, not the words – I had readied myself for those – but their method of delivery, a last token of her childhood. I suppose that was why I kept it, this and only this, for there had been plenty more.

I didn't cry, when I looked at it. It felt precious to me, instead, like a love letter, but I put that down to its decay. When I pulled it from its envelope, after Anja went, I was left with a dusting of mauve on my hands. Soon it would be gone altogether but that would change nothing. She was right, Rose. She couldn't get past, or over it. After a while she stopped asking but had begun, by then, to leave me in stages.

When she got to sixteen she left the school that I had chosen for her and enrolled in a nearby college – substandard – though she got the grades she needed, which felt like spite at the time but was more likely good sense. I had long lost the right to be proud of her; her achievements and attributes were her own.

Next came university in a far-off northern town that I never visited and from which she never really returned, though she came back to Queen's Park now and again. I knew this because I saw her once with Sarah, her old friend, smoking outside a pub one August afternoon in what must have been the holidays of her second year. They had both had their noses pierced, horrible, but they looked like what they were – middle-class girls playing at it. I didn't dare approach.

Instead I spent an uneasy evening wondering if she was staying the night in the big house three roads back, where Sarah's family lived a life beyond implausible in its perfection. A neat counterpoint to our careful little twosome in its depth and breadth; a rebuke almost, though the right-thinking parents would have been horrified at that. Five children – two girls, three boys – all beautiful, talented and kind. The father a lawyer of the good-guy type, the mother an ex-journalist who took a slot on Radio 4 instead when the children came. Yes, really. State-school educated and two, at least, up at Cambridge.

Their happiness spilt out of the huge sash windows of their three-storey home, all faded kilims and artefacts from foreign travel. They lived directly behind us and, aged about nine, Rosie said that when she bounced high on their trampoline she thought she could see our chimney, was it red?

She loved it there and who could blame her, but came home quiet. I made her hot chocolate and laid a blanket over her knees. Put a radio on in every room to make the house seem occupied.

The summer that I saw her was a hot one, the rest of which I spent in my back garden imagining that it was the Gaters' well-bred voices that reached me and their roasting meat I smelt and wondered if she was back there too.

I liked the mother, Lydia; had been dragged to a couple of their infamous Christmas parties across the years, but when I saw her crossing the park that October, looking exhausted, everyone safely back at college, I swear she dipped her head.

I waited for something bad to happen to that family, but it never did, at least as far as I know, and not that I would have wished it on them. Haven't seen any of them for years, although the clan will have grown, spread, accrued. And I came to discover that wanting and trying will only take you so far and I've never been one to beg. I gave up, in the end, simply to ensure my own survival. Stopped with the regular entreaties, and soon after received a note – a bitter page – citing the new depths of my betrayal. In doing what I thought she had asked – leaving her alone – I gave her the means to hate me more. That was six years ago.

Things were such with Rose that she would speak to me if I called, but never made her own approach.

I had not met her partner, and their child only once, whom she had too young, younger even than me, named Sam.

She dropped me a card when he was born and cashed the cheque that I sent her by return.

I chose not to take her letter back up to the drawer. Instead, the spare room; a place I rarely visited. Back it went, shedding more of itself on the way.

18

Paul and Maureen came by, though they didn't stop for long, heating up in the hall in their outdoor clothes.

Peter is feeling better; an adjustment to his medicines and some sessions that the two of them attend. Maureen's daughter Lauren has come to stay, with Lola and Jack – more trouble with her husband. Mo told me all this in a rush, with relish, her pleasure at being called upon burning through her veil of concern.

'How long?' I asked.

'Indefinite,' she said, with a loaded look.

She wants to throw a lunch, for us all, a get-together, the weekend after next.

'And Peter and Paul have said they'll come.'

A lunch for Lauren, her daughter, who's had it tough. There was nothing to say but yes. They shared a tight pleased glance and I saw that they had been expecting me to refuse. I have been walking less the last couple of weeks. The rain, but Anja too.

Anja's started at Paul's and he thinks she's smashing; he told me so, there on the doorstep. A magnificent cleaner, which was true – I had found myself upping my game to keep pace – and a lovely girl to boot. Peter seems to like her. Fresh blood, Paul says. He hears them chatting. A welcome distraction. And what a great laugh. 'I know!' I replied, but I didn't, I couldn't think when I'd heard it.

And she was upstairs all the while, and I wondered if she was listening. There was no sound from above and I had no sense of where she might be. Wherever it was, she was still; one move and the house would have given her away.

When they had left, at last, I called: 'Anja, you OK? Paul and Maureen have just gone. Did you hear them?'

'Oh, right. Sorry,' she said.

She was coming out of my office when I reached her.

'All done!' she said, and I followed her back down, counted her money out of my purse and rounded it up to the nearest tenner.

'I haven't got change. Don't worry about it. Get yourself a coffee,' I said.

'Thanks, Mags. See you later!' And off she skipped.

She sometimes stayed on for a chat. Not that time.

I switched on my computer, the swipes of her cloth still visible on the screen in the final seconds of blackness. The BBC homepage appeared, surprising me again. She had set it all up, and was right, I did like to see the headlines and the weather and a list of all the top TV that I might enjoy. Its currentness thrilled me. Breaking News appearing as I watched. I sat there, sometimes, waiting for something to happen before my eyes, but it hadn't yet. It made me feel part of it all, which I suppose was the point. I never clicked beyond that surface page.

She had organised me entirely over a fortnight, creating a bank of folders to sit on my desktop – largely empty – though I planned to get to it soon. 'Personal', 'Travel', 'Photos', though I had none, and a place for passwords, not that we named it as such. We had chosen instead 'Pet Stuff', another of her smart ideas. She offered to help with some physical filing too, but I said no to that.

I caught up with work, a mail from Nancy dated last week, and typed all afternoon, a few hours lost, not in someone else's problems, as Paul had once suggested, but in the simplest pursuit of accuracy. What about confidentiality? he asked. Did I ever know a person whose notes I'd typed? Did it make things hard? Truth was, I was barely aware of what I wrote and remembered nothing when it was done. The process is wall-eyed, deaf-eared, that's why I like it. The dog sat on my feet while I worked and when I had finished I took him out, just us, and felt the muscle of my brain unclench and ease.

I threw sticks, and wondered what Buster thought of as he ran and whether it would be possible to repeat this action until he tired of it. It was always me who abandoned the game and, sure enough, my shoulder tightened and I found I'd had enough. It took him a while to work this out.

He came to me, dropped the stick at my foot but I stepped over it, pretending not to see. A dog is an optimist – he will keep on trying. It took four rejections, four times that he watched me walk away, took the stick in his mouth and left the thing, once more, clear in my path. Head at forty-five degrees, ears stiff, tense in his efforts to communicate. Finally he let out a short surprising bark but when that didn't work, he understood. He left the stick, emptied of its magic, and took his place close by me, trotting evenly, his head and back and tail in a long low line. I talked to him, which brought his nose higher, and then he found a smell and was off, all forgiven.

We passed by the cafe on our route back home, but no one sat out at this hour. I wondered about the woman I had seen, if she had someone to go home to, unlike my mother. Unlike me.

'So few men in your life,' Chris once said, back when each other's pasts seemed meaningful. We might even have been in bed. He knew there was no father or brothers and assumed the rest, and was right, as it happened. I think he liked the idea that I was missing something that he could provide. Thing is, I never felt it as a lack.

There was another prospect for my mother, once, some time in my early teens. A neighbour died, making her husband available; my aunts brought the news in low serious voices broken up by the occasional whooped syllable that left me shocked, close to offended. He was nice, Archie Brown; my mum and he took a couple of walks and he joined us for a scrubbed and silent Sunday lunch, but in the end he chose a woman from his church. My mother sobbed bitterly when she heard; Fran only this time, Bet unsuited to that job.

'It's all his fault,' she shouted, and I knew she meant my father, for he had died in the pub – a heart attack, mind – and a rotten piece of luck, as he rarely drank but his father had, and mud stuck. She was good for no man after that. Our surname, Benson, carried my grandfather's disgrace and they were pleased for me when I threw it off.

'Kent, you'll be a Kent,' Bettie cried, when I told them of my engagement. 'The garden of England! Well how about that!'

She was prone to silliness and, as it turned out, of course, the name was only on loan.

I was tired by the time I got home and couldn't be bothered with dinner. Ate some cheese on toast with mustard and a splash of Worcestershire sauce. A couple of glasses of a decent Rioja. Switched the radio on low and got back into a book of good historical fiction. Thick socks and my toes as close to the fire as I could stand – mid-October by then, but still not cold enough to warrant it. Now and again the dog gave great big blows of satisfaction in his sleep, and I knew what he meant.

A good day; simple, solitary, absorbing. I remembered why I'd chosen my life, and reminded myself to keep hold of it.

19

Paul called, worried about Anja.

'She seems down, Mags, have you noticed?'

Peter had taken her to one of the Tates but she held her coat to her the whole way round and said nothing, except that she found it weird. He thought it might be the crowds, or the scale of the thing.

When I had asked, she said she'd had a great time.

They think she might be lonely. In need of friends her own age. Paul had mentioned it but she said: 'No way. I like to be alone. Or with you guys, of course.'

He sounded anxious on the phone. I could hear him moving through his house, the change in space as he passed from room to room. He told me that Anja and Peter had talked, when they were out; loosely, at an adjunct, but that he had learnt more about her life, what had happened. It was as horrible as you might imagine, but Peter would not repeat it; said it felt wrong, prurient even, to pass it on.

'I agree with him though, don't you?' Paul said, but his hurt sounded louder. 'Have you seen that bruise, on the inside of her arm? It looks like fingermarks.'

I hadn't but I told him she marks easily, as she had told me.

'Do the two of you. Go over those things?'

I said I didn't ask, or want to know. I thought about it though, when I got him off the phone, what it was that Anja and I discussed, and saw that it was mostly me and that maybe this was odd. I talked about the simpler times. Let her hide in that version of my life for a while.

'Tell me about your aunties, which was the one that did the cartwheels?' she would cry.

Bet, fifty-one when I last saw her and could still turn three in a row on the grass behind the promenade at Hove.

'You belong in the circus, you,' Mum would say, pulling me on, but Bettie caught up, hot and blowing; pinched my arm.

'Never wear a skirt, my love. That's my advice to you. It's skirts that held us back.'

I didn't reply – it was meant for Mum anyway.

'That's your advice, is it? The whole sum total of what you've learnt all your years on this earth?' She'd give a tut and shake her head, which was what Bet was after all along. And I loved a skirt, no one would get me out of skirts, with their shiver and their drama.

'That was Bettie,' I said to Anja. 'She was the youngest of the three. I think I told you that.'

Locked into position in that small powerful family. Her nerves a counterpoint to her jollity. The sort of woman who could have made a bad mistake.

'And there was Fran, too, wasn't there? She was your favourite. I know it!' Anja said.

She was right, of course, but there was less to tell about Fran. A tiny woman – I overtook her when I was twelve – a monkey of a person, strong and tanned and nimble, her arms covered in a downy fur that I inherited. She tried her best to moor us, to talk Mum down from her furies and Bettie, her fears. She was constant and level and sane, none of which makes for a story.

A woman seemingly without appetite, which could have put her apart from the others, but there was nothing in her to envy. I kept close and hoped some of her evenness would rub off; blunt my own sharp edge.

I tried, later that day, to speak to Anja, after I'd told her the one about Bet saving a tourist – a man! – by diving into the swell (she was a strong and fearless swimmer) and pulling him out while the lifeguard flirted. My childhood as seaside postcard.

We were busy as we talked; Anja bent down with a cloth, me cleaning the surfaces above. I preferred to help her now, as she worked.

'What about you, Anja?' I said. 'Tell me something about your growing up.'

She thought for a moment.

'What can I say? My mother and father worked hard. Everybody did. I am an only child. We lived in the country, near to a town. I played with my friends. There was a river. No aunties for me. I wanted a dog.'

She scrubbed the front of the cupboards hard, almost reckless in her action and I worried that she would knock herself, or rub off the paint. I stepped aside and she caught me with an elbow.

'Oh, sorry, Mags!'

She told me her age though I had read it in the paper.

'Don't forget that I am only nineteen. Not so much to tell yet.'

And then: 'I left all that behind. I am here now.'

'Yes. I suppose so. Was it? It must have been terrible for you. Over there.'

'It was not for long, Maggie. Six months. I got away.'

'But are there people where you are staying? People to help? For you to talk to, and so on?'

'It does not help. It's over and gone. Why would I want to talk?' she said.

'Of course.'

She looked down at her palm, picked at a callus at the root of a finger.

'Do you miss them? Your mother and father?' I asked.

'Not so much. We did not talk like you and me.'

She stood, with a click of her bad knee. She hugged like a child, her arms round my waist, her cheek flat to my front. She was short and I tall enough that this almost worked. Then she stepped back and sneezed, three giant sneezes, evenly spaced, that took her chin down to her chest each time. She shook her head, when she was done, like a dog, and looked up at me with glee.

'Phew. These sprays! They really get me!' and went back to work.

But she had a way of reading things.

My home is clean and blank. I do not gather and display. I am not defined by the things that surround me; that has been my choice. Yet Anja had an eye for the giveaway object.

Next day she came around to spend the afternoon; a new thing for us. It is noisy where she lives, and they watch stupid shows, she said. I was happy to oblige. We drank tea, where I would usually have wine, and the telly felt old-fashioned and communal and we talked at it, about it, in the place of other things. After a while, though, she became restless, trailing around the house, picking stuff up, as she would.

'I bet you love the ocean, Maggie. I see it all around in your home,' she said.

'What? What are you talking about?'

'Don't you notice it is all blues in here? The colours of the sky and sea.'

She had a tendency towards the romantic that was hard to read – naive or stupid, endearing or annoying, protection or escape; I wasn't sure. There were two blue rugs visible from where I stood, in the hall and the sitting room, and the curtains could be described as stormy, at a push.

'Hm. I suppose so,' I said.

'And all the boats of course.'

'What boats?'

My hands on hips. A frown. A touch of challenge.

'The pictures, see? There.'

She pointed at a couple of old Habitat prints, so shiny and thin that when I'd got them home, I wondered if I had just bought the frames; the images merely fillers. They were the closest to hand when I entered the part of the shop called Art, the first two in a deep stack propped against the wall. Still I'd chosen them above any other, I suppose. A touch of the Vettriano, I'd thought at the time.

'And the wooden sign on the string upstairs. That's so sweet.'

Some painted driftwood saying 'Bathroom' that Rosie had picked up. Anja played me now, with affection. Trusted me enough to tease. I acted my part.

'God. You can have that. Please. Take it off my hands.'

'And you have your shells by your bed, remember. Can you hear the sea in them?'

'Ahh, but they are from Cornwall actually. Years ago. A holiday. Not Brighton.'

'Brighton! Is that where you are from, Maggie? That's quite

close I think? I read about it in one of my guides. A train ride from here? Maybe we should go.'

'God, you're a right Lloyd Grossman, aren't you?' I said, and explained the concept of *Through the Keyhole*, which she liked.

'Come on. Are you hungry? I'll make you something to eat,' I said.

We went through to the kitchen and she watched me as I cooked.

When Anja had an idea, she kept hold of it, or rather she left it out in a prominent place for me to trip over. She gave it a day after that first mention and then announced the need for a change. Shall we go somewhere, Mags? Would I take her some place new? Of course I would. Great! She would think about where. Unless I had an idea?

I did not.

She wants to see the sea. What did I know of Hastings? A dump? OK.

A subdued morning followed.

Where else? she asked, next time. Somewhere fun. Not too far. Where was Blackpool? You're kidding! I said. Miles away. She took it well.

And finally: I've got an idea! Shrieked down from the landing. How about Brighton? The perfect place! (As if a sudden thought.)

I sighed. Let the girl have her way. OK, I told her. Why not? She knew enough of people, of me, to leave it there, to bank her win.

She left late, and at the front door said: 'Not at the weekend though, Mags. Much too busy. Let's go Monday.'

I nodded. It was arranged.

20

I met her at the station and we shopped for mags and pop, my treat. The gossipy ones that she liked, and the real-life stories too. Big bottles of Ribena and chewy sweets, renamed, but tasting the same. We waited just a minute for our train.

It felt like the holidays when we got on. There is something in the promise of a coastal town; they were right to call them pleasure beaches. Living there was different, of course, and the winters were long but you smelt it even as a child, when the weather changed, not knowing what it was but responding nonetheless, that whiff of licence that sent me baying through the house, an ordinarily placid girl, no matter how fast my mother slammed the windows shut against it.

It was here on the train, in October, even; the tourists brought it with them and I saw Anja's nose twitch. She looked up and around, unable to settle to the magazines or the years-old Maeve Binchy that lay age-blown on her lap.

She was different out of the house; watchful. She tracked a family across from us: a mother, father and two blonde daughters with pre-booked seats, their reservations rising stiff from the slots in their headrests. A lovely group who took their places calmly. The girls removed their scarves, which were laid in the rack above the windows, but kept on their coats, of a dark woollen blue. The adults read the papers and the sisters their novels about mice and ballerinas. In a while, they switched to colouring, a box each of pencils with their names stamped on in a square gold print. Martha and Alice – I strained in my seat to make it out. Halfway there and the mother produced two boxes of Tupperware and they all snacked on dried apricots and halved grapes. I willed the children to sulk or stamp but they didn't and I grew bored of them.

In front of us, theatre style, sat two young men. Loud, and of the visibly thuggish type. Morning beer, blunt vowels, a sudden way of talking. Bad dentistry. Anja followed them in the reflection of the window, attentive to their blasts of noise and unpredictable moves.

I closed my eyes, feeling weightless and mobile until the next chug or shunt spoilt things, and went back to my last summer by the sea. Nineteen. Same age as Anja. Sat on a bench in Steine Gardens, my toes dug deep into the grass, listening to a man tell me why I should go with him to his hotel that night. That he'd come all this way, straight after work, what did I say? I needled him for the unintentional rhyme but he was a good-natured boy and hadn't pressed me.

We had met two weeks before when he was day-tripping with friends and they strayed off the tourist path, found themselves in Kemp Town. He watched me dive again and again off the east side of Banjo Groyne, bare-faced in a one piece, a careful picture of unselfconsciousness. Impressive to the onlooker but easy if you knew when and where, though Mum told a story of a girl twenty years before who had missed the tides and never walked again.

We saw them arrive, three of them, three of us, and sniggered as they hobbled, shoes in hand, across the scalding pebbles and set themselves down close enough to send a message. Our feet were tough and smooth and we could cross the beach as we pleased and did so needlessly as they sat stranded on their towels. My one, Tom (his name appeared suddenly, spat out of some recess of my brain), plucked up the guts to speak.

'Where's the best fish and chips around here?' he said, looking straight at me. 'You girls look like you know your way around.'

We showed them how to dive and, later, lay on the beach where the electric railway ran overhead and threw stones at the wheels of the trains. The best sort of hit made a spark and a crack and the stone ping away so you hid your face and pulled in close to your boy to make him think there was something you were scared of. We messed around under there for a while and said goodbye. Tom was the only one who wanted to meet again, which made me feel proud but bad for my friends, though they didn't take it hard. A fresh trainload arrived each week.

I liked him less just the two of us, a fortnight on. The tone had changed, less cheek, more of what you might call courting. He had a habit of rubbing one side of his face, jaw pulled away from his hand, which made me think he was new to shaving though he said he was twenty-four.

I had no intention of going to his room but could find no way of telling him, so said I ought at least to call home first. Then I sat in the lounge with my mum and Aunty Fran and made my gin and orange last because getting a second depended on Mum's mood or my behaviour or rather her perception of my behaviour at the moment she came to make the two of them another. The time we were to meet came and went and I felt a sherbety mix of thrill and dread; power, really, I suppose. The door went and I jumped, but it was only Bet, having done her bit, fed her men and come over to us for her weekend. Mum saw it and recognised something of my state.

'Expecting someone, Margaret?' she asked and they looked at me, the three of them, slit-eyed.

A female household meant a girl without protection, so my mother made a point of vigilance. Not that she objected to boys per se, she just didn't want to see me spoil myself on the wrong sort of boy. In bed that night I felt guilty and tearful but when I told the girls next morning we howled until our knees went, though we avoided Banjo's for a while, just to be safe.

I started, and wondered if I had slept for a second and snored.

'Look. We're nearly there,' Anja said, and she was right.

We came into Brighton backwards. It spread up the hills in the minute before we stopped, white terraces broken up by the odd block of colour, pink, lilac and green. It looked like fun.

The station remained beautiful; lofty and Victorian but smaller too, as things often are when you come back to them and are used, as I am now, to the capital.

I showed her the roof, curved glass and iron, but she knew of it already and told me, instead, about the recent renovation that she'd read about in her guidebook.

We were still looking up when it began to rain. Instantly the noise became too much, a frantic drumming, each raindrop amplified. It set the seagulls looping, huge and clawed, fat on dumped chips, and she panicked, just as I had as a child when I first heard this sound. She grabbed my arm and we ran together through the echoing space. My god, when had I last run? My body announced itself, lungs and muscles and heartbeat. Her cry was a high short screech that took off up to the ceiling with the caws of the gulls.

We stepped out onto the pavement breathing hard and I recoiled in instinct against the smell of piss and perm solution, but it was not there; instead, a rising wet metal, which settled in the back of my mouth. I pulled her across to Divalls, where we used to sit and wait for our rare visitors from London.

It might have been the dash, but I felt a fluttery sort of euphoria. I bought two sweet teas and began to jabber, about how, in my day, the teaspoons had been attached to the counter by chain. The rain steamed us in, as it had done that first time in Queen's Park. She said as much, at the moment that I thought it, which turned my mind to lovers, and perhaps hers too.

We warmed our hands on our mugs, ate two heavy buns and it was time to go. The pier, I'd thought, but it was too wet now. We sat next to the window and I wiped myself a spy-hole. People rushed and dripped outside, and for a moment it could have been London, but the door went and the flat grey gloom of a wet seaside town slipped in. It settled on me and I wondered briefly what it was that I was doing here, in Brighton, with a pregnant teen on a soaking day.

'OK, we need a plan,' I said.

'Take me to where you grew up!' she cried, still buoyed along on our earlier mood.

'God, no,' I said, and heard it come out harsh.

What a suggestion. What a thing to say. I felt an affront, almost a hurt. I had a sudden sense of the house's proximity. I wondered if the front door was still blue, if someone had squared off the hedge, and if the new people stood out the front in hard-soled slippers poisoning any green that dared push itself up between the paving.

'Why not?' she asked and her face showed clearly that this had been her idea all along.

I thought of sitting here, at this same spot with my mum, aged sixteen, waiting for James, the son of an old friend of hers who had moved up and out. He was considering the university, she told me, taking the syllables carefully, and we were to put him up for the night. She slid her hands off the table.

'Do. Not. Show. Me. Up.' Marked out on my kneecap.

She laid them back before her and tapped a tune on the plastic cloth, aware of her nails, reddened to match her lips. They didn't suit her and when she was still, I could see the rim of her thumbnail, coarse and thickened, beneath the paint.

'Or where Frannie used to live. Or Aunty Bet,' Anja said, in a fond sort of tone. Favourite characters from a much loved tale.

'It's just. I don't. I don't want to do that,' I said.

I realised my mistake; the inevitability of her request. But I could not accede to it. The day assumed its real aspect. I felt the malice of the place all around.

She looked past me at nothing.

'It was a long time ago,' I said. 'They are not there any more.'

'So where is the harm?' she asked, and we lapsed into a thick silence.

'Have you got the guide?' I said, in a bit, and she reached into her rucksack and pulled out an exercise book in vertical stripes of cherry and pink.

'Oh.' She went back to her bag.

The *Time Out*, when she found it, had slippy pages, too much detail and illegible print. I couldn't see it helping but flicked back and forth in the absence of a better idea.

'There,' said Anja. Her finger moved fast, pinning open a page.

'The Pavilion?' I said.

'One of your princes lived there.'

'That's right. We can go if you like.'

She nodded and I was pleased once again to have pleased her.

Outside the rain had stopped and the air was zippy.

'Wait for me!' she said, and I did.

We started down the hill, like a thousand times before. It was the most direct way, but the coldest too, and the most populated, so I turned into North Laine. We zigzagged round the back of the houses and she exclaimed at the graffiti and the general bohemia of the place. No one I'd ever known had lived here, but still I wrapped my scarf up over my mouth, just in case. I put my arm through hers which I knew she liked and pulled her left and right until we got to the Pavilion.

We arrived, and I remembered straight away how much I loathed to sightsee. Nothing happens when I stand in an old building, my imagination fails, and I have always struggled to grant this place respect. But Anja was queuing for handsets, her hands wedged uncomfortably into her jeans pockets in a search for coins. I paid for two.

We lumbered stupidly, focused on the recorded voice. The palace looked cheap, gaudy and imitative, but the narrative had been refreshed and was domestic and gossipy. The experience had changed since my schoolgirl days. The classroom feel of the guided tour, with its back-row opportunities, long gone. What once was shared was now solitary.

I pressed pause, and looked instead at Anja, rapt and oblivious; there was more pleasure in that. Then we were done, another tea discounted and we stood back outside in the cold. She looked at her watch.

'Maggie, come this way. For the best bit. I don't know if you know.'

We turned the corner of the palace, and round the back, on the north side, we found the most beautiful ice-rink. It was huge, sat in purple alien light and smelt of frozen air and spiced wine. I was surprised, I'll give her that, and this feeling caught a touch in my throat.

'Do you want a go?' she said.

'Heavens, no. Don't be ridiculous.'

'OK. You can watch.'

The bar was long and temporary, a posh marquee theatrically lit in yellows and reds, chinoiserie borrowed from the palace.

I bought a drink and took a spot close to the edge.

Anja appeared, walking on her toes across the matting. She reached the ice and pushed off, quite hard, stiff-legged and top half lurching. She travelled for a bit, her feet parallel and static and then began to slow painfully. She came to a halt and I thought she might be stranded but she bent at the waist and baby-stepped to the side. She looked for me, and gave a wave involving her shoulders. I raised my hand and she started again.

I went up for more wine. I had to admire Anja's tenacity. Her approach seemed pretty sensible. For a while she pulled herself round the edge, with a focus on her legs, pushing out on the right foot, letting the left catch up and swapping, suspended and risky. It didn't take long for her to get it. Then she brought the top half in and for a while seemed to regress, the swinging of her arms over-emphasised and fitful. The trick seemed to lie with the core. When she stood up, back straight, she found her stride. A matter of minutes, and she was almost elegant.

'She's good, isn't she!' said a woman stood close by, and I blushed for the first time in years, whether in pleasure or having been caught at something, I didn't know. My face felt so livid that I raised a hand to it and sure enough its heat passed into my palm. I left it there.

'Is she your daughter?' the woman said.

'Oh no!' I replied. 'Just a friend.'

'Oh.' A wrinkle of discomfort above her eye and then she wasn't alone any more. She started to busy herself, make ready for someone's approach. The pointless rearranging of chairs and dirty china that some women do.

I looked, curiosity, nothing more and saw a man approaching; just a man, until I paid a bit more attention and saw that he was wearing my face. The same colour eyes, well-washed cotton blue, spaced just too close; the same pinch at the top of the nose, affirmed in my case by years of wearing glasses; my skin tone – sallow and thickish in texture.

But it was more the overall effect of him. The skew of his shoulders, the hang of his arms, the suggestion of chippiness. He headed straight for his wife, holding out two drinks. Bill or Charlie, it had to be. One of my cousins, Bet's sons. Why not? He looked about the right age. Charlie, I'd say. The younger of the two.

Behind him came two girls in their late teens, my mother's grand-nieces, then, though the sight of them would have seen her tightening, handbag to her chest, eyes markedly elsewhere. They were pierced, through eyebrow and nose respectively. The first had her hair shaved to the skin on one side though the top was long and well tended. Both had that pillowy slab of middle showing all the way round. Nice kids; relaxed, out with their parents. And as I watched, one of the girls took an arm across her chest and held a shoulder, a gesture I had seen so many times on Fran, to hide herself, but also to soothe; I had borrowed the habit myself, for a time. At that Charlie must have felt my gaze, perhaps as threat, for he looked at me as surely as if I had called his name. He knew me straight away and started visibly and in that breath I felt it too, the jeopardy in our encounter.

I turned back to the ice. I found Anja just as she fell; hugely, dramatically. Her legs scissored, one kicked up so hard and high that it pulled the other off the ice. She came down neatly, on the base of her spine. Elegant almost, ruler drawn. There was a jolt the length of her and then she lost her neatness and crumpled.

A memory started. Me all of ten, pushing Charlie in his buggy. Stopping far too often to walk round and check him, fussing with his blankets, looking down into his empty face, dying for someone to see us. And there was Anja, and her fall, and the two conflated and I thought of the baby; of Anja's baby.

I was up, floored my chair and staggered, splay-footed, across the rink. I reached her and she was smiling, propped on her elbows as if she lay in bed.

'Did you see that? Ouch! I'm gonna have bruises tomorrow!' she said.

I took her arm and pulled it, and she slid a little on her bottom and gave a silly giggle.

'Come on, Anja. For heaven's sake. Get up. Don't get cold. What about the baby?'

'Oh, I think it's OK. At this early time. I'm not hurt,' she said.

'Are you sure? It's not a good idea this. Come on now.'

Her hands travelled to her belly and she stopped smiling. She twisted her legs to the side and tried to push up.

'Do you think?'

'Just get up, Anja. Get off the ice,' I said.

I bent and took an elbow and one hand, gentler now, though I didn't feel it. I pulled her, and felt an answering tug at the base of my neck. She'd lost all knack for it. Together we lurched to the side.

I glanced up to see Charlie gaping openly through the plastic of the marquee, hands flat against it, and his wife too. I tried to put my expression back in order, drop the anger out of it, and the shock. He looked slack-faced and stupid; unevolved. There was a quickness in my mother and her sisters, my best inheritance, but he was dull. Anja watched her feet and said nothing. She was sobbing by the time she grabbed the barrier, great fat tears that fell straight down on to her arms, my fingers, the ice.

'Do you think I have hurt the baby? Oh my god. I did not think.'

She was on the verge of panic and I was terrified she would fall again.

'Silly girl. Calm down. Hold on,' I said, and knelt to her foot.

The lace was stiff; tubed and waxed and double-bowed, and each time I tried to work at the knot, a flake of my nail chipped off. Finally it was undone and I loosened the criss-cross the length of her boot and took the heel. She sat, face elsewhere, vague and compliant.

'Help me out here, can't you?' I said, the knees of my jeans soaked and a horrible stretch across the shoulders of my coat.

She wiggled and kicked and, between us, we pulled her foot free. It felt warm and damp and heavy in my hand. The carpet around us was drenched.

'Come on,' I said. 'Don't stand here. You can hop across to a dry bit. We'll get there.'

She put her arm across my shoulders and I slipped my own around her middle, for balance. She wore an anorak and a bobbly woollen jumper but her waist beneath felt thick, arced, muscled. A couple of clumsy steps and we made it to a seat.

'Thanks, Maggie,' she whispered, very close. Her breath felt warm in my ear and I smelt the mint of her gum; crunchy pellets that she chewed one after another until the whole pack was gone. She let me go, easing her toes carefully onto the ground.

We travelled back apart, abashed, and said our goodbyes at the station.

Back home, and the skin on my face felt raw, stripped by that wind I'd forgotten, racing up off the sea. I found some cream in the back of a cupboard, took the crust off with a tissue and rubbed it into my cheeks.

I made a hot whisky with half a lemon squeezed in and a cord of honey dissolving at the bottom. A couple of pips floated on the surface and I breathed above it while it was still too hot to drink. I felt the steam kick in the back of my throat.

I went, we went to Brighton. Simple, irrefutable, though from home, clear-eyed, the fact of it astounded me. An outing, an adventure, a day outside the norm. She wanted to go. I wanted to make her happy. For a time, it had seemed that simple.

I pinched the web of empty skin between my finger and

thumb. I could no longer trust myself, and I was all I had. How could I have passed outside the orbit of my own safe space and sensed no warning, no presage of danger? I felt bewitched.

And yet. And yet. There was no one for Charlie to tell. No one who cared that I came back, asked why, or who I was with.

Still I could not help but wonder what he knew, what he had been told, way back when. It must have had some punch; that much showed on his face. Someone leaves. They never come back. This takes explaining. Unless, of course, you are a family inured to your own disgrace, fleet and reactive. All that is required, in that case, is to look away. Leave things be. Nothing could be easier. A lie is only hard to sustain if it is bothered. My people have long known not to pry.

My drink had heated me and, in a while, I felt numbed. The television began to grate and for a moment I thought that the picture and sound had slipped out of synch, but when I switched it off and on again, things remained the same. So I lowered the volume, and watched the phone instead.

Later, I thought I felt a change in the air, a tautening, like the pull on the string of an instrument, and imagined that it was sound racing towards me in great throbbing waves. I held my breath and waited, but there was only silence.

21

Anja changed things. I could not be alone in the same way. I missed her when she wasn't there – that was the truth – and I was coming to be used to, to depend upon, companionship once more. It was wet outside, she was not due for hours, it all felt dull.

It took me back to an older time, this restlessness, this constant motion. To Purley, where I lived with Chris, a funny place, near Croydon and desirable, I think, when we arrived. Road upon road of housing – villas, they called them – even the vet's was in a house, and the cottage hospital where I gave birth.

The first home I'd owned (joint), the first proper house I'd lived in (a roomy semi-detached), and everything chosen by me, from scratch, on a very fair budget. Yet it never felt other than impossibly strange. I didn't know how to live in it and spent my days travelling room to room; indoor miles marked out by the holes my heels left in the carpet, hoovered up before Chris got back.

It wasn't the baby. Looking at her scorched me. She made me feel strong and brave, her and those speedy diet pills that I was taking – everybody was. It was just that the suburbs didn't suit. Its bosomy embrace made me want to bite. Blame my mother. You can't have it both ways.

I lost the knack of female friendship about that time. The

114

other women found me brittle, I found them dumb, their conversation narrow. Subsumed by motherhood but so unsure. I didn't need to talk about my baby, I knew it all on instinct. I touched her and she burst my heart.

Chris didn't mind, he liked that I was apart, of finer stuff. I didn't care much for housework so we were the first in our set to get help. Our set? Mostly airline – close to Gatwick – and couples on the up, transplanted from London, busy bringing their vowels into line and hiding unsuitable relatives. I didn't cook, but Chris didn't really eat. The funny hours he kept, and a dread of getting fat. We lived on biscuits and cheese.

It got dark though at one stage, I can't deny it, and it was Chris who saw and pulled me out; one swift hard yank.

'Are you not happy?' he asked, from the upright chair he favoured. 'You seem to be drinking a lot. And this. I mean, what is all that?'

He had paused from his crossword and with an up and down swipe of his pen, drew attention to a pile of magazines stacked beside me as I lay on the settee. The weeklies that my mum sent when she'd finished with them, plus old swollen novels picked up from car-boot sales, all wrapped in used brown paper that she ironed flat under scraps of worn-out sheet. Women's stories; pulpy tales of sacrifice, graft and redemption, that I lived in as I read, and forgot completely when I was done. I dropped them off at Oxfam in batches, and the great shelf of bust on the woman behind the counter, dressed in discontinued shades, somehow made me sad. She showed me I was lonely.

'Can you at least sit, Maggie, when I'm talking to you?' he said, but I looked straight ahead at my toenails, signature red, propped up on the sofa's arm and then at the cobbled ceiling above me. I stretched my hand high and imagined my arm lengthening up and up and the blistered feel of the paper beneath my fingertips; popping each bump like bubble wrap. He got the doctor in, and different pills. Told me when it was time to stop and suggested a host of new interests. Bridge, which I almost liked, a cooking course – abandoned, exercise of various sorts. Even drawing. He was shockingly middle class.

It was the piano that stuck. The first one that I ever touched was in the hall of his parents' house. We stayed there the Christmas I was pregnant and on the night of Christmas Eve I left the stifling sitting room and sat at it, the keys cold and textureless, almost liquid beneath my fingers. I didn't dare make a sound, pressed just enough to feel the first spongy give. Michael came out, his brother: 'Do you play?' he asked.

'What do you think?'

'Nor me. God, my mother's a bitch.'

She had been asking about his work, his weight, his drinking.

'Don't say a thing. You know the Chinese believe that if a pregnant woman speaks ill of someone, her child will look like that person?'

'Oh god. All right. Not a word.'

Michael had a Chinese wife so beautiful and kind that even I wondered what we'd missed. It infuriated the family, that piece of luck; a violation of the way things should be. She left him later, and everyone relaxed. Chris came out, said: 'Great idea!' and played a piece straight through from memory.

And Chris remembered it, the following year, when I was ill. That moment of interest. We hired a piano first, to try, and when I liked it, his mother gave us hers – huge, polished, barely movable.

It was delivered to our house in a van. A good twenty minutes with the back open, the instrument shrouded and the men sitting on the pavement, drinking tea with Chris and deciding how to get it in. He was good with trade, neither spoke down nor lowered himself. Entirely comfortable in his privilege. They set up ramps of planks brought along for the task and off it came, still draped in cotton, though anyone could see it for what it was.

Me cringing in the hall, full of shame.

Halfway up the steps and the sheet caught on a nail knocked into the front door to hold a wreath. The piano was exposed with a flourish. I have to admit, it looked like show. I panicked and slammed the door, which can't have helped.

The three men carried it, gingerly, into the hall. Back and forwards, a final tip and with a run of notes, it was settled in the lounge, which it filled, people forever stepping round it.

And from that day, anyone who missed its arrival could view the instrument from the pavement. I wasn't much liked by that point and the piano, I think, was the final straw. People took it personally. I had to buy nets in the end.

I tried to teach myself from books, at first, but it was Chris, again, who found someone. Ben, even younger than me, a music teacher from a nearby school for boys. The first creative person I'd ever met. I looked away, at first, when he played, embarrassed by his emotion.

He told me I had a pianist's hands, which was true, though I knew the compliment as fingers fit for diamonds.

Twice a week he came, when school was done, in teacher's clothes, grey trousers and a white shirt, his jacket on the back of his chair and his tie stuffed into his bag. The baby at my feet in her basket. Hours used, and I like to think it made my daughter musical.

I wondered, should I buy a piano? For something to do? There was more of me again, and that can be exhausting.

Still a while until Anja was due and I decided to walk it off. Struck a brisk pace, despite the rain which fell hard and slanted. It seemed to subside and I lifted my face, breathing in long and deep. An eddy of swollen raindrops drenched me. I shook my head and moisture seeped beneath my collar. It did not help; I got home angry.

There she was, waiting; pathetic in the wet. Crammed into the porch, behind thick ropes of water where the guttering had gone.

'Oh god, I'm sorry. How long have you been here?' I asked.

'Twenty minutes. It's OK!'

Her nose, her hair, her eyelashes dripped. She seemed to think it funny.

'Did we change the time? Sorry, I totally lost track.'

I stepped up next to her, a twist of cold rain finding its way straight down my front. I tried to unzip a breast pocket for the key and elbowed her as I did. It was like standing behind a waterfall. The rain on the stone banged and clattered, a harsh metallic sound, and the air was full of an ozone smell of burnt-out electrics.

We got in and she steamed like a horse.

'Where's your coat?' I asked, but she didn't reply.

I could read 'Don't worry, be happy!' on the top beneath her sodden anorak, and when she took off her shoes – canvas trainers, in this weather – her socks showed damp at the toes and heels.

'Give it all here,' I said and she cackled as she did it. 'I'll put them in the airing cupboard. Come upstairs.'

I chucked her stuff in the bath and took her through to the spare room. It smelt of baked air and new carpet.

'Let's see if there's something under here that's any good,' I said.

I knelt by the bed and lifted the valance, disturbing dusty strings of lint and desiccated insects. I reached for a handle, blind, and yanked out the huge shallow rectangle of rough white plastic.

'Some of Rose's old things. I thought they might be useful,' I said.

I pulled the zip three sides of the bag and flipped back the lid.

'Go ahead. Take what you want,' I said.

'Thanks, Mags, that's really kind.'

She waited until I stood, and riffled through, fast and expert.

'It's nothing,' I said. 'Hold on. Wait there a sec.'

I took the steps to the office. She had been in, cleaning; had left a spray on the desk. I opened the top drawer.

Two sets of keys lived there, in small square envelopes of the sort that used to carry payslips. Always on the top, alongside my passport and the paperwork ordered in ascending size. Not that time.

I dug around repeatedly then lifted the whole lot out. The envelopes slipped easily to the floor from somewhere within the pile, and I felt a relief at things being where they should.

'Here you go,' I said, when I got back to her. 'These are for you. Now you can come and go as you please.'

'Oh, if you don't mind. That's great! I'll make sure I don't lose them!' she said.

She stood for another of her hugs. Too tight, this time; I felt her breasts pushed hard against me through her flimsy top. It almost hurt and I wanted to push her away but didn't dare. I was limp in her arms until she let me go.

She left the room with a black roll-neck I'd never seen. The rest of the clothes were shoved back roughly, the last inches of zip gaping open, bulging insides. The radio downstairs went on, over, and up. Her own tuneless song began.

I took everything out and started again. When it was all done nicely, I went down for the Hoover. If you suck out the air before you seal, you can preserve the things inside for ever.

22

Maureen's party, later, and the need to be there by midday gave the morning an edge, though I know how bad that sounds.

I stood at my wardrobe.

It had been a long time since I dressed up and I wondered if I could reconnect with that pleasure. I used to love, adore clothes, even as a child, forever trying things on, folding, re-arranging. Vanity, yes, but also in appreciation of their power. The perfect outfit can make things happen, of that I have no doubt.

My colours are blues, greys and black. Red, here and there – a mute red, mind. Pink – the darker end – though I might be too old for that now. Yellow in the summer but nothing approaching mustard. I know this; any woman with a sense of herself understands what suits her.

One of my last (and favourite) memories of my marriage is a Colour Me Beautiful party in Jan of Jan and Ian's front room. The worst-dressed woman I ever saw sat next to a gin and Dubonnet, cheese straws criss-crossed on a napkin, say-ing things like 'unique colouring', 'personal palettes' and 'wow factor'. When Jan came to find me in the kitchen later (a drop in volume next door warned me of her approach), drinking my gin (neat, by the fridge, like it might save me), I said, 'Just fuck off, Jan, why don't you?', which she did, and called Chris, who came and drove me home in silence. Not eloquent or clever, but it did the job and was magnificent in the response that it drew, a sort of retraction of the skin all over her face. She would probably pay for it nowadays.

'It's quite all right, Maggie, just a surprise, that's all. I don't think I've ever been sworn at before,' she told me, next day, when I went round to say sorry.

'Well, it won't happen again,' I said.

'No, it won't. First times don't. No harm done.'

If you squinted, the wardrobe into which I looked could have been mine from any one of the past four decades. Closer though, and that illusion receded. It was the smell, most of all. Damp and dust – essence of underuse. It would have to be jeans, that went without saying. The question hung over the top.

I thought of a blouse; new, or rather never worn. A burnt sunset with a shallow boat neck and a beautiful drape that I bought tipsy after a Christmas lunch with Nancy as 'most accurate transcriptionist of the year', straight out of the window of a shop in South Molton Street. I couldn't see it on the rail and thought maybe I'd left it on the train.

I sped through the hangers, setting them swinging with their anxious clatter, until something slipped to the floor and when I went to pick it up, found my top, puddled at the back. I shook it out and brought it close. It exhaled sun and peach and freesia over a darker blend of chocolate, vanilla, plum. Cheap and blunt, fingerprint distinct. It could only be Anja.

I held the blouse before me. It must have been too small for her, her back was broad and her shoulders muscled. At the armpits I saw a pinching, a splay of wrinkles pleating the thick silk. I turned it inside-out and where the sleeves were stitched

122

to the body, the seams wore a dusting of old deodorant.

I dropped it; I felt disgust. I put my head into the wardrobe and breathed in deep, the tickle of my garments on my cheek. Only that one then, it seemed, though I paused at a few.

I took a shower, and stepped out vulnerable, into altered space.

I pulled out drawers, I searched for clues. Clumsy in my towel.

I stood before the mirror and saw the ghost of her in my glass. I knew the way she looked at herself, pivoting slowly, one side and the next. Focused, unashamed.

'Checking for your best side?' I said once, from the sofa, embarrassed to bear witness. Forced to speak.

'Of course,' she said. 'Everybody has one.'

I'd seen her trying on faces, dreaming of an audience I couldn't imagine. I had thought, do I recognise her? Do I know this girl at all?

I crept through my home, feeling for her presence. In the bathroom, a green-ringed cup from one of her teas. A matted hairband on the floor, another by the fridge. The carpet on the stair darkened by her heavy tread.

She was all over, of course, and with my permission. At my request. I paid her to get into corners, root things out, spot stains. She was comfortable in the places that no one else would go, not even Rose, when she had been around; my flesh, my blood.

The bathroom cabinet with the pills I no longer swallowed, the drawer that housed my underwear.

'I can help with that!' Anja offered, one day, as I pulled clothes from the machine.

'I've started,' I said. 'Don't you worry.'

But another afternoon, when I got in, the drum had been emptied. I thought of telling her no, but heard the slight in it.

Maybe I'd issued an invitation outside my knowledge. I had long forgotten the rules of proximity, and it is different, of course, for the young. It is always hard to share, I told myself, and I am out of practice. These things take time. The blouse would wash.

I found a discarded make-up bag and plundered its contents. I tweezered my eyebrows and moisturised my face. One upward comb of mascara and a blink on a tissue. Vaseline on my lips and, on a whim, across my brows. I wiped that off. Chose a collarless shirt in grey, just heavier than sheer.

I glanced once more in the mirror in the hall, and saw myself, a blue-eyed brunette on her way to a lunch. Buster noticed the change and padded nervously. I took a bottle from the rack and the chocolates Anja brought that very first time.

My coat, a smarter one from the wardrobe, had one pocket pulled out when I came to put it on. Unusual, for me, that haste, that lack of care, but not unheard of. Perhaps the work of the dog, in search of some reward.

23

I pushed open the gate and saw Peter and Paul in the window. They stood hinged, as usual, but too fixed to be comfortable. I rang the button doorbell with its harsh old-fashioned buzz, and Mo was there before I'd dropped my arm.

'Hi, Mags. Come in. Thanks for coming. Lovely. I'll take those.'

A new Maureen, in hostess mode. She had made an effort, in bootcut trousers of an unkind fit. The stretch across her bottom had thinned the material to expose a webbing of white elastic. From a distance the effect was of one long panel of shine. Her top I'd call tomato, with a prominent batwing sleeve. Fat pearls in her ears, too big to be real, and a broad-heeled black-patent court. She looked overheated, poor thing.

I followed her into the sitting room wondering what I'd learn of my friends that day. She had too much furniture, Mo, but had pushed it all to the side to leave a vacancy in the middle that no one wanted to fill.

'I thought I'd ask Anja,' she said, as we came into view of her guests. 'Well, I got the boys to,' she added, and pointed.

She sat, in her slippers, at one end of the sofa, her hands folded on her lap like someone's foreign exchange student. Her eyes rolled dumbly from face to face, content, but absent. Nothing of the girl I'd just imagined, thumbing through my things either in insolence or intimacy. She noticed me and crossed the carpet – Chinese, cream, an inch or more thick. She kissed me, three kisses, right, left and right. Always that way, with Anja; she had told me so when I mentioned once how hard it was to keep track of people's greetings these days.

'Hey, Maggie. How are you? You look nice!'

Like me, she had dressed up, in a pink hooded top with something written across it in silver, too abstract for me to read, and a generous slick of glittered lip balm. The effect was one of youth, and playfulness. No artifice in it. My idea of her earlier was baffling.

I thought she was about to speak but then Paul was there, and so I went to him, two kisses – that was Paul – and on to Peter, who waited at a distance, amused at the jumble of welcomes and my confusion. There was a squeeze at the end of his hug which reminded me how much I liked this man. Anja tucked herself back into her corner of sofa. Lauren sat at the other end, gripping hard on its arm. Someone put a glass in my hand and I took a long, welcome drink.

'Hello, Maggie. Long time no see.'

Lauren peered up at me with an appraising look and no intention of moving.

'Oh, hello down there, Lauren. I didn't notice you. How are things?'

'Oh well. You know,' she said.

She dropped her eyes, raised her brows and thinned her lips as if it were all my fault.

How funny, I thought, such a sharp little shaving of Maureen – the bit that sniffed and judged – but none of her generosity. Mo had mellowed across time, a lifetime in the city kept her adapting, but Lauren lived in a small gated estate in Caterham and her views had narrowed and set. She wouldn't change now, unless something huge happened. I'd met her before and thought her a pain, but never seen this hard edge of challenge.

She wasn't speaking, but held the focus of the room with her distaste. Maureen watched from the doorway and Paul looked around aimlessly. Something by the Carpenters started in the kitchen, the radio up loud to establish the notion of fun. Maureen glanced back to it, embarrassed by this exposure of her efforts. So I sat between the two women, felt the brief touch of Anja's leg against mine.

'Oh dear, Lauren. Been a bit tough going for you lately, has it?'

'So Mum's told you. Well, yeah. It has, to be honest,' she said.

She began to talk, and our party jerked back into action.

Maureen came to me with the bottle, out of thanks.

It was the usual stuff a woman complains of in a man. She talked in great loops that left no space for comment, pausing only to snatch a glance at Peter, angered by him in some way; his self-sufficiency perhaps. He sat alone propped on the windowsill and drank his wine with consideration and an easy look.

Paul was crouched before Anja, speaking about London; places she should go, what not to miss. She keyed it all into her phone.

Anja was different with a man, I saw that straight away. She had moved to the ledge of her seat, straight-backed and attentive. Her voice was loud, she was more assured. It had nothing to do with flirtation.

I moved deeper into my chair with some comment about my back; all the better to watch them. Still Lauren spoke, angled over her knees.

Paul was talking about farmers' markets, air miles, ethical

eating. Anja liked Nando's, Coca-Cola, food that was a brand. One time a fox got the rubbish and I found a pair of grease-proof pockets among the mess strewn the length of the lawn. I was puzzled, as I picked them up, followed the trail around the back of the shed and I found a ripped-up box, a Happy Meal. After that I often noticed the spatter of ketchup through the skin of a bin liner, or came across a pod the dog had hidden and licked clean. She made no move to hide this habit, though nor did she eat in front of me. Perhaps she thought I would not have approved.

She listened hard as Paul spoke. Her eyes roved his face. Her response was perfect although she cannot have cared about his argument; I wasn't sure she even understood. His certainty sounded childish and irrelevant; an insult, almost, and I wanted to shut him up, stop him making a fool of all of us. But there was also his satisfaction, his pleasure at being heard, and her face pin-bright, reflecting his conviction back at him. I caught her look for an instant, and thought she saw me see all this, but I couldn't be sure. She laid a gentle hand on my thigh. She could be anyone, this girl.

Mo came back with a 'Bugger! Oh sorry!' as she tripped over a child I hadn't noticed. A neat stream of nibbles slid to the floor. There were two of them, a boy and a girl, lying on their stomachs wearing earphones the size of buns, watching a single thin screen that they had propped against the wall. The child – the boy, Jack – curled up his leg and held it where Maureen had kicked him and then pushed off with the other foot to lunge for a sausage roll. The girl saw and grabbed for one too.

'Get off, the pair of you, they're for the grown-ups,' their mother said, and shook a foot at them, but they couldn't hear, merely looked at us with big round eyes and went back to their screen.

'Don't worry, loves, there's plenty for everyone. My famous home-made sausage rolls!' said Maureen, trying to pick them up off the carpet, clumsy in oven gloves.

'D'you want another one, Jack?'

She spoke loudly and waved a clubbed mitt at him, scattering pastry.

'Oh well,' she said, and left a pile of food before each child. Maureen's dog Sammy was up from her bed at that, seeking her chance.

'I wish I'd thought it through. He was always a bit of a bastard, to be honest. And now they're stuck with a crap dad,' Lauren was saying.

She paused, which was probably my chance to speak. She followed my gaze to her children.

'Oh, don't worry about them. They can't hear a thing. I wouldn't slag him off in front of the kids.'

She folded her arms, insulted.

'Mum?' – called in the direction of the kitchen.

'Where's she gone?' – muttered to herself.

'Can I have another drink?' – the drone of a child.

Lauren pressed a hand into the seat and was off, wandering listlessly after her mother. I shuffled across towards Anja.

'Mind if I join you?' I said.

Paul gave a wide-eyed look after Lauren and I said, 'Don't!' and Anja said, 'What?'

'Well, it's nice to see you out of the house, Mags, anyway,' said Paul.

'It's nice to be out,' I replied, unsure if that was true.

'And Peter's feeling much better as well, aren't you?' he said. It was their decision not to hide things.

'I am.'

'God, you're a regular district nurse,' I said.

Their happiness brought out the curmudgeon in me. It always had, it was the shape of our friendship. Well rehearsed and good-natured. Anja grinned on, not following, or hiding it.

'Christ, it's hot in here.' Paul flapped the collar of his shirt and blew out his bottom lip. I touched a radiator, up full whack for the guests.

'Peter, would you open the window?' he said.

He unscrewed the lock and shoved up the sash, exposing a long inch of air. The cold snaked in.

'I'm gonna get more wine.'

Paul came back with a bottle of red and poured Peter and me huge glasses.

'Anja, what about you? Where's yours?' he asked.

'Oh. I.'

She looked round her.

'Don't worry. I'll find you another. It's red for you too, isn't it?' he said.

'Actually, no thanks. It's OK. I'll.'

She reached back for a tumbler, empty but for one hump of ice.

'Get something for myself from the kitchen.'

'Oh sorry. You not drinking? I don't know why I thought –'

He looked round for Peter with a question on his face.

'Are you driving? Oh no. I suppose not. God. I'll shut up now.'

He picked up her glass and sniffed it.

'Apple juice? I'll fetch another.'

He walked away, and I could see colour spreading round the back of his neck.

She gave me a dart of a glance.

From the kitchen I heard Lauren say: 'Not too much of that. I bought it for the kids.'

Peter asked after the dog. He'd had a Lab when he was younger; it was Paul who chose the terriers. Anja clawed through her bag. From the other end of the room Maureen called: 'Righto. Shall we eat? I'm just going to put it all down on the table and you can help yourselves.'

A huge vat of chilli with Maureen behind it like everybody's mother. We fussed; settling spoons and moving mats under hot dishes just in time. A terracotta bowl of jacket potatoes with a cross cut into each, bucketing steam. An unambiguous salad – lettuce, tomato, cucumber and onion. Celery sticks in a half-pint glass of the tankard style; a pot of salt next door. Home-made coleslaw – another speciality. And Heinz salad cream in a squeezy bottle; I hadn't even known you could still get it.

The accessories last: sour cream with chives snipped on top, a huge mound of grated cheddar.

She'd put out the good plates.

'Dive in, you lot!' said Mo, still standing. 'What about the kids, Lauren? I've done them some fish fingers.' Three each. Sliding about before her on blue plastic plates.

'Put them on the coffee table, Mum. They can eat over there,' Lauren said.

Maureen almost sat, until: 'Blimey. The garlic bread!'

'I'll fetch it, Mo, don't worry. You get started!'

I plucked the tea towel from the back of Maureen's chair just as she sat.

'I'll help you, Maggie.'

Anja had followed me. The kitchen was in chaos. I bent to the oven.

'Could you get me something to put this in?' I said, as I pulled out the tray of hot bread. I felt a defencelessness knelt there before her.

She went straight to the right drawer and took out a bowl. I pulled the loaf apart along the cuts, burning myself briefly every time.

Anja stood by, and when I was done, she took hold of me, my wrists, rather hard.

'Maggie. I haven't told the others,' she whispered into my face. 'I don't want everyone to know. About the baby.'

I flexed my hands, and she let me go.

'It's your choice, Anja. Really. But what about at the hostel? Won't it help your case? How's all that going, by the way?'

'I don't know,' she said.

'Well, shouldn't you look into it? Can't we find out? And what about the doctor?'

Lauren eyed us from the table, tipped onto the back legs of her seat.

'I'm fine. For now. I need to think.' Anja's voice was taut.

'Well, if you're sure.'

'I am, Maggie. Please don't tell.'

'No, of course not. Don't be silly.'

I felt annoyed by her and implicated in something.

'And if you choose to drink. Anja, honestly. Do what you want. It's none of my business.'

'D'you need a hand in there? Everything all right?' Lauren called in a sing-song voice.

Anja went back to the party with her best oblivious grin.

I loaded up my plate. It really was delicious. The dog patrolled the table and Lauren shooed her away.

'This is amazing, Mo. Just like my mum makes,' said Paul.

'Back on low carb from tomorrow though,' said Peter.

There was lots more wine and we ate, and for a while we all seemed to enjoy ourselves.

'How old are you, Paul?' That was Lauren.

'Me? Forty-two. Why d'you ask?' A different tone. An anxious note.

'Christ, you don't look it. Don't you keep young? Ten years older than me and you wouldn't know.'

True, with her roots growing through and her cracked hands. She must have shared my thought, and scissored the ends of her hair with her fingers.

'Local, are they, your parents?' she said.

'Who, mine?' said Paul, a child, pretending not to hear, hoping she'd go away. She watched him steadily, moving accurate forkfuls up to her mouth.

'No. Not really. St Albans. Not born and bred like you, Lauren.'

'See much of them, do you?' she asked.

'Yes. They get down when they can.' His knife clanked against the side of his plate.

'It's nice though, isn't it? Getting everyone together like this. We do our best, don't we? Eh?' Mo called weakly from her end of the table.

'And what about yours, Peter?'

She swivelled on her chair and I saw that she was drunk.

'Both dead, I'm afraid,' said Peter.

'Oh dear. Then again, you're older, aren't you? Still. Awful.'

Maureen stood up and started bothering dishes.

'Tell you what. Shall I? I'll heat this through a bit. In case anyone wants more later. Or another spoonful before I go? There's loads!'

Everyone said no and she left us to it, hiding in the kitchen. I lost a bit of respect for her then.

'What about you, Tanja? Where are you from? Originally?'

'Me? It's Anja! Don't worry – nearly got it! Albania, thanks.'

'Oh right. Don't know much about that. Oh Christ.'

Lauren knocked her glass with a ring and we all watched it roll a reckless circle. She caught it and a little wave of wine lapped up the side.

'Bloody hell. I think I better slow down!'

She looked delighted, her first real smile of the day.

'Where are the kids?' she said, and stood, staggering briefly as her hand slid along the table on a coaster.

'Oi, you two. You can't eat and play on that thing at the same time.'

She set off with her drink.

'Shove up!' she said.

They made a space for her and she sat down in between them on the carpet. The small one, the girl, pressed her face deep into her mother's hair.

'What you watching then?' she asked.

I ate more of what was left to fill the space. Anja texted deftly. Suddenly Lauren was getting her children into coats.

'You can't just sit about in here all day. Come on! Let's go to the park while there's still light!'

She couldn't find their bits and went again to her mother.

Maureen's voice was low in the hall.

'Yeah but, Mum. Two men? Really? And the cleaner?' Lauren said.

Another few minutes and they were gone, Lauren's voice falling off into quiet down the road. Maureen brought in a raspberry pavlova and some single cream. Another bottle under her arm. She thumped down onto her chair.

'I don't know what to say. She was horrible. She isn't always like that. Maybe it's the stress.'

Paul barked out his amusement and Peter took her arm.

'Please don't worry, Mo. We've all known worse. She's under a lot of pressure.'

'And she's drunk,' I said.

'Well, I know but. I expected better. Honestly.'

She tutted and rubbed a finger across an eyebrow.

I knew what she was thinking and it wasn't of us. She was taking it personally, as a mother will. Asking 'What have I done?'; 'Why is she doing this to me?'; 'What is it that she's trying to say with these behaviours?' And of course, these were the right questions, but the answer would not be simple.

It's a funny thing, a daughter who won't conform, who turns to hurt you. Poor Maureen had done nothing to deserve it, as far as I could see. She was simply kicked, like the dog, when times got tough. My mother once said: 'People will take as much as you're willing to give. Don't leave yourself with nothing.' That might have been Mo's mistake.

But I don't think she withheld, the cardinal sin, which I was found guilty of. And I had, of course, withheld a fact. A key fact. The fact of Rose's paternity. And that was my choice, though it never felt like one. And that choice took on greater meaning; it came, for my daughter, to define me. She said, later, that there had always been something hidden; that she had known it from a girl. That hurt, that rewrite of our history, her childhood – peach-tinted days – and I am no romantic. More time passed, and I saw that maybe she was right and I was sorry – that it was true, that she had seen it, and that it had mattered so. But she wanted all of me and, in being denied, refused me entirely. Children will just eat you up, if you let them. Especially girls.

I felt a sudden roll of nausea and went to the loo. Pushed open the slit of window and raised a tilted head to it. I could hear them chattering again.

When I came out, Paul was sat in front of a computer; Maureen's laptop that her son had given her for a birthday.

'I've rearranged it all, d'you see? Now your email is here. Much better. What else?'

Maureen stood at his shoulder, her glasses on, her forehead clenched.

'Do her a home page,' I said. 'Anja's done one for me. I've got the BBC.'

Peter had begun to clear. Anja was picking up gobbets of food with kitchen roll and I saw Maureen reach and squeeze her at her waist as she passed. 'Thanks, love,' she mouthed, and then: 'No. I know what I want. Facebook, isn't it? Mia told me all about it.'

Paul blew out through his lips.

'Do you even know what that is? Are you sure she's going to want her grandma poking about on her Facebook page?' he said, with a pitchy laugh.

I saw Maureen bristle. A flick of the head that lifted her fringe, which she resettled between two fingers; her tell, I'd spotted it years back. She moved off. Peter had noticed but Paul was too busy at the screen.

'You've got a page, Mags, didn't you say?' he asked.

'Oh, I don't know. Someone else did it for me,' I said.

'Shall we have a look at yours, and see if she fancies it? OK, email address?' he asked.

'I don't remember,' I said.

'You must do! Surely it's on your phone?'

'I haven't got that sort of phone,' I said. 'And it's not my usual email anyway.'

'Is it the Yahoo?' Anja called. She appeared at the edge of the room, a big bowl under one arm and a tea towel across her shoulder. Hot from work. Upper lip shining.

'I know your Yahoo address,' she said.

The comment settled oddly on the room and I felt a fool, as she spelled it out clearly; old and silly. Perhaps something worse.

'Password?' Paul asked, eyes down.

'Yes. Excuse me,' I said and reached across him to type.

'Right,' said Paul. 'Here we go.'

A page appeared; entirely unfamiliar. Nothing recognisably mine.

'This is the newsfeed. A post from one of Maggie's friends. See?'

I pulled up a chair. The square of photo that identified the writer was inconclusive. I saw Susan's name, from the walks, but the image next to her was, inexplicably, a cat.

'And here she's posted photos. '

Mallorca: a ghastly group shot. We stood outside a cafe in anoraks and with a hiking stick each. The challenging day. It was

137

hard to see, at first, which one was me; I looked like a man in a pair of stretched-out glasses. A couple more – scenery, a meal, a drinking game that I must have been in bed for. Unusually, it looked less fun than it had been. As a postscript she suggested a 'rematch', this time in Morocco.

'And you can search for friends here. And there's a timeline, where you fill in your history so people can find you. You've been tagged in another photo, Mags. Here we go. Wow. When was that? You look. I don't know. Kind of powerful,' said Paul.

He clicked on it, and the picture enlarged. It was years old, black and white; a shot of my daughter, really, having won a North London spelling competition. A professional had come to the school, sent by the local paper. I, the proud mother at her arm. Rose looked herself: serious, decided. I wore an attitude I'd long since shed: pride, and something close to arrogance. A hair's width of eyebrow. A creeping fret began.

'What? Where did that come from?' I asked.

'You can find out. This was posted by – Kate Williams. Ring any bells? She says she went to school with Rose. She must have scanned it in.'

'But she isn't my friend,' I said.

'Well, maybe only we can see it. I'm not sure on all that. Peter, can you come over here a min? He's better on this than me. You've got loads of friend requests. Have a look. I'll go see what he says.'

Paul got up and I moved the screen close. Mo's mouse-pad span the page the wrong way and the faces on the screen lurched and swam, little nightmare glimpses that set my heart stop-starting. I got the knack, and things got worse. There was Julie from that office job; a girl, no two, from my school; sweet

Jesus, was that Ian? Horrible breaches in the skin of time. I pressed delete, delete and delete and Paul was back.

'Christ, Mags. You don't mind! Peter will look at it now, if you like.'

'Hold on,' I said. 'Give me a minute, would you?'

'Of course. Are you OK? You look. A bit.'

He peered into my face, blinking hammily, and I saw that he, too, was drunk.

'I'm fine, just a second.'

He left me and I went through to the end, no longer reading, just clearing out. And then I saw that I had a message. A mail.

I opened it and found it was from Kay, another receptionist from the surgery. A woman I had sat beside for years but knew next to nothing about, save how she took her tea; a woman after my own heart. A journalist had been in touch, she wrote, asking all sorts of questions. She hadn't said a thing, mind, but thought that I should know.

I rose, walked back to the loo and threw up and up, till there was nothing left; running the tap to drown out the noise.

When I came in Paul asked did I still want to look? But I told him no.

Lauren returned with clamour and fuss and some story about ice-cream. I joined them in the kitchen, dried some pans, and said I needed home for the dog. Peter offered to walk me.

Outside it was darkening, a yellowing moon, a thick wet cold. We talked vaguely as we went and he saw me all the way inside. We made our brief goodbyes.

The dog scratched madly at the kitchen door, and when I let him out he almost knocked me down. I knelt to him while he nudged and whined, and breathed in the hot leather of his ears. When he was finished, I removed my coat and looked in a mirror. A silty rim of mascara had settled beneath my eyes. I wiped my mouth and took a long drink straight from the tap. Then played my message, two days old. Two days it had lain patient inside the black box of my machine.

'Margaret. It's Chris here. Chris Kent. Call me, please. It's important,' and a number. His voice higher and thinner, due to anger or age, I didn't know. It had been twenty-eight years.

It was him. I had struggled with this knowledge two full days.

I felt powerful and afraid, like a child who believes it can pull a plane out of the sky with its look. As though my own dread had given him life, summoned him to me, in some horrible inversion of a wish.

I listened one more time, and pressed delete.

If he wanted me, he would come. There was only the present, and the present was Anja. I would keep my eyes down.

24

A little context. Chris and I. The day he threw me out. August 25th, 1984.

A hot hot day, and flies, everywhere. A weird infestation that summer, and all that anyone talked about; the women at least. Tiny flies, smaller than the house fly, which vanished with the rain but always came back.

I had woken dry-mouthed and woozy; pretty standard for that time. Chris long gone and the bedroom full of a buttercup sun that lay on me heavily, slowing things down. My daughter by my side, still asleep; three years old, her dark hair in a sweaty curl at her ear, an affront to Chris's blondeness that we joked about. Colouring from my mother's side, coarse and outdoorsy, which I hoped meant she'd be tough. But her skin was pale; shaded to blue at points, the veins at her temple and wrist so close to the surface they made me shudder. I watched the pulse in her eyelid, for a moment, as she slept.

Dinner at home for eight. I lay back and closed my eyes.

Later I got up for the bathroom. Flies hung suspended in loose groups, in the doorway, in the shower; wheeling at my approach. I flicked on the long tube of light above the mirror and saw tens, maybe hundreds, crammed into the space between the bulb and its casing. Up close they boiled gently, clambering across each other, going nowhere. My stomach tumbled, and I reached for the spray, but the smell of it made my head hurt, and what a job to clean. A tight twist of tea towel shoved the length of the unit, nudging the desiccated bodies along until they rolled out the other end. And there were always more. I left them as they were.

By lunchtime I'd done that thing that women do, and maybe men, for all I know. Convinced myself that today will be the day that makes the difference. A clean slate, a new leaf. If only I try hard enough, all else will follow. To say that I was hopeful would be an overstatement, but there was the possibility of hope. A tealight of hope, not so much that tonight would make him happy – Chris was a man who asked for very little – but more that I could eke something out of it for myself. Lean back at its close and feel part of things, instead of fidget and twitch, sitting on my hands to stop myself from yanking out the tablecloth.

First, the menu. It seemed important to get this right. I pulled a chair across to the back door and sat there shoeless, smoking; Capital on the radio, the little one pushing herself across the grass in a plastic car and an early *Delia* and a couple of *Good Housekeeping Guides*, optimistic gifts from our mothers, heavy on my lap. I read about the principles of the supper party – a cosy and informal affair, relaxed, no fuss – and liked the sound of it. Smoked-salmon roulade and duck and blackcurrant sauce were my choices.

I went to Sainsbury's with the buggy and a basket and kept to the role, in lipstick and tights. Received my approval and enjoyed it; saw others' pleasure at the sight of a mother, well organised and smiling, still beautiful, and determined to be that person.

Back home and I defy a soul not to enjoy the assembly of a smoked-salmon roulade:

First, beat the cream cheese with the mayonnaise and lemon zest. Chill in the refrigerator for thirty minutes.

I lacked the relevant tool, so skinned the lemon with a potato peeler and chopped it as best I could, supplemented with a squirt of juice.

Lay out your salmon and spread the mixture over it. One and a half tablespoons per slice.

Sprinkle evenly with dill.

On top, add a layer of chopped prawns. Press down carefully. Then plenty of fresh ground black pepper.

Roll the slices starting at one short end and place seam down on a plate.

I had to read that twice.

Cover and chill.

Half an hour before you serve, cut each roll, on the diagonal, into eight neat slices.

Tip: Use a very sharp knife and a sawing action. Dip the knife into lukewarm water between each slice so that it cuts clean and neat.

This works.

Fan the slices out attractively, slightly overlapping. Add a garnish of lemon twists and sprigs of dill.

Serve at room temperature.

In between all of this were the ducks, poor things; eight of them, with puffed out chests and newborn ribs. Pounding them with a mallet and scoring the skin made my head swim; I was squeamish back then, but would lose patience with that person now. The sauce I shudder to recount. Blackcurrant, cassis and butter, separating slowly in its boat on the side.

Chris was around and about, smiling at it all out of the side of his face. A few holes of golf, and home; a kiss for his daughter. A run to the dry cleaner's – he liked to look after his uniform himself – and to pick up the booze. Content, humming, apart.

What do I remember of her that day? 'Row row row your boat', which my mum had taught her the week before. Cauliflower cheese for lunch. The way she talked to herself as she played and stopped when I drew near. No apology or regret but still, she stopped. Later, I heard her plinking away on the piano, and crept in to watch. Her posture pulled me up.

In her stiff straight back and the tip of her head, her look straight down her nose, I saw myself. I felt that I had a clear view, as if in a mirror, for the very first time and I mean that; these were the days before everything was photographed. There was my hauteur, my chill, and I wondered when this had happened and understood briefly why people seemed to like me less these days.

I left her, honestly, thinking only of myself.

The day got hotter. I closed the doors and windows, covered the fruit, and sprayed. Ten minutes later I went round with a duster and hoovered up all the crispy little corpses.

I thought to arrange the dining room, but struggled to imagine what supper party might mean for the table.

There were fresh flowers that Chris had picked up. Calla lilies, the big ones with no smell. Bright red thistles, dyed, surely, and heliconia – the lobster claws – which I loathed but he thought romantic. They are pollinated by hummingbirds and the occasional bat, he told me; nonetheless, they remain ugly.

I took the flowers to the kitchen, sawed off their ends, a job in itself, and split them into three small jugs. Spaced them down the table. Got rid of the placemats and candelabra. Pulled in two coffee tables and lamps. Quite pleased with the effect. Chris appeared: 'No cloth?'

My mother phoned.

'How are all the preparations going?' she asked slow and clear, her tone set for an audience.

'Fine thanks, Mum,' I said.

'What are you cooking?' Big spaces between the words.

'Smoked-salmon roulade and duck and blackcurrant.'

'Ooh. Smoked-salmon roulade and duck and blackcurrant.'

A noise from somewhere behind her. She gave a snort.

'Who's that? Aunty Bettie? What does she say?'

'You're not to worry about your Aunt Bet.'

'What does she say?'

'She says you'd be better off with a pork chop.'

We laughed together, forty-five miles apart.

'I've got to get on. I'll call you in the morning.'

She was talking to her sisters before the phone met its cradle.

It was too hot for a bath, so I freshened up with a flannel and put rollers in the bottom and front of my hair. I could hear Chris reading a bedtime story.

He sees a bonfire smoking
Pigeons in the sky
His mother cleaning windows
A dog going by.

I knew she liked to see me, all dressed up, or perhaps I liked to show her, but I'd need to rush, they were almost done.

It was a slippery dress in purple blue that slid over my head in one slick move. Boxy, high-necked, tight at the wrist, with big gold buttons running up the front. A play on the power suit, I see now. At the time I imagined myself Diana in it. So fine that the hem caught on a calf, a missed prickle of hair. I shook myself, and it dropped down into place. I felt like a girl under its swish as I moved to the doorway, but Chris was there with his finger to his lips.

I pushed past him and went in. Sleep had plumped her but I saw a fist clench once, and again, so maybe there was time. I stroked that hand, her cheek, her eyelid though I knew it was selfish. She made no response. I whispered her a message and left, full of her. Went to the kitchen and drank my first Martini of the night, mixed by Chris, the proper way.

'You'll find a pilot knows his cocktails,' he told me once, and that much was true.

The first was the best, as always, and on an empty stomach too. It took me inside myself and I buzzed around, all fiddle and primp; called through to Chris to put some music on. He liked the old stuff and so did I, at that point of the evening, at least.

I did my make-up last in the hall where the light was best.

I watched my face before I began; observed my pupils shrink in the last blast of sun – a bit in love with myself, I'll admit, that was the Martini – and did my thing, which was subtle, and led to an overall effect of gloss and shine. Nothing you could put your finger on, a look that worked by contrast, for Jan and Moira would be made up from the paintbox.

Moira read it as a rebuke: 'I wish I could be more like you,' she told me every time, at a certain point of the night.

'What do you mean?'

'Don't know, really. Natural. But I don't think Tony would be so keen.'

She was a nice person, stunned by the demands of her two young sons. Thin-skinned and always tipped into glum by the evening's end.

'Buck up, Roo,' Tony would call across when he saw her droop, but he never came over.

We could usually talk her round.

I was ready and wanted them to get there so I could have my second drink and suddenly they had.

Chris opened the door to the six of them.

'Look, we're all here!' A rising hilarity. The Franks had given the Millers a lift, and Jan and Ian's cab pulled up at the very same minute. They seemed amazed at the coincidence, and I felt the edges of my good mood shrivel.

'Come in! Come in!' I pretended, and we all went through to the lounge; candlelit as I'd moved out the lamps.

'Ooh. How atmospheric!' said Moira, and gave a tremble.

'I love coming here!' said Sue on receipt of her Martini, a bridge of cocktail stick across it, spearing two olives.

Jan refused hers and Chris mixed her a Campari instead.

Our territories were marked out in snacks; two separate clusters at each end of the room.

We ladies gathered at the piano and picked from a mound of pastry clubs, spades and diamonds. I watched Chris wince as Sue put her drink straight down onto the wood. I moved it, when I got the chance, onto the runner that I'd laid there for the job.

The men stood by the window, looking outwards as they talked. They finished their nibbles and Chris went off for more, coming back with a bowl of crisps to show he still had the common touch. He brought the bags of salt with him and tipped them on in careful sprinkles that made him look a clown.

Good old Sue passed back and forth, for handfuls, and to fill us in on the subjects of their chat. Business, in general. The miners' strike. The condition of the golf course. We rolled our eyes, and discussed the royal baby (born the following month – Harry – I watched them leave hospital on the TV). The flies. A mutual acquaintance's awful birth.

'Food any time soon, Mags? We're starving over here,' Chris called.

He was playing it bluff and manly, unusual for him, but I did my bit.

'Of course. Of course,' I said, and trotted off.

'Can we help at all?' said the ladies, as one.

'No no no. You enjoy yourselves. Nothing to do. Just give me a second.'

The salmon lay sweating under cling film. A small group of flies had found their way in and drowned in cream cheese but I dug them out with the end of a nail and smoothed flat the grooves I'd made with a fingertip.

Everyone came through and I stomached the praise. We ate the roulade with packet Melba toast and an oily white wine and picked the lemon rind from between our teeth discreetly.

'Swap round, swap round!' I cried as I cleared the table – a trick I'd learnt from Jan – and went out for the ducklings.

She appeared in the doorway as I fried them off in two pans as the recipe required.

'Here, I'll do this one,' she offered, and took a handle, giving it an abrupt shake which dislodged the flesh that had just begun to stick.

'See?' she said. 'And perhaps a bit more butter.'

She took a fish slice and pressed down on each breast for extra sizzle.

I did as I was told. We both stepped back to save our faces and the front of our frocks.

'That's a lovely dress,' I said, just as I thought the opposite.

'Thanks. I got it down the boutique.'

'It suits you,' I told her, which was true.

Her looks – and she had them – were rather small scale. China teeth, a narrow nose, children's ears. Her neck was long and tight, a visible cord of ligament running its length, but I knew she thought it a good feature from the way she styled her hair, curved out and away, lacquered stiff, and through her choice of neckline, square tonight. She laid her hand across her collarbone as she stood. As a habit, I felt it showed stress. Still the yellow of her outfit worked with her colouring, dark and pale with plain chocolate eyes. She had split nails that she complained of during kitchen chats, worn very long and accurately painted. She travelled in a fug of Giorgio by Giorgio Beverly Hills.

149

'That's them,' Jan told me and the duck went in the oven for a final fifteen minutes.

'What else?' she asked.

'Shit, I've forgotten the potatoes,' I said and I had, completely.

There was supposed to be galettes, but I hadn't read on far enough to even find out what they were.

I felt genuinely surprised and tried to think back, but the booze had obscured the earlier part of the day.

Jan looked at me, amazed, and released a slip of giggle.

'Maggie! How about rice?'

'I'm not sure. I think so. Look in there, behind you.'

She boiled it up in time for the duck, made a curious garnish with two carrots, a spring onion and some thoughtfully stationed peppercorns and gave me an exaggerated wink as we carried it in.

The duck was bloody as intended and I ate it in a rush, drenched in sauce.

The conversation flowed. The men teased, the ladies bridled for effect and each burst of amusement got louder till I excused myself. I took the plates through and scraped them with the radio on low. Bobbed around the kitchen, taking my time.

I got back to the end of David describing the economy – his prerogative as bank manager. The jerk of a shoulder that he could suppress in calmer moments had sprung into life. Sue listened intent and nodded seriously as he spoke, one hand on the back of his chair. Her lipstick had travelled to the right of her mouth but it didn't shame her, somehow, as it would have the rest of us, perhaps because she wouldn't have cared if she'd known.

Chris and Tony, so similar I wanted to say so. Pilots to the bone; neat in cashmere V-necks and pressed shirts and their pretence at deference. Then Chris shook a wrist, jangling his watch, which told me he wasn't listening. Ian was rather drunk and holding himself very still in denial of it. He looked on with both hands gripping the table. Every little while he gave the smallest list, overcorrecting every time.

I'd have liked to have known him better, Ian. He was a salesman, in the print, I think, which didn't seem to provide the rich seam of anecdote that their brand of male friendship called for. Still he held his own, earned a good wage and beat them all at golf, which appeared to count for something. But he always seemed at a distance, and I thought I heard a faint chord of unease in him, which made him interesting to me.

The other women watched with no role in it, Moira resigned and Jan looking for a way in. I saw her think of her jelly, and jump up from the table.

She had agreed to do the pudding last week and brought it with her in a large rectangular Tupperware.

'No peeking, and not a word from you, Ian,' she had said, when they arrived. Stowed it in the fridge after lowering a shelf.

'Or shall I show you? No. Why not leave it as a surprise.'

Now she crept into the room, her wrists straining, and stood back from the table waiting to be noticed.

A loaf of gelatine in tiers of red, green and yellow. Fruits – strawberries, grapes and pineapple – suspended in their relevant stripe. The wobble and bounce of a *Carry On* film that made me honk and earned a look from Chris. Everyone oohed as she lay it down, and cut thick wedges off a tinfoil-covered board with a cake slice she had brought from home. She poured a dribble of cream on each and we passed them round.

At first there seemed no taste to it, just texture, smooth and evasive, dodging my teeth. Then a sweetness and astringency that filled my mouth with saliva. We looked at each other and exclaimed.

Later we left the dining room, us women clustered in the kitchen, smoking and exchanging intimacies. Jan stood by the window, drying the glasses with a fresh tea towel, breathing on their outsides and rubbing again. Music started from the lounge and the men called for us to come through. The others went in, skittish, but I crept upstairs, pretending I'd heard a cry.

I sat with her, the pump of her chest under my hand, listening for the odd bubble of sound from below that broke in her room. Sue's voice, in particular, seemed to travel.

'Let me choose, let me choose next,' she called and I heard the girl in her, and that was something new.

Halfway back down the stairs, and the acoustics changed. I paused. A quietness landed, a blanketed hush.

A curl of worry. I got into the lounge. Sue and Moira stood close, Sue borrowing Moira's anxious face until she noticed me and dug out a grin.

'Oh, there you are, Maggie. Come on over. Come on. What should we play?'

When I was close enough, she pulled me to her, leaving her hand on my arm. The same song started but she made no move to change it.

Across the carpet, Tony and David bent to Ian. He looked set to stand, clutching the arms of his chair, until the loll of his head tipped him forward. He dropped to one knee and I thought I understood.

'Oh, it's no problem. Are you not feeling too well, Ian? Don't worry!' I said, in a lively tone.

'Come on. It's all right. Let's get you home. Where's Jan?'

I pushed between the men and hoicked him under an arm.

'I'm here. Just leave him, Maggie. I've called a cab.'

Then everyone was moving. The Millers and Franks gathered their things, there was a jumble of goodbyes and they were folded into their car, leaving silence and a sense of aftermath.

Chris paused at the front door, wearing a distracted expression that made no sense. Then he looked up and past me and I swear, I felt Jan at my back. I turned, and there she stood, with her still way of being; her drunken husband just visible behind her.

'Let's go into my office,' Chris said and Jan followed.

I felt confused and syrupy slow, but did what I was asked in the absence of a better plan.

Inside, he stood behind his chair.

'Look, Maggie. Let's get this done. I don't want to spend another night in this marriage, and I'm sure that you don't either.'

Not out of the blue, exactly, but still, a jolt.

'Come on. No nonsense. We can make this easy or difficult. It's entirely up to you.'

I've never flown in a plane that Chris had captained but there could be no one better in a crisis. He was so disciplined, so lucid.

He snatched up his hands and reached for a cigarette from a box on the desk that I hadn't known existed.

A flash of irritation at that; at the times I'd had to get the baby up and out when I'd run out of cigs and all along he'd had a stash of his own.

'Why is she here?' I said, though I knew the answer by then.

'We're together, Maggie, why do you think?'

Jan's eyes led the rest of her in a kind of spasm towards the door. Chris saw it too and said: 'No, Jan. Stay here. Not after the way she's behaved.'

I found I couldn't take my eyes off her.

I remembered her tears, late; Cointreau tinkling in heavy bevelled glasses. Her and Ian and their problems. The way she passed on gossip, with an appetite she never showed at the table.

'Maggie, I just need your agreement, OK?'

And she sat, crossed her legs and locked her hands and in that moment I saw her quite differently. The badminton round robin, of all things; that suburban staple. Jan in her ready position, the spectacle of her resolution set against the stripe of creme blush, the girlish skirt, and her weirdly splayed fingers, to mind the nails. She always won. And I realised then that she wanted to be here. She had been asking Chris's permission, with that glance; thought she knew men and their weaknesses and that without her he might not see it through. But that was not Chris; he would never start something that he couldn't finish.

In another room, Ian coughed richly and finished with a swallowed belch. The wheel of his chair gave a sharp squeak and I wondered if he was about to appear. Instead I heard him piss, long and deep.

'Concentrate, please, Maggie. I know you're drunk but can we just get this done?'

'Yes. Fine. If that's what you want,' I said.

'Good. At least we're in agreement.'

He and Jan risked a look.

154

'I'll leave tonight,' he said. 'Stay at the hotel.'

A place near Gatwick that he used for early flights.

The doorbell went and she ran to it; a provocation, perhaps, but I didn't respond. It was the cab.

'Chris. D'you mind?' she said, and he went with her and heaved Ian to his feet.

He woke briefly and mumbled, 'Thanks, thanks a lot', as though they were strangers.

Chris held his head like a policeman as they bent him in to the car and moved to the front window to give the driver some instruction. The taxi pulled away, leaving the two of them in the street.

'I'm going to pack a bag,' Chris said, when they came inside.

'What about you?' I asked.

'What do you mean?' she said, and I had to admire her lack of apology. She was wary, together.

'She's coming too,' Chris replied.

I didn't have the stomach for a row. Chris took the stairs in twos.

He was down in a minute, all business, with the solid mid-size bag he liked and an emotion rose in me; a sort of child's feeling of injustice, of it all being just so unfair. Chris saw it, he knew me, that I can't deny, and was angry.

'Don't start, Maggie. I'll make sure you're OK, I will. If you behave. But you do need to behave. There will be terms. There is a baby to consider now after all.'

I looked for Jan and felt hate, hot but positive. She had the good grace, at least, to drop her head.

Chris watched, and waited, but I found I had nothing more to say.

'That's that then,' he said, and left, trailing Jan.

When they were gone, I found myself in a light-headed excitement. It was true, I didn't want him, or any of this. I would miss none of it. I looked in on my child and felt a rush at the idea of a better life. I wanted gone.

I went downstairs and saw my keys on the hall table. I jammed my thumbnail between the rings, ripping it back to the quick, and worked the house set round. I lay these on the sideboard. There were two more bundles, the car – his now – which I edged off too, and the spare for my mum's. That I kept, thinking then that I would need it. The fob was featherweight and tinkled as it swung. I crept into the lounge.

There was a long jellied stain on the piano. I reached a finger, felt its gluey touch, and flared out lines to make a Christmas tree. I almost wiped my hand down my front, but at the last, on a whim, sucked my finger instead, tasting sweet jammy alcohol.

Then I took a key, the gold one – the Yale – and stabbed at the instrument hard; once, twice and a third time too. I made three edged dents in the wood; the first suggestions of cracks running outwards.

A stupid thing to do. A regret that I carry to this day.

25

November. London deep in rain. I was afflicted by memory. Assaulted by the past at every turn.

I pulled my knee removing a boot and it was the day that I slapped Uncle Stan.

No uncle really, just a cruel, if perceptive, old man, but he slighted me – I can't remember how – just that I'd been given a drink and he'd taken the rise. I'd hit him before I knew it and when she got me home, my mother slapped the back of my leg so hard there were pinpricks of haemorrhage for weeks. Her ring gouged a neat chunk from the bend of my knee; more than forty years later I can still feel that knot of mended flesh.

I brought a mirror downstairs and tried to find it but could not contort myself enough to see.

The knee got worse and so I took myself to the doctor's on the bus and saw the young man in front, a student, perhaps, pull up 'Prufrock' on his screen; my favourite poem from a distance-learning course I never completed. I read it clearly over his shoulder in a large exotic font; he plugged in his earphones to listen – what a thing! – but it was another of Eliot's verses that started up in my head.

I was thirteen again, stood on the makeshift stage of a late-summer talent show on the beach, performing 'The Naming of Cats'.

Thirty-one lines but the challenge was not its length. That poem has a life of its own. Its syllables run away with you; trip you up, if you let them, but I had finished, word perfect, and looked out across the audience, breathless from beating that last, impossible line.

His ineffable effable
Effanineffable
Deep and inscrutable singular Name.

I could still call it up, it came to me instantly.

An eddy of applause and then a sharp throaty sound from a single spiteful girl. A silence began, a contagious sort of silence; a ripple of embarrassment that spread like blown sand, in shuffle and glance. Half an hour later, the prize awarded to a pair of bendy sisters, there was Mum, yanking my arm, my feet struggling to gain traction on the stones. We got off the beach and she took my chin in that fierce grip that I loved.

'I have never been more proud of you, Margaret,' she said. 'You were. Brilliant.'

An ordinary word but one I'd never heard her speak. Too much pleasure in it. Too much commitment. She realised this at the same moment as me, and looked away, embarrassed.

That recollection physically hurt. It stabbed low in my stomach, a twist of pleasure pain that made me gasp there on the bus.

I put my hand down to the place. Mentioned it to the doctor, when I got there – I thought it might be the startings of a bladder infection – but next day it had gone.

And there was Anja. I called her and she came and I wondered if I was using her like the men before me, because I paid her, with as much as she would take, in gifts and treats and things for the baby, and she made me feel good with her youth and her simplicity and her ready laugh as against my age and weariness and mistakes.

She knew something was up; she was softer, kinder. Trying to be what I needed, I supposed.

She made me forget myself, just like the Lou Reed song.

Was that so very bad?

26

Monday, and she wasn't due, but arrived in tears, banging on the door, wild-eyed. She had seen a man who worked for Goran. He had come up behind her at the bus stop, too close, and when she turned, he smiled a slow growing smile. He got on the next bus, her bus, but she stayed stuck to the pavement and watched him as he moved through its body, still wearing that lazy grin.

'It was to warn me. Do you see?' she said, standing in the hall, sweating and crying and moving from foot to foot.

'I don't know. It seems possible. Are you sure it was him?'

I tried to catch up. I'd been expecting a package of books. She was certain. It was his smile. Its leisured passage up his face. All the girls had remarked on it. Even in their context, he stood out as a creep.

I saw him in my head. Simple, or a sadist.

I watched her travelling back. The changes in her posture and a collapse of the contours of her face. He never came close, she said. A family member, working on the outskirts of the business. She gave a shudder.

'We should go to the police, Anja, straight away. I'll call them for you now, if you like. What's his name?' I said, in some imitation of action.

But Anja didn't know and pushed past me to the sitting room. She sat, shoving away the jab of Buster's snout, crying with an insistent rhythm, powering along under its own momentum.

I laid an awkward arm across her shoulder, but she didn't respond. Her body throbbed, rigid.

'Anja. We should call the police. They've probably got one of these Photofit things and you can pick him out.'

'Yeah but so what? What did he do? He's just a guy.'

'But you've seen him with Goran. It might be important. Come on. We should make an appointment,' I said.

'What will I get from that?' she asked.

I didn't know, other than it felt loosely like the right thing to do.

'Well, it might help your case, I suppose. You know. Get everything agreed.'

'OK, I need to think right now,' she said, more to herself.

She stopped crying. I tried to think too. I stroked the dog and waited.

'Nothing. We do nothing. That's the best plan,' she said.

'Well, yes. If you want. As long as you're OK. I suppose you're safe there, are you? In that place you're staying?' I asked.

She answered with a sideways look and a shrug.

'They say, my case worker, they will help me if I press charges or not,' she said.

'Right. Well, that's good to know,' I said. 'So. What are you saying? Are you having second thoughts?'

A knee-jerk of moral indignation that I tried to hide.

'Who knows, Maggie? I have to think for my baby right now.'

'I understand. I do. Look. Whatever you decide.'

I patted her knee. What else was there?

She nodded.

'How about I make a tea for us both?'

'Yes, please,' she said. Then: 'Maggie, do you think I could have a bath?'

I saw gin, coat hangers, razor blades.

'There are only showers in my place,' she said.

'Oh, how awful! I couldn't stand that. Get up there. Yes. I love a bath,' I said, though I hadn't taken one for years. 'I'll bring you a fresh towel.'

Thank god for a task. I rushed to the kitchen, put the kettle on and three teabags in the pot. Upstairs to the laundry cupboard where I chose my largest towel, in aubergine, of the sort you get in a smart hotel. I'd bought it as a treat but barely used it; far too heavy and it never quite dried through.

I laid it outside the bathroom door. Steam had moistened the paintwork and I could hear water running and smell the first hit of scent that lifts when bath foam meets hot water. She would have used the glass-stoppered bottle my daughter bought, its contents originally rose-scented – a joke of sorts about her name. I had refilled it with something thick and purple and marketed as relaxing. Laying claim to lavender, but closer to travel sweet.

I went down for the tea and as I came back up, bent over the scalding mug, I realised why I was hurrying.

'Anja?'

I gave a mouselike knock.

'I've got your tea, I'll just leave it outside, shall I?'

'I'm already in. Could you bring it to me, if you don't mind?'

I am not comfortable with other women's bodies. I pushed open the door, and immediately my glasses fogged, which helped. There was nowhere to rest a drink within arm's reach of the bath, save its rim; I knew this from experience.

'I'll just put it there,' I said and reached in from the furthest distance feasible.

Her face, raised to me, looked boiled, but that was as much the tears as the heat and I thought again that those whose features hold in trying times have an advantage. But it is the same for me and so I felt a solidarity too.

Her hand broke the surface of the water and grabbed for mine, transmitting a fierce heat. We stayed like this for a while; my back beginning to hurt, the ripples steadying and the suds splitting out into scum. She looked ahead at the islands of her knees.

'Anja, do you think it's time to talk to your parents about this?'

The prints of my subconscious all over it. I felt a certain easing but also a shame.

'They are not bad people. But it is not their problem. She will only worry.'

'Well, you are their daughter. I'm not sure they would see it that way.'

'When it is better I will call,' she said.

'OK. I'll leave you to it. Do you want to stay for some food?'

She said yes, and I went downstairs and opened a bottle.

I had been thinking of an omelette for myself, but when I checked, the eggs wouldn't stretch. I poured myself a couple of inches of wine and swallowed it in three long gulps, my mind rushed and jumpy.

I tried to recall what I had cooked for Rose. Cod in butter sauce was her favourite – frozen, boil in a bag, a dish I would no longer find, nor choose to eat.

There were things in the cupboard that could work in combination and I remembered a meal a lover once made; whore's pasta, he had called it, in Italian. I hadn't taken offence. Garlic and a tin of tomatoes. Capers, and an anchovy, whizzed. He'd cooked it in a previous kitchen but the blender hadn't travelled, so I chopped the fish instead, feathered and acrid, sticking to my knife. No herbs, alas, but I put what I had together and when I came back later, the ingredients had rearranged themselves into something new. The smell was deep and meaty; a surprise. I recoiled, though my mouth filled with saliva all the same.

She shuffled in in her slippers that lived here and I thought perhaps she'd started to show until I saw the knot of towel at her chest. She wore the White Company robe that I'd bought her but pretended to find lying around and her hair was wrapped in a hand towel with the bits she had missed falling dark and clotted beside her face. All that bleached-out cotton made her skin a yellow grey. She looked bulky and uncomfortable. She hugged herself and I saw a ripped nail snag on a thick white thread.

I went to her, touched an arm.

'How about a drink? One won't hurt.'

She said OK, and sat at the counter. I poured her a large one and she held it like a bowl, inhaling it first. She took a long slow mouthful and I tasted it too, in my imagination; the pleasure of that first rare sip.

'Do you want a look at the paper?' I asked.

I pulled a *Standard* from the pile, knee-high, stacked by the bin. She flipped the pages steadily, got to the end and began again.

I mixed the sauce and pasta in the pan and lifted a heap into two shallow bowls. Grated a thick pile of parmesan onto each and handed her one, a fork stabbed in it. We ate side by side, inelegantly, bent over our food. When she stood there were slashes of red on the collar of her gown that I'd never get out. You could barely taste the fish.

Eating seemed to have done for her. She took her bowl across and when she'd stood at the sink for a while, it became clear that she was crying.

'Come on. Let's go in,' I said. 'Shall we see what's on the telly?'

I unclawed her hands and she wandered away from me.

When I went through, Anja sat on the floor, leant against the sofa.

'Just chuck the dog off,' I said, but she didn't move.

Their heads were close and, as I watched, he put his nose in her ear and she rubbed her face up and down his broad muzzle. He licked her, tears and snot, serious and careful, and she let him. Her turban slipped askew and her hair fell down.

'Give me that,' I said. 'I'll put it on a radiator.'

She held it out to me feebly.

'Maggie,' she asked, 'do you have a brush?'

I did. I got it from its place in the kitchen drawer. She didn't look my way when I came back in, her eyes set on some quiz show with a howling audience. It felt most sensible just to sit.

I took my usual spot at the sofa's near end, bottom deep in the sag of cushion, knees high. Buster raised his head at the disturbance, saw it was me, and lay down again, beginning an exaggerated stretch that ended when a pointed claw made contact with my thigh. He slept once more.

Anja began to move. She pushed up on her hands and shifted herself the length of the sofa, face still tipped to the screen. She reached me – her shoulder touched my leg – and bent an arm behind her to release her hair, trapped between the cushion and her back. She stretched it out, set it gently on the chair by my side, where it rested, like beached seaweed, dampening the wool.

'Maggie,' she said, at the telly, 'will you please brush my hair?'

I started with the ends. I reached across myself and passed the brush through the hair that lay on the cushion, but the bristles snagged on the upholstery. I spread the limp strands across my palm, and began again but that did not work either; the strokes, this time, impeded by my flesh.

I took the hair; gripped the bulk of it in a tight fist against her nape, a makeshift ponytail, and worked on that, but after a bit she shook her head gently – I let go – and took her fingers to her forehead. She scraped her nails quite hard across the dome of her head which I read as a rebuke of my own half-hearted effort.

So I did it properly. I leant back and took hold of my leg under the knee. I pulled it in towards me, then across. My feet found the floor either side of her. I moved forward in my seat, took her head gently between two hands and said something along the lines of: 'Right.'

I started again at the base of her head, the brush flipped on its back, and worked where it all looked tangled in short actions until the teeth ran smooth. There was a patch of bald and I realised that this was what she did with busy fingers when she didn't think I looked; bothered, twisted, yanked and then worried at the bare spot. I paused on it with the whisper of a touch, but she jumped, and I moved on.

Next, I reached over the top and began a long strong motion

166

all the way across the curve of her skull. My hand followed the passage of the brush and we fell into a rhythm, brush and stroke, brush and stroke.

Each strand was thick, thanks, perhaps, to the dye, but there was not much of it. For the second after I brushed, the hair lay complete like a body of water, and then collapsed, strands toppling left and right, revealing her scalp to me in tiny white slices.

Sometimes a noise burst free of the TV and I looked up, but the colour and the motion seemed too abstract and I went back to my task and the animal texture of the girl beneath my hand. She didn't move; she didn't speak.

When I started on the side, I felt her effort against the brush, a resistance to keep her head from tipping, and so I held the other side steady, in my own scooped palm. Her head was weighted and unstable, though her neck, deeply furrowed, looked strong. She had a mole at the back that I was careful to avoid.

'All done?' I asked, but she shook her head, and I carried on.

It is a mother's job, to brush a girl's hair. Mine did so, daily, but it was rushed and functional, brought to a close with the brutal twist of elastic, the aim to keep the hair out of trouble, nothing more. My mother brushed her own in a different way, and I liked to watch.

Her hair had been long and dark, down past her shoulders, and she enjoyed the bite of the brush, I could see it. When she was done, it bushed around her narrow face like a capital A. I touched it once and it felt fibrous and connected, like candy floss, but she slapped at my hand and tutted at her reflection. She had a way of putting it up, a technique of twist and pin that tucked the whole thing back in on itself. At the end, she was left with just the shape of her head and a subtle thickness where the hair gave way to neck. The grips were perfectly invisible, and I never saw the whole dislodged.

'Did your mother do this for you?' I asked Anja, after a while.

I felt a sensation in my palm; a heat, a glow.

'Yes,' Anja said.

'And did you like it?' I asked, hoping, I think, that she would say no.

'Not one bit. She did it every morning. She counted the brushes. An old wives' tale, no? It was boring.'

She made her face heavy, new to me; a face designed for her mother.

'But I like it today,' she said.

'What kind of woman was she? Is she?' The hair was getting greasy now, overworked, but still I went on.

She gave a big sigh that lifted her shoulders.

'Tall, with a nice figure. Her hair is a natural red. We are not similar.'

'And what was she like to know?' I said.

Anja had to think.

'Kind. But always worried.' A break. 'I was not proud of her.'

'Few daughters are,' I said.

The rim of an ear was lined with stubs of scar tissue – abandoned piercings. I thought of touching them, rubbing my thumb across the ridged surface. I wondered how that would feel.

'I am ashamed of this now.'

She pulled up her knees and wrapped her arms around her calves.

'Your mother would not want that, I'm sure,' I said, although I knew no such thing.

On the television the audience roared. Buster whined in his dream.

'But she was weak. I – despised her?'

She mouthed the syllables carefully, twisted to me to confirm her choice of word. I gave a nod and felt a complicity.

'Even as a girl,' she said. 'It was lonely.'

'It's always lonely.'

'And soon I will have a child. I could not stand it if things were the same.'

She pulled away and her hair slipped out of my hand like something alive.

What to say? I took my time.

'Sometimes the space is too great. Perhaps it was that way for you and your parents. But it can change. You have the chance of a fresh start.'

She said nothing, but looked at me with those depthless eyes.

'I need a refill,' I said. 'Can I get you anything while I'm in there?'

She said no.

In the kitchen it was colder, and I was aware of my flush, the banging of my heart. I saw myself in the window above the sink.

Back in, I sat at a remove.

'Oh look. You like these, don't you?' I said, and groped for the remote control.

A group of handsome boys danced in a line. We watched in silence and soon they were done. The dog stood, stretching out each leg until it trembled, and moved off to a cooler spot. Anja climbed up next to me, sitting on the bottom of her legs, as she did. She laid a hand on my knee.

'What happened to you and Rose?' she asked.

'She. We drifted apart.'

'It is hard for me to understand that. Knowing you.'

I feigned interest at the screen.

'There was an argument?'

'No. No argument. She asked something of me that I couldn't give.'

'What could you not give your child, Maggie?'

She started to cry in gulps and swallows. I felt her anger rise and the beginnings of a distance between us that I couldn't bear.

'Look, I'd made a promise. For good reasons. And the truth would only hurt her. It was complicated.'

'It was about her father, wasn't it, Maggie?'

'Yes, Anja. It was about the father.'

I looked down at her hand on my leg, white, well filled, young. Her nails were alternate pinks, a neon and a pastel, the remains of a home-made manicure. She wore a silver ring on her first finger.

I took it, and the heat in it surprised me again, and the feeling of spongy give.

'It doesn't have to be that way for you. You'll find the right words, Anja, you will. I didn't. But you will.'

I wanted to say: 'Don't think badly of me', but I didn't, thank god.

'Will you brush my hair some more?' she asked.

I moved back towards her.

27

Let's go back again. August 25th, 1984. Chris and I. The day he threw me out.

A hot hot day. I had woken dry-mouthed and woozy; pretty standard for that time. Got up for the loo, tugged the end of the string by its knot, heard its neat perfect click. There were the flies – I will have mentioned those – teeming, seething. Just that year. They never came back.

Then I was sick, in one conclusive heave, and that was not standard. My period was late, only a week, but I knew it for what it was. Pulled on a dress over last night's sweat and strapped the baby into the car.

We took the short drive into Croydon, a clear run with the radio on and the windows open. The breeze rushed in, pimpling my skin and raising the hairs on my arms and when we parked at the back of the shops and I climbed out into the sunshine, the morning's heat pressed down on me. The road smelt gorgeous; it gave, a touch, under my sandals and for a second the horizon tilted. I was excited, against all logic. At having a secret, and the danger of it, but most, I think, at the promise of change. The surety that from now, at least, things would be different.

I went to the boot for the buggy, eyes busy behind my sunglasses, my stomach empty, though I had no appetite. Trippy and insubstantial.

And she felt it all; Bella, my firstborn. She always did; she was witchy that way. She reached for my hair as I bent for her strap and wound a long strand round one finger, laughing at me openly.

My mood travelled through her, expanding into joy in her own tiny self. She sang 'You are my sunshine' at me, and I joined in too, stuffing my face under her chin at the sad bit. She screamed with happiness and yanked great handfuls of me as I pulled away.

'Actually, big girl, maybe you should walk today.'

'Yes. please,' she said. 'I am three.'

Not a baby any more, as Chris was always telling me.

'You infantilise her' – a quote recognisably his mother's.

True, but just the way it was. Such were the parameters of our love.

We took a lap of the shop to check for anyone we knew and bought a test from an approving pharmacist. I felt calmer on the way home and recited nursery rhymes to Bella all the way, patting at the stiff white paper bag on the passenger seat now and then, to feel for the box inside. I didn't rush, enjoying the last few moments of before.

I settled her with some toys and locked myself in the loo. I read the instructions carefully, despite having done this every month for the year it took with Bella. I had known to wait, and with a toilet in sight, was suddenly desperate.

I rushed to undo the stiff plastic of the packaging. Unstoppered the test tube and clicked it into its stand. Readied the cup beneath me, and found I couldn't go. I tried to concentrate, to isolate the muscles that needed to relax. My urine, when it came, was a sharp toxic yellow with a wisp of cloud twisting through it. I filled the pipette with a bubbly suck, and carried it over to the test tube, ready with its half-inch of chemical. I squirted in my sample, and watched the liquids mix.

Bella banged on the door and I felt a blast of irritation. I said nothing and she quietened. A lorry passed outside and the shelf shivered in its fitting. I watched the finger of liquid ebb and ripple and steadied the tube with a finger. The instructions were clear. Keep the sample still. Any vibrations might affect the accuracy of your results. When the surface had flattened I left the bathroom and lay on my bed, summer coming in through the window, the radio down low while my daughter bounced and chattered. She knew this mood and liked it best, when I was still, so she could get to me. The fact that I was absent posed no problem; an advantage, even.

I watched the clock empty-headed and when it was ten minutes over, got up to find a bright ring of colour suspended in the liquid like some crazy type of science.

Then Chris's car outside, back from golf, and I shoved all the bits back in their box, wrapped it in loo roll and ran downstairs, stuffing the bundle right down into the bin – not about to make that stupid mistake.

I was washing my hands at the sink when he found me and I watched his mouth take shape in anticipation of speech when a dull thud sounded behind him, which was Bella's head meeting the skirting board as she tipped heavily down the last of the stairs.

He reached her inside the long pause of her inhale and I was about to call out when her cry finally came, though it was smothered by his shirt. A great big bump appeared and then a lollipop, which he had bought on the way home, held back until the medicine went down. No harm done.

A better father than he was a husband. I wondered if it was me.

I went back to the day. It was mainly preparations for that evening, the dinner Chris had arranged on our behalf, but my piano lesson first.

I ran through my practice before he arrived, like a schoolgirl, and drank up my praise when it came. The room was stifling, the crispy old velvet of the piano stool sticking to my cotton dress.

I felt sorry for Ben, sopping in his shirt, which he plucked away from him in a nervous gesture. A half-circle of sweat showed through in the space above his vest, and his hair at the back was darkened, like Bella's after a nightmare. I had imagined him an émigré, a Jew with a tragic story, but he was a local boy, from Carshalton. I played 'Ave Maria', still new, before I'd heard it on a hundred TV weddings, and a miracle to me. It brought Chris to the door but Ben hadn't noticed, listening with his eyes shut, and he jumped when Chris spoke: 'That's beautiful, Maggie. You're really coming along.'

Afterwards, I offered Ben lemonade; fresh lemons in a tall glass jug stirred with a long metal spoon. We talked, sometimes, while we shared a drink but Chris joined us today and conversation limped.

And all the time there was the baby, my knowledge of it. I nearly told Ben, after the piece, but common sense prevailed. I bent to it now and again and warmed my hands there for a while, and then turned back to the world, bland and smiling, before anyone noticed that I'd gone.

It receded, though, during the party. I was distracted, hot and tipsy, trying to keep to the timings and make it all look effortless. Until Jan, until the very end of the night. I was exhausted, no longer vigilant, the smell of her menthol fag brought my hand to my mouth and she said: 'Maggie, are you all right? Are you sick?' Then: 'You're not.'

We were sat out the back on the wooden kitchen chairs, just her and me, the others behind us, indoors. I dropped my head, legs wide, the top of my arms along my thighs. All around was the sound of scores of couples enjoying identical evenings.

The noise of it rushed me and I thought that I would vomit, but it passed and things returned to their appropriate distance. I glanced at her briefly. Down again. Rubbed my eyes and my temples.

'I see,' she said.

A little time and I straightened. I looked out into the dark of the garden, the air hot and solid, and saw a lit square of orange appear in the night. Someone sat, on the loo, I imagined, and I watched them, framed by the window in perfect profile like a face on a cameo. A matter of seconds and they stood and the night was sealed shut again. I turned to Jan, feeling like I'd imagined it.

She sat posed, stiff and awkward, and I thought maybe she was ill – something to do with my food – and then realised.

'Oh, Jan, I'm so sorry. I know you and Ian. Have had problems. I mean. That you've been trying for a while.'

She gave no acknowledgement.

'I should've. Sorry. It was thoughtless.'

'It's all right, Maggie,' she said, and got up from her chair.

She walked back inside and I thought how little I liked this woman and wondered why I had spent an evening trying to please her. Then I remembered that I hadn't, that I had made fun of her jelly, and snorted a giggle out of my nose. I sneaked up the stairs to my daughter.

Coming down, there was that sense of something wrong that people talk about. Not intuition, I don't think; it was more physical. An adrenal response, a chemical awareness of danger. I didn't look to my husband; had I done so, his absence would surely have told me something, particularly coupled with Jan's. Nor did I trust enough in my own instinct to ask. I went along with things until the truth was unignorable.

And even then, standing in his office, my thoughts crawled. About him and Jan I found I cared very little. I hadn't known, or even suspected. I wondered when I'd last even looked at him.

I felt my humiliation in retrospect, though, as I worked out how it must have played. Jan leaving me in the garden, going straight through to my husband. Pulling him away from our guests with a look or a proprietary hand.

Unless she started it there, in front of them? Perhaps they'd all known for months, talked it through, decided on their allegiances. Chris saw some of this on my face and moved to close it: 'Don't start, Maggie. I'll make sure you're OK, I will. If you behave. But you do need to behave. There will be terms. There is a baby to consider now after all.'

There was a question in that, I saw it straight away. A window of doubt that I could have prised open, if I so chose. Our sex life was infrequent and at my behest, but it was not dead; a shame for Jan, but there you go. The dates were ambiguous and I could have made them work. I could have called it his, but I would need to track back, make the weeks tally, offer some kind of surety. He would have made his own calculations, though his face gave nothing away, and he wouldn't get it wrong, or broker doubt.

I took a deep breath and tried to count. In the meantime,

conjure offence, audacity, hauteur. But my mind was dull and sticky. The moment stretched and snapped. I abandoned all effort and watched him fill up with disdain.

'That's that then,' he said, and went, trailing Jan.

He stopped at the door.

'One last thing, Maggie. We're going to have to talk about Bella.'

He told me he'd be back the next day.

28

A productive morning, not that I worked. I'd taken a break from all that – Nancy was fine, there were plenty of transcriptionists. I had been trying to understand Anja's case. Researching things. Seeing if I could help.

There is a process, but it is not simple. At the moment of her escape, Anja became a Potential Victim of Trafficking. She told them what had happened to her – I knew that much from the policewoman – but they could not take her at her word. Her goal was to be acknowledged as a fully-fledged victim. The moment she spoke up, a countdown to that decision began.

This first stage is named Reasonable Grounds. Five days in which to determine if her story was credible, plausible. That they thought, but could not prove, that all she said was true. There was space for conjecture, gut feel; imagination even. What a job. What a week. We had long since passed that milestone.

The next stretch was hers for 'recovery and reflection', that thing she said to me the first day that we met. This was how she seemed to use it. A couple of days on, and the man on the bus was forgotten. Her balance was back and like a child she found delight all over – a funny in the paper, something nice to eat. She floated free of this drama, or so it appeared, all the serious work taking place elsewhere, someone else determining her future. Her outlook made no sense to me; I did not see how she could live with the unknowing. If it were me, it would be different. Everything would taste bitter. I found that I was souring on her behalf.

All working towards a Conclusive Decision. If they found in her favour, they believed it more likely than not, that she, Anja, had been a victim of trafficking. The language was snaky and congealed. I wondered how it worked in practice. She would be granted leave of one year, while she helped the police, to be extended if required. The target for this decision was forty-five days.

I reached for my diary – in name only, its pages went unfilled. She had been here two months; more. That milestone was long passed. Why had she not said?

I read on. My world listed. When the court case was over, regardless of outcome, she had no right to remain. It became a question of asylum, then, which hinged on risk. The degree to which a woman was seen to be in danger; of reprisal, discrimination, of violence or of re-trafficking should she go back to where she once called home. This process was ongoing. Her case was complicated but she could hear news any day.

It made my head spin. How could she be so passive? So ill prepared? We should have told the police about the man, the threat; that much was clear. Perhaps it would all fall to me.

I had missed lunch by then; would have done better, perhaps, to name this sensation – an anxiety cut with something sharper, blood thrumming in my ears – as hunger. But I did not. Instead I paced the house, trailing the poor dog, stuck as ever with some version of my mood. It did not suit him – he is naturally disposed to caution – but it is the fate of all dogs to share the burden of their owner's emotion. He clamped his ears to his head, nosing frantically to distract himself, trying to throw me off his back.

I went to my notes written in a fresh pad from the drawer and the pages that I had printed, having finally unjammed the thing only to find it inexplicably switched to photocopy.

There were helplines and guidelines, offices to visit and numbers to call and I tried one, but after ten minutes holding, lost patience. I slammed the phone into its cradle which made a plasticky snap and I thought for a second that I'd broken it, but the impact had merely opened a seam along the mid-line where the batteries go. It snapped back flush with a click.

Buster was whining for a wee and I thought of his walk and the others, my friends, who would be wondering, soon, what was up. Which led me to Peter, who had started in the Law, and his pro bono work and the shame he felt in abandoning it when the pressure became too great. Peter, of course; he would know what to do.

They would be at home now, the two of them, having eaten something wholesome at their reclaimed table. Paul would get up to air the dogs and Peter go back to his work; I knew the shape of their routine. It would breach the terms of our friendship to arrive uninvited, but I found that I didn't care.

I put Buster in the garden, perplexed but compliant, and went out. The temperature had dropped and the air swiped the breath from me. My eyes sprung tears. I broke into a jog of sorts – I was cold, had thrown a coat over my shirt as I left – and arrived at theirs panting; tight-chested and chilly with sweat. My knock was hectic and uneven.

Peter came to the door.

'Maggie! What a surprise. Come in. Paul's not here though.'

'I know,' I said. 'That's fine. I wanted to see you, actually.'

He took my coat off somewhere, and gestured that I walk through.

The hall opened into a huge room at the back that Peter had designed himself. It was all glass out to the garden where the lawn had been replaced with a rough grey slate. There was a smooth curved stone something set to one side, water turning over its surface and, as I watched, a bird swooped down and took brief sips from the deepest point – a knot of current where two fast streams met.

He took a while. I wondered if he was phoning for Paul.

There was plenty of seating, though no obvious place to sit. A row of high plastic stools were tucked under a bar-like stretch that signified the border of the kitchen. A bench ran the length of their table that I would struggle to get into, or out of. He must have come to the front door from elsewhere, for it was dark in here, an unlit winter afternoon squeezing out the edges of the room. Then he was back and pressed a button on a panel in the wall. Light rose in another portion of the space and a sofa was revealed, uplit by a stream of small bulbs set flush into the floor. I took myself towards it.

'I've come to ask a favour,' I said, before I sat down, and he had the chance to ask.

'OK,' he replied, though his tone was more of a maybe.

'Well, it's for Anja really, not me' – a lie, I saw, as soon as I had said it.

'It's about her case. I think she needs help. Better representation. Or at least some more advice. I'm not sure she's quite. Getting to grips with things.'

'And she's asked you to do this, Maggie?' Peter said.

He was drumming the pad of his thumb with his first finger, an exposure of nerves.

'Well, no. I thought I'd speak to you first. I didn't want her to get her hopes up or anything.'

'I mention it only because I've already offered. And she told me no. Quite clearly.'

When did they talk, she and Peter? I thought she only worked an hour or two here, once a week. And Paul said he stuck in his office all day. Could it be that she stayed on afterwards, as she did at mine? Drank tea? Lifted her legs and laid her head down on this sofa?

I looked down and next to one of my old hands lay a single coarse hair, deep red until the last half inch of black. I reached out and edged it with a nail. It jumped out of reach at my touch.

'Oh right. I see.'

He watched me, saying nothing. I pulled at a thread of burnt orange, an expensive thick-weave linen.

'Mags, is that OK? You see my position?' he asked.

His voice was kind and he seemed unembarrassed to say no. This reassured me. It allowed me to go on.

I said, 'Peter, I want you to do it anyway.'

He frowned.

'I'm not sure, Maggie. That doesn't feel quite. Ethical.'

'Ethical?' It came out as I'd thought it, incredulous, dismissive. 'Don't look at it like that. She's a teenager. Think of yourself at that age. She doesn't know what's for the best. She doesn't understand.'

'Well, yes. That's possible,' he said.

'And I think she's hiding from it actually, from what happened and from what might happen next. As friends we need to help her, Peter. It's our responsibility.'

Did I believe this? I felt conviction as I spoke but would have said what was needed to get him to agree. I was ready to expose her child; that would have come next, if required.

'Don't you see? She has lost her trust in others, in everyone, given what she's been through. We need to act for her,' I said.

I saw in his silence that I had gone just far enough.

'What's to be lost in asking someone, Peter? We don't even have to tell her, if we don't want. Or depending on what we find out. But at least we'll have a clearer idea of how things stand.'

'Yes. All right. I have someone I can call. Leave it with me.'

A decent man, Peter. I admired his decisiveness and the ease with which he could change his mind.

'I'll let you know what she says, Mags, but I want you to be careful. You're thinking like a mother here. Which I do under-stand. But keep yourself safe, OK?'

I kissed him on the cheek. Just once; my way.

'Thanks, Peter. Let's see what your friend recommends,' I said.

'OK. We'll talk.'

He stood. 'I need to get back to work now.'

'Of course.'

I pushed myself up.

'One thing though,' I said to him, at the door.

'Would you not tell Paul? I mean it's not a big deal, and if you're uncomfortable please forget I said anything. It's just that I'd hate for him to worry on my behalf. That's all.'

An irrational request that I did not know why I made. I felt a disproportionate pleasure when he agreed.

On my way home I succumbed to a daydream. One minute I was walking, fast, the wind slapping my face, hair trapped in my lashes. The lack of dog a presence in itself, a ghost limb, my hand flexing for the lead. A general sense of purpose, I suppose; a mood of qualified optimism.

Then a change. A soaring of the heart. That is accurate. It was new to me.

For the first instance, I could not place its source, until I saw us together, Anja and me, in something like a vision. We were doing what we always do but there was a permanence to it. Someone to take meals with, hold on to a story for. Nothing dramatic.

It burnt out soon, this emotion, snuffed by logic. Implausible. Stupid, even. It was the strangest thing. But a warmth remained.

I felt it still, when I got home, opened the door, expecting her off-tune whistling, the natter of the radio. When there was silence, a sorrow began, deep in my chest, but I knew the ways to keep it down.

And it was not as if I was alone any more. The past was back, pushed up against me.

I sat in front of the television and it reached across; ate from my plate. There was something in my bed now, where once there was just space. It was not company, on that much I was clear. I wished that I could kill it, but I had forgotten how.

29

I had told myself caution, caution, but when Friday came and I heard her in the house, I knew that I would speak. I clicked the dog off his lead and he ran to the kitchen for a drink. His laps were huge and noisy and he came back through to me dripping from his chops. I slid my shoes under the rack and called up into the stairwell.

'Hi there, Anja, is that you? Shall I put the kettle on?'

'No, thanks, Mags. I've only just started. Later would be great,' she said, still out of sight.

From her voice, I thought I placed her in my room.

But I couldn't wait.

I went on up and she passed me outside the bathroom, mouthed a brief greeting. I stood there a moment trying to find the words, and walked through to my study, saw its unusual disarray. I heard her behind me.

'Everything OK, Mags? I guess you left in a hurry!' she said, pointing at my desk.

'Oh! Just wanted to get him out before it got too late. I'm fine. Everything's fine, thanks.'

I looked down and bothered some papers.

'And how about you? How are you?' I asked.

'Yeah yeah yeah, good,' she said and I knew if I didn't start she would be off, putting right my mess.

'It's just. I've been meaning to talk to you,' I said.

I heaved my bottom onto the edge of the desk. She paused in the doorway and threw her damp cloth cleanly into the bathroom. I found it later, stuck dried onto the basin. Her face was clear but careful.

'I've been wondering, Anja, how is it going with your case?' I said.

Straight away I knew my tone was off; too measured, leaking concern. I remembered this from dealings with my daughter. Girls sense these things and they do not like them.

Her eyebrows, dark and pencilled, dipped towards her nose in a deep dissatisfaction. She held herself still, and ready.

'What do you mean?' she said.

'Well, the referral process. I suppose the decision has been made by now? And your asylum claim. I mean I really think we could put some work in there.'

The words fell, too practised, between us.

'How do you know about all this, Maggie?' she asked.

'Oh I don't really. I was just on the computer and I had a bit of a look. I want to help, that's all. No big deal,' I said.

Under my hand lay a sheet headed 'UK Border Agency' in red, white and blue, but I didn't dare move.

'I have a solicitor,' she said.

'Oh really? Because I thought that you only got legal help for the asylum bit? So I assume you've got conclusive grounds –'

But she had started towards the stairs. I raised my voice.

'We should have mentioned Goran's man. And the pregnancy. I've been meaning to bring that up –'

She stopped, took an exaggerated pause and spoke into the empty air ahead of her.

'It's OK, Maggie. I'm dealing with it. I don't want to talk

about this any more now, thank you.'

I said nothing and she corkscrewed at the waist. Her eye, the one I could see, was a single dark tone, and then she moved and its surface was broken, a sharp cube of silver, a flash of outside refracted through the skylight.

I saw an immobility there that must have driven her mother mad. Rose had worn a version of that face, leached of feeling, denying me access, but she would run when it happened, dip her head and take off to her bedroom where she knew I wouldn't follow. I had been glad to let her go.

Anja, though, was different. She held her position; let the silence stretch until there could be no mistaking her invitation. I felt the pull of the fight; a rolling, like lust, in the hollow of my stomach. How pleasing, I thought, to hold up her belligerence, her ignorance; to list its implications. My argument unfurled, lucid in my head, and I knew that I could win, and felt a brief taste of that satisfaction.

A heat started in me, dangerous and spreading. It raced down corridors, certain of its route. I left Anja, in pursuit of it; closed my eyes as I barrelled towards its source.

I knew her before we got there; Helen of course, my mother. Hands gripping her skirts, eyes on fire, transported. She was articulate in her fury; a glamour to her – her only glamour. Never more compelling than in the arms of a rage. She would have come for me then, with a slap or a yank, more welcome than the cut of her tongue.

Anja registered the break in our connection and took it as retreat. She moved down the steps bouncily and I watched her vanish in slices. I followed; shocked, contrite, and nearly lost my footing in socks.

'Anja. I'm only trying to help. Please,' I called.

She had gone through to the sitting room, and stood at the shelves. She picked up my stuff and used the tea towel that she carried over her shoulder to flick at the dust. She knocked the shepherdess, but caught it deftly.

'Can you not let me help you?' I asked.

'Oh, Maggie. What do you know?' Easily, smilingly.

'Well. How these things work,' I said.

'What things?'

'Official processes for example,' I replied, hearing my own ridiculousness.

'No. You don't. Here in your comfortable life –' Slow and rhythmed.

She held her hand before her, circling it on her wrist, and took a long lazy look at me. She moved off again. She wiped the edges of the telly with exaggerated care. When she crouched to the satellite box, I could see her tattoo and the top of her pants.

'Anja. If you mean. I can't begin to know what it was like for you in Italy. Of course I can't,' I said.

She strolled across to the skirting.

'It was not how you think,' she said.

'Of course. Not for one moment. I couldn't imagine –'

She stood up, knees clicking. Rolled an ankle with a hand on the opposite hip for balance.

'No. I mean. Goran was my boyfriend.'

I thought of the man at the airport. A young man still, fit and strong. Powerful. Exciting perhaps.

'Maybe I was stupid. But there you go.'

A twitch of shrug. A convincing toughness.

She began to sway gently, shifting from foot to foot, pretending a lack of interest in me.

'I was with him for a year, though he was away a lot. He said he was a salesman.'

She huffed a short breath out of her nose.

'And did he come from your town?' I asked politely, as if enquiring about the usual courtship story.

'No, he just arrived. He said there was a cousin in the next village.'

She faced me plainly then, and with a question. She had expected shock, perhaps even hoped for it, but I just saw my daughter in her. Rose's teenage efforts at worldliness; her casual acknowledgement of some scandal, or expression of adult opinion, and the watch and wait to see how I would react. I had consistently failed to register outrage; not so as to disappoint her, I simply never felt it. Human frailty rarely surprises me.

'I don't suppose you're the first, Anja; nor will you be the last,' I said, a sudden tiredness upon me.

But she did not want to be absolved, or made typical.

'I left with him because I wanted to, you know,' she continued.

'Yes, I see that,' I said.

'He came with me to the house when I told my parents.'

She lifted a cushion from the seat of the sofa and propped it against her thigh. She gave it three hard slaps. Clouds of dust burst around her hand.

I pictured the scene, her pride at her lover, her disdain for home and the old life she was throwing off. Her certainty and her excitement. The way her parents recoiled.

'My mother cried and my father said "Just go", but I didn't care.'

I wondered how these months had been for them.

'You poor thing,' I said. 'It must have been awful.'

'Some of the other girls, they will never be OK. But I am. I am free,' she said and her look was narrow and proud.

'You are.'

But my agreement seemed to deflate her. She dropped onto the seat and rubbed the creases from her forehead.

'But would you let your daughter leave? With a man that you did not trust?' she said, at last.

Always the mother who shouldered the blame.

'What choice did she have, Anja? Be honest. Would you have listened either way?'

It came out sharp and she looked up at me, surprised.

'But she did not try. She would not stand up to my father. She was too worried about shame.'

Her voice was shrill and I watched tears gather at the water-line of her lower lid. So I sat and threw an arm around her but the set of her shoulders was unyielding.

'I'll make you a cup of tea. And run you a bath, if you like,' I said, in the end.

'Thanks, Mags,' she replied. 'I can do my own.'

She set off towards the stairs and paused for a moment at the bottom.

'Mags?' she called, though she knew I was still there. 'One thing. I've been meaning to ask. Could I keep some stuff here? A few bits? Just so they can be safe? A lot of people come and go where I am staying.'

'Of course you can. Bring them next time. No problem at all,' I said, happy to be able to help.

'Thanks,' she said.

She carried on up and did not falter as the phone rang and Chris's voice came at us from the hall. Her step remained sure.

Thing is, we understood each other, Anja and I. And that is rare.

30

Low light, white sky, nature in November shades I'd never wear. A beautiful day for walking. The dog pulled and I'd forgotten my gloves, but I didn't mind. I caught step with my friends, slipped back into the old grooves. I waited for them at the usual place.

We had a good walk, a long one. Buster tried hard with the other dogs, but Sammy is a loner and the Jack Russell sisters have no space for anyone else, particularly such a large and enthusiastic male. He cantered towards them and they waited till he got close and twisted away unkindly, separating easily as if they'd planned it. I watched him lurch on the spot, like an old rocking-horse, unsure of his next move. The two dogs circled back and he realised they were teasing him. He cast me a look, and set off on his own. He didn't seem to mind.

Maureen shouted for Sammy who paced the railings by the swings, her head following the children's dip and soar. I noticed the absence of strain in Mo's voice and knew that this was Lauren's work, filling her mother's time, needing her again, and was happy for my friend.

Paul has said nothing, so I guess Peter must have kept his word. We walked some more and the feeling between us was gentle. They didn't mention Anja and so nor did I. Yet she was never far from my mind. It was almost like being in love.

It was funny to be touched again. I shrank from it at first, her gummy grip. She was mucky, like a child, with bitten-down nails and bloodied cuticles. Yet her skin was white and smooth and filled. She laid her palm on me softly and left it there. I blushed hot at first, but later, remained calm. She slipped an arm through mine as we walked.

Her smell was fleshy up close, but not unpleasant. She did not the hide the fact that she was human, alive. There was no shame in her. My own aroma is good sense and hygiene, a layering of gels, sprays and liqui-tabs; my pheromones indiscernible beneath them.

I came to enjoy the proximity of another, and found that it was contagious. Paul jumped, first time I knocked against him with a shoulder, my initial, rather clumsy advance – he thought I had slipped – but soon he rubbed my back and touched a hand. Maureen hadn't noticed, I was sure, and yet she responded nonetheless. Her behaviours changed; she warmed and mellowed. Funny how we read each other's signals, just like the dogs.

I left them for the butcher's to get a chicken and couple of decent steaks. Someone opened the door just as I arrived and I breathed one deep rusty lungful and stepped aside to let a woman out with her buggy.

I found I stood before a new shop, or a shop I had never noticed before. Its window was a landscape of sweets, floss clouds, marshmallow hills and huge lollipops for trees. It sold things for babies; a shrunken jacket was laid against the scene, looking puffed out and inhabited; a silver spoon stuck out from the egg-yolk sun and a string of elf tooth boxes formed the tail of a kite. Rippling from a flagpole, in front of which a teddy flew a plane, was the most beautiful lemon blanket.

I went in and spoke to the lady, who took me to the plinth

where they all lay stacked, in the obvious shades and my yellow, a raspberry and a teal.

Up close, the cashmere was fine and downy. She spoke of its versatility, its refusal to moult or pill and finally its price, one hundred and twenty-five pounds, and we both stroked as she talked, a softness under my hand that seemed impossible in nature. I imagined Anja's baby underneath it, tucked in tight and sleeping, face turned and perfect. And next, I'd bought one, and the box was almost as good again: square, shallow, an untreated cardboard secured with a thick velvet ribbon of aquamarine. I raced back through the park, my heart pounding, the meat forgotten.

She wasn't expected until later, and I was unsure of how to fill the time. The box I placed on the sofa, in the kitchen, and finally back in its bag. A bath, I decided; that is what Anja would do.

It was a long time since I had lain immersed in water. How altering, and what a marvel, weightlessness. Every now and again I moved my feet from the end of the bath, laid my head back and achieved a moment of perfect balance, suspended like a spaceman.

I added more hot until my chest felt shrunk, and pushed away all thought of guilt and wastefulness.

My hands before me were no longer my own, their usual patterning, a geometric repeat like the veins of a leaf, had vanished.

I lifted a leg out of the water, and observed it, for the first time in years. The calf muscle hung low off the shinbone, wobbly in its bag of skin. I straightened it, my back held, and ran my hand up and down its length. Hairless now, a few soft bristles aside. My skin contracted beneath my touch, which felt more alien, even, than Anja's.

Tears came next; no sorrow, or emotion, nor a sound. Just an emptying. I closed my eyes, loose-lidded, and moved lower in the bath and let the tears slide through their crack and down my face, until they merged with the water.

When Rose was small I would lie in a similar bath, about a mile away, doing just the same. It relieved something, like letting a vein can, for some. I would slip into the warm and the tears would flow, like milk, and when I sat up later, the bath blood cool, water sheeting off me, I felt eased.

It was a strain, those early years, though no one would have known it. I made myself seem free and unencumbered. Other mothers were intrigued, they told me later, at the point that they believed us friends. My absence made me interesting. I was without need, like the boy they couldn't get or keep at college. And I built relationships with these people, of a sort. It is easy to take care of those you don't really care for. I found the words; I helped. But I was wipe clean, and nothing of their problems stuck. This was how I knew it wasn't real. They drifted away over time.

Things changed when there was Maureen, Peter and Paul. What was it, five years back? If not total honesty between us, there was, is, a lack of pretence. An underrated quality in friendship, in my view.

And then came Anja, and what was it that we two shared? Could I say I was myself with her, that exalted state, whatever it may be? I am not sure. But who would want that anyway? With Anja, I could be someone else; I could start anew. And what is better than that?

I hauled myself out, dried, dressed and waited.

When she got to me at last, I felt shy and sensitive; the seams of my shirt abrasive on my skin. She brought the outside in with her, on her coat, in her hair – old food and perfume, half-dried wool and something musky. It was all I could do not to take a step away.

'Oh, Anja,' I said. 'By the way. I picked you something up.'

I handed her the bag.

'Thanks, Mags!' she said, and reached inside. She took the gift, and let the bag slide to the floor.

The packaging held no interest for her; she didn't see that the box had been hand-folded, nor the message that I had chosen, inked on to one corner in the shop with a wooden backed stamp. The woman had run its curved surface back and forth across a moist black pad and pressed it onto the cardboard with the care of a child. 'From Me To You With Love xox,' it read, in a cursive that looked neat and aged.

Instead, Anja tugged at the ribbon then chucked it onto a chair. She ripped the box in her efforts to get inside, and revealed a first glimpse of the blanket; one buttery tuft. She grasped this corner, pulled, and the packaging fell away. The blanket dropped before her in a long liquidy ripple. She took a second edge and held it up, a rectangle now, as wide as her arm span and halfway down to the carpet.

I saw that she was confused as to its point. To me, too, the gift seemed all at once insane; ridiculous and profligate. I wished that I could tear it from her hands; hide the thing. She looked at me over the drop of cashmere, and back down.

'It's –' I started.

'A scarf'! I know! Thanks!' she said, and flung it behind her

196

head. She pulled an end and wrapped the length another time round her neck, loosening it roughly at her throat.

'It's awesome! So soft!' she said, and buried her nose deep into the wool.

There were two inky prints already visible and I saw the weave gape where she had tugged.

'This'll keep me so warm. Let's go for a walk and try it!'

I put the box by the back door and ripped off the sticker that showed a baby heart next to a bigger one. The colour didn't suit, the yellow drained the life from her.

I found my coat and went back out.

There is a place I walk when I don't want to be with others. Gloomy, full of dogshit, but it does the job. I took her there. Daylight was failing and the grass was studded with rubbish, frozen where it fell, but we strode, and the grip of my disappointment let up. I thought, how indoors we are, Anja and I; and watched the other walkers look twice and try to work us out.

Anja's mood was airy. She fingered the blanket at her neck, kicked leaves with her useless canvas shoes.

'Have you ever been in love, Maggie?' she asked, after a bit, swinging her arms, her mittens flapping beyond them.

'Oh, I don't know. Not to any satisfactory conclusion,' I said.

'But you know what they say though. It's never too late. Right?' said Anja.

She was given to cheering cliché.

'Indeed they do.'

'Peter and Paul are good, though. Don't you think?'

'They are,' I said, although the truth was that I found it hard to watch; the care they took, the mutual respect. My instinct

197

was to jeer. Could this be real? I had come to believe that men were not like us. Their happiness was a shock to me, an insult almost. Like hearing the world is flat, after all.

We walked some more and I felt her mood next to me tilt.

'Anja. Whatever it was that you had with Goran –' I began, but didn't know how to finish.

She waited.

'Well. I'm sure you're aware. That it was not love.'

'But I did love him,' she said simply.

'Yes. You may have done. But what he did –.'

She interrupted: 'He could be kind sometimes.'

Buster came and bowed to me to show me that he wanted to play. Then he saw our faces and moved along.

'At first we went to Tirana. It's the capital, you know?'

I said yes, though I didn't.

'There were parties,' she said. 'I thought it was his thing. To share.'

The path was muddy and trenched. I held her hand to steady her as she stepped up and walked its flimsy lip to avoid the worst. My own boots sucked and bubbled.

'And then he told me it was business,' she said.

The ground became firmer, and I let her go.

I saw him travelling with panache, orbited by girls, raising a finger for more drinks.

A small dog cantered over and the fussing of him absolved me of the need to reply. I think she read my silence as rebuke.

'Maggie, I was alone in a new place,' she said, her voice pitching upwards.

'Of course. I'm not. I'm just listening.'

Her phone beeped but she silenced it, low in her pocket.

'You really don't need.' I tried, but she wouldn't let me finish.

'I know, and maybe you don't want to hear, but there is more,' she said.

'OK,' I replied, long and inflected, and it made me think of my daughter again, her confessions; that she had hidden sweets, been mean, told a lie.

'I did not work for long. It was not his idea for me. He said I could stop if I helped.'

Her meaning was clear but it seemed that she wished me to ask.

'Help with what, Anja?' I said.

'Getting more girls.'

What did I feel? Sadness, mainly.

'You are the only person I have told this to,' she said.

'Well. Thank you. For trusting me. That must have been a terrible decision.'

She shrugged.

'Less terrible than working.'

'Yes. I suppose so.'

A fine frozen rain began, like the flimsiest of snow. It chilled me, where it touched my skin, but failed to translate into wet. There was traffic, a drill not far, no human sound.

'He said there would be someone else, if I didn't,' she said, with the beginnings of a whine.

'And I'm sure he was right.'

Then: 'Mags. Do you think the other girls will tell?'

'The police? Who knows? But you are not to blame. We do what we have to, Anja. In the situations we find ourselves in. You didn't choose it. Most of us are. Never tested, I suppose.'

'It was not for long, Maggie. And there was only one girl and we left her when we came here. Maybe she went back home?' she said.

'Let's hope so. I hope so too.'

'So now you know,' she said.

'Indeed. Anja, you survived. That's the main thing. And now you're here.'

'Yes, I am. Thanks to you.'

'Oh, not really,' I said, but she was at me. She took me in her fierce embrace and her breath was rushed in my ear, her chest heaving, her face still wet.

'You would fight for me, Maggie. I know you would.'

I felt her belief inside me, in my heart.

'I would Anja. I will.'

She held me there for a long time and I closed my eyes against the stares of passers-by.

'Let's get back,' I said.

We walked fast, our arms linked tight. It felt colder as we pushed out into the wind, and warmer again as our bodies heated. I wanted to get home as if something more waited for us there, beyond the yellow of a fire, a full glass and companionship. She matched my speed and began to pull me on, younger and strong. The dog jogged close with a wide wet grin. Anja hummed beside me and then the bravest of a group of boys called 'Lezzies!' at us, from a safe distance, and we roared, we really did, in a way I could barely remember, my mouth stretched huge and stupid, the noise catching in the top of my throat. We heaved and rocked and in the end I got a stitch. When it had passed, I felt a little bereavement.

'One thing, Anja,' I said. 'There's one thing I've been meaning to ask.'

'Yes,' she said cautiously.

'It's just. Why me?'

She gave a rolling chuckle. 'What do you mean?' she said.

'At the airport. How did you decide? Why me?'

We were on the street now. Home in five minutes.

She was silent and I saw that she was considering her answer. I took to counting our steps; a nail must have come through the sole of a boot, for my heel marked out a sharp metallic beat.

I went back to the fantasy of my involvement; a scene I visited for comfort.

Anja gets off the plane; no plan but alert to opportunity. Every nerve sings. She is looking for someone. She will know her when she sees her.

Next we are in the loo, standing in line. She studies me up close, sees the hump of bone at the top of my neck that aches from the journey; a whorl of scalp where my hair is flattened, the slope of one shoulder bowed in testament to every handbag I've ever worn. But she doesn't see vulnerability or feel pity. She doesn't see middle-aged woman at all. She sees someone who will change her life, who is strong and brave enough to help. She is wondering, should she? Dare she? She needs to find a way to ask. She wills the question into life. Somehow, miraculously, I hear it and look across; I see that face. Our connection is made. Everything is agreed.

Still Anja hadn't spoken.

'You were just there, Maggie,' she said, in the end.

'I felt sick. The pregnancy. I got to the toilet and I thought I would throw up and they would know. I was panicking. I splashed water on my face to try and stop myself. And I looked up and I saw you in the mirror, and you were staring at me so hard that I felt frightened. It sounds so stupid now.'

'No,' I said.

'I was terrified. I couldn't move, all of a sudden. I thought I might even die. And so I said a prayer – the first time in years – I prayed to god to help me. I even whispered the word out loud, I think. When I heard a knock on the door I nearly passed out! I saw it was you and I ran.'

'But you grabbed me, Anja.'

'I'm sorry, Mags! I just needed to get away! I know this is crazy but for a minute I thought you were with him.'

I thought how fluent she had become, how expert her English.

'But soon I saw that you could help. That I could hide better with you beside me. And the weirdest thing of all, it was so easy! All I had to do was decide. It was up to me. Just me. It was amazing to know that, Mags.'

My vanity exposed; I might even have laughed out loud. How could it have been otherwise? I knew this world. Blind and indifferent. But it was still the world that delivered me Anja.

'Why don't you stay tonight?' I said, all in a rush. 'The spare room's made up. It wouldn't be a problem. Not at all.'

The idea had been growing as she spoke. Now it filled my head; the neat clean bedroom, sheets fresh out of plastic, hospital corners.

'That would be great actually, Mags,' she replied. 'I do feel tired.'

'Come on then. We're nearly there.'

31

I put her in the sitting room.

'Hold on. Let me just go and air it for a sec. Then I'll show you up.'

'I know it, Mags! I clean in there all the time!' she said.

'Of course. But you're a guest now. Just give me a moment. I'll check it's all OK.'

I took the stairs in twos. The door needed a push across its dense inch of carpet. The air inside was still, unbreathed.

I pulled up the sash window and a bit of London rushed me, the deep release of bus brakes and the shriek of a girl who must have slipped. Next door's nanny was smoking in the garden and I leant out and inhaled. I took in just enough for something to happen – a tightening behind my temples, the briefest sense of alteration.

I went to the airing cupboard and fetched two towels that I laid on the chair.

I straightened the covers, plumped and then levelled them.

There was a carafe with a glass on the bedside table. This, I rinsed and filled.

I turned the radiator on and the bedside lamp, rubbed the surfaces with the elbow of my sweater. There was nothing else. The room was small and otherwise empty. I caught sight of myself in the mirror. My hair had bounced and I looked a little manic.

Then I stepped around the bed and opened a wardrobe door. There were a couple of old coats and a tangle of dry cleaner's hangers, which I straightened, ready for her things. An old box lay on the floor, of the sort you assemble yourself. I toed it in to a corner, but its old position remained, marked out as an absence of dust.

On the other side, my summer things hung. This door was stiff, unaccountably so, and when it finally opened, I saw an edge of sundress fall away, bearing an imprint of hinge. I carried the box across and watched it vanish beneath decades of hemline. All things settled, I reached for it anyway. Empty but for shoes. Four little pairs of shoes.

I lifted the lid at arm's length and felt inside, something of the lucky dip in it. First, I pulled out the mary-janes, black patent, the length of my palm. Their pink soles were unblemished, the only sign of wear a swipe of scuff on the back of one. I imagined her sat at a table, feet swinging, her shoe catching the leg of her chair. Had I scolded her for this? What would the occasion have been? I couldn't picture her in them at all and didn't know why I'd chosen to keep them, though they were beautiful enough.

A school shoe next; Rose's first. I had written in these, her name along the side, though the NS of the surname was rubbed away; an early sign, I realised, of her high arch, which remained undiagnosed for a good few more years. These shoes were better, worn and kinked, the leather stiff and curved back on itself. Evidence of life. When I pulled them straight, I heard a crack.

But my favourites were the smallest ones, two almost identical pairs. Bought years and miles apart, for two distinct girls. The repeat, when I noticed it, had astounded me. Both long outgrown, I'd been packing things away when I found them. At first they had looked the same but when I brought them closer, their differences were revealed. The bigger ones had a more textured grain, and a citrus zing to the smaller pair's cream. It pleased me to spot this; it bled them of their power. For years they had lain there, untouched, bound together, top to top, in a shroud of crunched brown paper.

I unwrapped them now, with deference, half expecting them to have crumbled or even disappeared. But they were just as I remembered. A common enough shoe really, of leather so thin you felt that you could rip it. Made with just three pieces; the broad clubbed front, a back panel – elastic frilled around the ankle, and the sole, of a rougher suede. Something elfin about them, knife cut and hand stitched. Never meant for the carpet, let alone outdoors.

I rubbed their softness on my cheek, breathed them in. I ran my finger inside each one, as if to ready them for real children's feet. Anja called from downstairs and I felt a kick of confusion.

'Can I come up, Mags? I really want to go to bed.'

'Sure. Course. I'm all ready up here.'

I shoved the box back into the cupboard. The shoes, I laid on the wardrobe floor, where shoes are meant to go. They sat upright, stuffed with a little of the paper to keep them firm, and it pleased me to see them there.

'I've put a nightie out for you, Anja. I left it in the bathroom,' I called, and she came through a minute later, her arms outstretched, wanting to share the joke of how she looked; ordinary enough in mid-calf, spotted cotton.

She got straight into bed and lay on her side with a shudder.

'Do you want a hot-water bottle?' I asked, but she told me no.

'There's water here and a glass. I'll just change the clock,' I said, but didn't have my glasses, so she did it herself. I found myself reluctant to leave.

'Oh and, Anja, see? I've left some wardrobe space for you here. In case you want to hang up your clothes.'

I opened the wardrobe, gestured with an arm. One shoe had toppled, but I left it.

She sat up.

'Oh. I think I left my stuff in the bathroom,' she said.

'Don't worry. I'll get it for you. Shall I pop it all in the machine?' I asked.

'Oh yes, please, Maggie. If you don't mind.'

She sighed and slid back under and I patted the lump which was her shoulder. Her eyes were already closed.

'Nunight then, love.'

'Good night, Maggie.'

'Sleep tight.'

I'd got to the door when she called to me, gently.

'Will you tell me your story, Mags? One day?'

'One day. Not now though. Time for sleep.'

I took her clothes from the bathroom floor, hooked her pants out of the leg of her jeans and put on a wash.

When I checked later, she was sleeping, so I went back down and poured a whisky. A man's drink, my mother used to claim, which was why I'd said yes the first time it was offered. When I sunk my nose into the glass, though, there had been a wonderful recognition. I'd smelt it warmed on Frannie, all those years, when she'd crept back up for one last goodnight. I've loved it ever since.

32

Putting the key in the piano that night made me cry. It opened something up.

I raced from room to room, the ruins of dinner everywhere and when I noticed my shoes, on their sides, pigeon-toed, I grabbed them and very nearly ran. I wanted Frannie, but Mum would never forgive me that, and so I called her instead, whispering even though I was alone. Her voice was tipped with worry when she answered and sharpened as she listened. When she had the barest facts she said she'd come.

'Don't leave the house. Bet can drive. We'll be there soon.'

Those next two hours, while they drove to me, were almost sweet. The mother of a small child is rarely alone and I moved around the house feeling ghostly, filling time. I tidied up and sat in the corner of the settee to wait.

It was still warm. I had no need of a jumper and the air seemed swollen and pillowy, as if I could take a pinch between two fingers. I closed my eyes and must have slept for a second or two, before my neck collapsed and I was jerked back into life. The silence outside was complete, the birds hadn't started in my suburb and there was no traffic, but I could hear the mechanical chug of the dishwasher in the kitchen, found a rhythm in it after a time that I began to anticipate.

The street was behind me through closed curtains and theirs was the first car in a while. I heard a change of register as Bet shifted gear, and a rev that tore up the silence. Two yellow headlights hit the opposite wall as they pulled up the short steep ascent of our drive. It was just after four, daybreak in less than an hour. I couldn't have borne it in the sun.

Mum was all business. She patted my arm: 'OK?'

I followed her as she unbuttoned her coat, making straight for the kettle. Bet came afterwards – 'You all right, love?' – and sat herself uncomfortably at the small square of kitchen table. Mum put a biscuit tin in front of us that she'd brought with her from home.

'So who's this Jan then?' she said, into the fridge.

'Oh no one, Mum. A friend.'

'Funny kind of friend.'

'More of an acquaintance.'

'Well. I'd expected an air hostess or someone from abroad.'

'There's been those too,' I said.

She looked at me, acute.

She brought across three mugs and milk in a jug from the night before. I went to pour it then remembered they liked it added afterwards. The beginings of a rind had grown over the surface and I tipped the jug in gentle circles to see how long it would hold.

My mother approached with the pot, took the lid off at the table and stirred. It would already be too strong for me but when she spooned in two sugars, the way I'd drunk it as a child, my mouth filled with saliva and I found I couldn't wait. I opened the tin. Something dense and oaty with dried fruit spooned through.

'Go on, eat one. It'll do you good.'

She took her tea away with her, blowing on it as she went.

'What did he say then?' she asked, straightening the tea towels that I'd left to dry on the handle of the oven.

'That he wants to be with her,' I said.

'And she's got a husband has she? A house, this woman?'

'Yes.'

'That's good. That's something. And what have you said?'

She was looking at me now, still a long way off.

'Hold on.' Betty cocked her head and raised a finger skywards.

'I thought I heard her. Shall I go?'

We listened but there was nothing, just a faint electrical hum.

'Yep. You do that, Bet.'

I heard her creaking up the stairs. Outside the darkness thinned.

My mother pushed out a rectangle of window above the sink.

'It's so hot up here, Maggie. I don't know how you can stand it.'

She wiped her hands on her pinny, and I wondered if she'd travelled in it; I hadn't notice her put it on.

It was a densely flowered cotton and clashed with her skirt underneath, in the same style as for ever – A-line, stiff, calf-length. Her ankles were still trim above doll's feet in courts so closely fitted they looked custom made, and I had a picture of myself as a girl, fat legs paddling in an effort to catch up, the snap snap snap of her heels as she pulled away. A wild lunge and the prize of a fistful of acrylic. She would swipe my hand off without acknowledgement and get on with what she was doing. I did the same, occasionally, to Bella; a reflex, but afterwards I bent to her, full of horror at the inevitability of it.

209

I laid my forehead on the table, felt its tacky laminate kiss.

'What's up, Maggie? Come on. Get a grip. There's your daughter to think of.'

'I know there is, Mum. And another.'

'What? What d'you say? Sit up, girl.'

'There's another baby, Mum.'

Everything changed.

'You what?'

She came close to me but I kept my head low. It had started to throb to a huge expanding beat. She put her finger under my chin and lifted, a move that I remembered. This near, the whites of her eyes looked lumpy and congealed and I had a sudden presentiment of losing her.

'What are you saying, Maggie?' she asked hard into my face.

'I'm pregnant, Mum. You heard,' I said, and jerked my head away. 'Don't do that to me. I'm not a child.'

'And you've told him? And still? Well.'

She didn't wait for my reply but pulled away and stood at the back door looking out, arms crossed under her bust. Instantly furious. This was an affront of a different sort. It required a new approach. Betty was back but didn't come in. She waited, trying to read the room.

I could see my mother thinking and the moment that the outrage dropped out of her and a worse suspicion rose. There was a collapse across her shoulders and when she came, she was terrifying.

'What else is there to this, Margaret?' she said.

She approached slowly in her well-worn shoes.

'A man might look elsewhere for some things but he doesn't leave his child. Not a man like Chris.'

I said nothing. I found that I had stood.

She got to me, and slapped my face hard. The sting of it felt like a burn, but it was over fast, and cleared my head. When I faced forwards again, she was still right there.

'You stupid, stupid girl. You selfish girl,' she said.

She was moving, kneading her hands.

'Who? Some idiot, I suppose.'

I swayed gently on my feet but didn't think that she saw.

'Now where are we?' she muttered to herself. 'Nowhere, that's where, thanks to you.'

She seemed exhilarated, almost, her anger gaining pace. The pattern was familiar, but she'd hit me early. It was hard to know where she could go from there.

'You think you're the only one, do you? You think you're the first?'

Turning on her toe as she reached the end of the room.

'Your marriage boring, is it? Out here among all your fancy things?'

She flicked her hand around her, looking for proof, but it was just an ordinary house. She opened the fridge again. She was in luck.

'Oh, that's right. With your dinner party and your duckling breasts, wasn't it? With blackcurrant something or other. It's a hard life, Maggie.'

I remained still. Any hint of response would mean defeat.

'You don't know you're born, you don't. Still that's probably my fault.'

An aside again, as she marshalled her argument. She had a gift for rhetoric. Should've been a lawyer, or else on the stage.

'But do you know what the worst thing is?'

She'd stopped and raised a finger, inches from my face.

'You're stupid. And I wouldn't have had that of you. Do it, do what you like. But don't get caught.'

'What do you know about it?' I said, to her back.

She paused.

'Pardon?' she called, her head looking straight out over her shoulder.

'I said, what do you know about it?'

She let the phrase hang there, gather meaning.

'Me? What do I know? Well now.'

I had to respect her control. She slowed it right down. At least a minute passed, my mother feigning thought. She gave me time and space. This was the moment for me to say sorry, to sink to my knees before her.

But I did nothing. I felt the queasy suggestion of consequence but held my gaze steady and watched surprise flash briefly in hers, and harden into a total commitment to beating me.

'You know what, lady? I am done with you,' she said, almost a whisper, with a twitch of her head either in emphasis or outside her control.

She gave me the longest second and said: 'I don't want to have to fall out with you, Maggie,' which surprised me; it was more than I had expected.

I didn't bite. I don't know why. Perhaps I am as proud and vain as they say.

She took her tin and left. Bet hugged me, her face wet, leaving a big dark smear of it across the collarbone of my dress. My mother was already outside, standing by the car in the first light, stunned.

Her coat, she forgot; it still lives in a corner of my wardrobe. It would have annoyed her, and I get some morsel of pleasure out of that.

33

I was awake before six and listened, for a while, to the family in the house next door. Their baby was new and still in their bedroom; it cried for a bit, and soon the older one began and when the parents' efforts to hush them grew too loud, I got up. I crept past Anja's door like a cartoon burglar. It was ajar, but dark inside.

It had been strange to have another person in the house. She was not a good sleeper and there were noises in the night. What I thought at first was a call for me and had me out of bed in an instant turned out to be the back end of a nightmare. She was sat up when I got to her, eyes open but not awake. She let me ease her back beneath the covers and I sat against the wardrobe and watched for a while till I was sure that she was sleeping. It didn't upset me. Bella had been the same.

Later I was disturbed by an adenoidal snore of astonishing build and evenness. She woke herself, I think, at its upper reaches, as she fell silent for a while, and the cycle repeated. None of which mattered. I got plenty of time for sleep.

In the early hours, I decided that I must see Peter. He'd had almost a week, and not a word. I texted him as early as seemed decent, and he told me half past eight. Paul would be out with the dogs, although it felt wrong, all of a sudden, to have involved him in that collusion.

He answered the door in slippers, his hair wet and combed,

and the scent of coffee bean behind him. He offered me a cup, but I saw on his face that the news wasn't good, and said no. We went through to his office this time, a move that was not hard to read.

'It's OK, Peter,' I said. 'I already know from the Internet that these cases can be tough,' as if it were no big thing.

'Yes,' he replied. 'That's what my friend told me. She emailed last night. I was about to call.'

He went to sit behind his desk and then changed his mind.

'OK. The odds are not great. Maybe two-thirds of asylum applications are refused. More among women. But these things are complicated. Each case is different. A lot of it is luck. Lawyers are important and you get another shot at appeal. But you just never know. So you should be prepared, basically.'

'I did think as much. It's fine,' I said.

'Right. I was hoping you wouldn't be too disappointed.'

Relief plain on his face.

'Disappointed? Well, it's not really a case of disappointed, is it? It's her future. It's her life we're talking about here.'

The room was pale and smelt of paper. Next to me stood his drafting table, empty of work, its huge blank face angled like an easel. Its surface was a cold white lacquer, so smooth that it felt soft underneath my finger. Above it, I noticed a photo of Peter with a child. Could it be his? Would they not have said?

'I know, Mags. But it's just. You know, these aren't our decisions to make, are they?'

I said nothing.

'And also Kate, my friend – I mean, she's not a psychologist or anything but she did say that it's not necessarily helpful for you and Anja to get so closely involved at this point.'

I thought of her at home, sleeping soundly in my spare bed.

There was something inviting in the pearled and poreless surface of his table. Tilted up, it seemed to dash the light right back at me. I had the idea that I could dive down into it; vanish beneath the waxy surface. Clips like tiny wipers were spaced around the frame to hold his plans in place and, as I touched them, I wondered if a man this particular would mind. A huge drawer of polished walnut ran along the underside, a nice note of contrast. There was a cut-out for a handle and I reached one finger inside and pulled, with just the tiniest of pressures. The drawer slid open with more force than I thought I had applied.

'Sorry,' I said, and pushed it shut. It hit the back of the socket with a satisfying bounce.

'Not that there's anything wrong with it, of course. With your relationship, I mean. It's just. Well, obviously it's unsustainable, isn't it, so it might become difficult for you, for both of you, at some stage. I think that was her point,' he said.

'Thanks, Peter. I appreciate it. I really do. You did what I asked. I had better be off now. Thanks.'

'Look, Mags, you don't have to go. Stay for a coffee. Please.'

'I need to go now. Really. Thanks anyway though.'

I took a step towards the door but felt the hem of my coat tug. It had caught on an exposed nail in the crossed legs of the table. It was a decent mac, from M&S, but I yanked at it anyway and it tore with a pleasing cottony shriek.

34

She was up when I got back, and looking to take my lead. We skirted each other, like some sexless one-night stand. I hid in function, said I'd just popped out for milk, although the fridge was full and I didn't carry a bag.

'Let's go for a treat!' I cried, at last. 'The cinema!' I hadn't been for years. She agreed and went off to google.

She chose the film while I walked the dog; a romcom, which we got to on the bus. It was shouty and brittle and there was too much of everything; a bottle of water so large it would be stale long before I drank it and popcorn you could wade through. I felt irrelevant, out of time, swallowed by my huge chair. Anja texted throughout, her phone held low. I have no idea with whom.

That night, back at mine, I saw her sweetness again. She made a cake. A woman at the hostel teaching life skills had showed her how and she went out to buy what was needed, and baked it in an ancient tin.

We ate at the coffee table, on our knees, with tea out of teacups and milk from a jug that she poured. A big slice of Victoria sponge filled with value jam and an underbeaten icing. Grains of sugar lodged between my crowns but I didn't show it. Her efforts moved me, but mainly made me sad.

She felt unfamiliar to me then, her difference singing out of her clearly. I watched her chuckle at the telly and she looked to me to share, but I couldn't raise a grin. I heard her curse in her own language when she cut her hand, and it all just seemed so very strange. I wanted to tell her to pull up her trousers, that no one wanted to see her arse, but that would have been unkind.

It's hard, this business of being with others.

Finally, she asked me, 'Maggie, is something wrong? You seem unhappy today.'

'No. I'm fine,' I said and then, 'It's just. I think we need a lawyer. A good one. That'll make all the difference, you know.'

She rolled her eyes, almost in parody.

'If you want to stay here, Anja, we need to be doing more. It's as simple as that,' I said and got up, propelled out of my chair.

'It all takes money,' she said, in a slow bored voice. 'And I have no money.'

'No, of course not. But I do.'

I was thinking of the amount that my mother had left and what I'd saved from my time at the doctor's. That sum put by for Rose that I'd never found a way to offer. There were Premium Bonds, if needed. More than enough. Surely.

'The question is who. How to find the best possible person.'

But I wasn't talking to her any more. I went out to the kitchen. There had been a friend, a woman from when Rosie was at school. I had her number in the book.

Then Anja was behind me and she seized my arm, yanked it with a strength that pulled me from the drawer.

'I don't want your money, Maggie,' she said, and her voice was low and aimed.

'What's the alternative? I have been to Peter and he told me that our chances are not good.'

'You went to Peter?' she said.

'Yes, I did. And I'm sorry if you don't like it, but someone had to do something,' I said, as if this were pure undeniable common sense.

I realised my mistake; I saw its impact on her. A flinch that she cut short as soon as she felt it, and a shrinking – I swear. She withdrew before my eyes. I witnessed that first step away from me and, god knows, it is easy from there.

'Mind your own business, Maggie,' she said.

'You are simply naive. You are being a child. This will not go away, I can promise you that.'

My voice rose and tumbled.

'It is not your problem,' she said, and that hurt, because it was not true.

'Not my problem? You make it my problem, Anja, when you come here with your drama.'

I jabbed a finger. Most likely moved towards her. I am a Benson, after all, and we Bensons do not shrink from conflict. Losing my temper was physical, a pleasure. I felt the freedom in it. It showed me I was alive.

But Anja saw it too. She narrowed against me.

'My drama? Is that right? Is that what you call it?'

A puff of scorn.

I said nothing, waiting for her to come.

'OK, Maggie. As you say,' she said.

And she left the room; she ambled. No rush.

I said to myself, let her go; but still I caught her in the hall, the scruff of her coat in my hand.

'What are you doing?' I said.

'Thank you,' she replied. 'For everything. But I am not yours.'

When she opened the door, there was Paul.

'Hey. You off?' he asked, but she stepped through the tangle of his dogs and was gone.

'Maggie? Is everything?' He looked slow and stupid between us.

'Good luck, Anja, yeah. Best of luck with it all,' I shouted, bent out of my door, one socked foot dampening, but she didn't turn back.

I stepped inside to a ringing silence, and wished for Frannie.

'Stop,' she used to cry, twisting a tea towel in my mother's wake. 'You must stop, Hel. We'll have the social round.'

And my mum would sit down at the table, head in hands, and start her journey back to us.

Warm sweet tea and the slow road of recovery.

35

Time passed more slowly without Anja.

The first day I woke into was bright and beautiful but I couldn't acknowledge it. I took the dog out, and again later. He seemed pleased with the extra walk but I caught him watching me a couple of times, though he put on his best jolly face when I did.

My groceries arrived; identical, bar a handful of items, to the week before. I recognised the man who brought them, around my age, smart in a way that made me sorry for him. Combed hair, belted trousers and a habit of knocking his wrist against the phone that hung from his belt that I found affecting. It felt difficult with him in my kitchen, and when he had gone and I was putting it all away, I acknowledged briefly the oddness of before and after. Not how changed things were but how relentlessly the same.

I cooked some of what I'd bought to freeze for the week ahead – a habit carried over from busier times. A spaghetti Bolognese updated across the decades and a beef stew into which I'd learnt to add Marmite.

My friends had been calling, and Chris, once more, but I'd unplugged the landline. From then, like Anja, I only worked with mobile.

Mo came, and I told her I had the flu.

'Christ, you do look bad,' she said, and offered to take the dog. She had to pull him from the house, legs locked, claws scraping and his head bent to me, swivel-eyed until the last.

When they were gone, I dragged an armchair into the garden room and sat and watched for the fox and his wife who were living under the house behind's shed. It was cold, the wood of the French windows crabbed and cracked and the glass uncertain in its frames, but I unearthed a plug-in blanket and an old blow-heater from the attic.

I thought of the things that she had brought here to keep safe. I reached out to help her, when she first lugged it in – an old Bag for Life – but she hesitated and I moved my arm back. 'Oh, thanks, Mags, here you go,' she said, a second on, and it was heavy when I took it. 'What've you got in here, the Crown Jewels?' I almost replied, but coughed instead. When I lowered the bag, the handles sagged and I saw a T-shirt uppermost, stretched across and tucked firmly down the sides. 'I'll put it in the spare room, shall I?' I said. Now she was gone and my fingers twitched to feel inside. I was on my knees, one hand stretched under the bed last night, before I stopped myself.

Buster came back in love with Maureen, a further reminder that I am easily replaced. She offered to walk him next day and I said yes.

Later, I took a bath too hot for me to think in and was in bed by nine, though I'd switched on the lamp by five past and gone downstairs for the dog; an occasional lapse, an old woman's weakness.

There was the usual failed negotiation. I wanted him on the bed but he did not consider that his place. He jumped up, pawed and circled, but would not settle. He lay on the floor, in the end, by my side. I hung my arm down so as to rest my hand on the soft top of his head, but that could not be sustained.

No Paul, which concerned me, as I knew he would be worrying.

And all this time, I expected her back. I thought, at least, that she would call. I should not have shouted, I knew that. But I had not anticipated abandonment. I texted: 'I'm sorry for what happened. Please let me know that you are OK. M.'

Was I sorry? To be honest, I was fine with the row. I didn't dwell on the words exchanged; they were merely tools, chosen to do a job, and subsequently laid aside. The question of their truth was beside the point.

I do not bear a grudge, when it comes to a fight. Least said, soonest mended. Benson family lore.

But perhaps it was different for Anja. When I went up to bed there was still no reply.

The third day was warmer, but wet – a hateful combination. I was glad to miss the park; the dressing for it, then hosing down the dog. His stink and the steam of his towel on the radiator.

And all the better, without Buster, to watch the foxes.

They seemed a settled couple. There will have been pups in the hole, the Internet said; if so, they were kept well out of sight. Grown up and gone now, not that Mum and Dad appeared to mind, sat on high, taking the air. One of them, I didn't know which, was bold. It looked at me and didn't look away.

That afternoon, I slept in the chair; a deep dark sleep, something about the localised heat of the blanket, and in that last second of disorientation before I woke, I felt my need for her. And I knew that I could will it away, this emotion, as I had done so many times before, but instead I held on. An idea came. She cleaned at Peter's about this time. I could go and find her there. Say sorry. Make it OK. Was it that easily done? I went, my heart buoyant.

I waited on the corner, sat on a low wall outside a dark house like a teenage suitor, but an hour passed and still she hadn't come. In the end I knocked. Their outside light was dazzling and I stepped closer to evade it and heard a metallic scrape behind the peephole and the heavier clankings of mortice lock, night latch and chain.

'Maggie, it's you. I've been calling,' said Paul, eyes rushing.

'Oh, right,' I said vaguely. 'Try the mobile. There's been something wrong with the landline.'

He took both my hands, dry and spindled under his touch.

'Are you OK? What's been going on?' he said. 'We've been worried about you.'

His smell was clean and grapefruit and he wore a round-necked jumper of a thin dark knit. I thought of reaching for him, turning my head into his neck, closing my eyes, just for a minute.

'Oh, nothing,' I said. 'I've just been ill. Did Maureen not say?'

I heard myself, woolly and distracted.

'Come in, come in,' he said, putting an arm round my shoulder and steering me gently. The warmth of their house swamped me and I felt slower still, and clumsy.

'It's just I haven't seen Anja. For a few days. I was wondering if she had been here,' I said.

'Peter. It's Maggie,' Paul called out into the house, his voice loaded, and then Peter was in front of us.

'Good to see you, Mags,' he said. 'We're glad you're here.'

We paused in a snaggled row in the hall.

'You go on,' Paul said, with a little shove. Peter went to him,

224

and behind me, they came to some agreement. When we gathered again, Paul looked grim but resolute. Peter lowered the radio and I felt a giggle rise at the portent of it.

We stood in a shifting triangle. I realised that I still wore outdoor shoes.

'We have seen her, Maggie. She came yesterday instead of today. We've been trying to phone you,' said Paul. 'There's no easy way to say this. But she stole from us.'

They moved together subtly.

'What?' I asked. I was not sure what I'd been expecting, but it was not this.

'Yes. Cash. It's definitely gone. And there was no one else here. We're absolutely sure. We wouldn't say so if we weren't,' he said.

'Cash. What cash?'

'Just money, Maggie. In an envelope.'

'For what, though?' I asked, a picture assembling.

'What do you mean?' Paul said.

He looked exasperated but Peter flashed him a glance and I knew that I was right.

'I mean what was the money for? Why did you have an envelope full of money lying around?'

'For builders,' said Paul.

'Builders? You're not getting anything done. This place is bloody perfect.'

I swiped a hand before me in a theatrical gesture that wasn't mine. I took in the room, but found my point almost immediately disproved. There was a large red stain on their white carpet seeping through a thick shell of darkening salt. Spilt wine, recent; kicked over, perhaps, in alarm at my arrival. The empty glass stood on the bar, sediment curving up its side.

'That's not the issue,' Paul said.

'Where d'you leave it?' I asked.

'Maggie —'

'Which drawer? A drawer she always goes in, I suppose.'

'You're being deliberately obtuse. The thing is, she took the money. Several hundred pounds. Out of our home. She broke our trust,' Paul said.

'You set her up,' I replied, and heard the violence in my voice. 'Did you think that you were helping?'

A kind of tremor travelled through me; a stimulus that demanded some response.

'It's not that,' Peter said, taking a step towards me.

'Because that is the most patronising.'

'Look at least you know,' said Paul.

'Know what?' I said.

'That she —' but he paused there.

'That she what? That she is desperate? That she has nothing?'

'No, Maggie.'

My argument was finding form. Pulling away from me. Peter saw it.

'OK —' he said, wide palmed.

'And nothing to lose? And no one to look after her?' I went on.

'You're making excuses, Maggie, I'm sorry, but.'

Peter broke in: 'Look. We would never call the police. We don't want to get her in any sort of trouble. We wouldn't dream of it. We just needed to be sure. To know what sort of person she is.'

'And what sort of person is she? Come on. I'd be really

interested to know,' my voice rising, fractured.

But they could not answer. I wanted to knock that glass. Hear it smash, see their shock. Destroy something that was theirs. But I had not learnt nothing across the years. I left them pleading in my wake, a thick wad of disappointment in my throat.

36

I walked home fast, the park churned and empty, my mind caught on a loop. I opened the front door and the house was all dust and dog. I decided to clean. The old trousers I changed into felt tight around the waist; this, I thought, is what happens when you become one of a pair.

I bent under the sink, impatient for the monotone of the task, but the box, when I reached for it, was full of unbranded products. She must have bought them cheap, from god knows where. I felt the bottles in my hands. They were alien and ugly, their plastic thick, opaque and hard to squeeze; their packaging brute and the names on them functional and obvious. The product inside ran liquid and clear and uncompromisingly chemical and I wondered how long they had been there, unknown to me, and what else there might be, of hers, in hidden places in my home? My mouth tasted acid. She was everywhere around.

I went down on my hands and knees and got into all the nooks.

I wiped the kitchen cupboards; found an abandoned toothbrush and used it to gouge age-old dirt from between the tongue and groove.

I cleaned the glass with newspaper and oiled the stainless steel with Johnson's.

My eyes ran and my cuticles throbbed and the skin on my

fingertips cracked. I found some rubber gloves and started on upstairs.

There were a number of her hairs curled into the plughole, red and black-rooted, suds clinging to them. I dug them out with a tissue and flushed them away.

I went through the basket and binned three of her socks.

I pulled the door to her bedroom shut. That could wait.

My head was ringing and my back in spasms and I sat on the top step for a moment and I think I might have cried, had the letterbox not rattled.

I waited; silence settled, and it happened again and this time the flap stayed open. I saw a slice of movement behind it and felt fear and next, how ludicrous, how very unlikely.

A man's voice called: 'Hello.'

The possibilities narrowed.

A handle twisted brusquely, the one that no longer worked.

Another small stretch of waiting.

I edged down the stairs and stood by the door, listening to the stranger's sounds. That got me nowhere.

So I tiptoed through to the sitting room and pressed my back against the last part of wall before it gave way to window. I peeped around meekly.

There was the back of a man in a raincoat, immediately expensive, my age or younger. He started down the path and I ducked, not that this helped, leaving me head and shoulders above the sill. He opened my gate, stepped through, and pulled it shut hard behind him. It banged on the latch, as it does, and then he stopped. I watched him kneel to the fitting. It was dark and my vantage obscured, but the care he took and the suggestion of ownership pissed me off in a very specific way.

The man straightened and saw my shape in the pane. I stood, my back yowling, and opened the door; to Chris, my ex-husband.

He rubbed his gloved hands, gave an exaggerated brrrr.

'Hello, Margaret. At last. I'm cold. I've been waiting out here for hours.'

Textbook Chris. A bad start. It was as if we had parted only yesterday, in the worst possible way.

'Are you alone?' he said. 'Before I come in?' He peered over my shoulder.

'Yes, Chris, I am,' I said.

'OK. Fine.'

I took a breath, looked at the floor. Felt a tight bud of fury in my chest.

'Shut the door, Maggie, will you, it's freezing.'

He slid off his scarf in his own matchless way. Pulled down his shoulders, dipped his nose and tugged. The scarf – cashmere, though the move worked better with silk – moved cleanly across his skin and over the curve of his neck. It dropped, weighted by the plush of its tassels, and he snatched for it with the hand that still held the near end. He raised the scarf to me, neatly halved, offered up like something won. Then saw my face, and buried the gesture in removing his coat. He followed me to the kitchen and settled his things, slippy and uncertain, on the narrow width of counter.

'Hmm. Very nice,' he said, with a cursory scan of the room. 'Did you not get any of my messages, Maggie?'

His tone was neutral, ambivalent.

'Of course I did,' I said.

He looked the same. He had aged well. Kept slim, no hair

loss, his bone structure holding. I cruised the kitchen, moving things needlessly.

'This is the first time I call you in, what is it, in all these years?'

I paused at the window, watched the hoppings of a bird.

'So did you not think it might be important? Did I not make this clear last time we spoke?'

'Hold on a minute, will you?' I said.

I left him. Stood in the hall for a minute. Pinched the crook of my elbow as hard as I could, something I hadn't done since I was a girl. My focus narrowed on the pain. When I stopped, the skin was marked with two crescent imprints. I felt more space and went back through. He looked angrier.

'Can't you just sit? Do you not want to know why I'm here?'

Fear then, the feeling I had been trying to keep down. Fear, after all; not fury.

He blew a breath through pursed lips, and told me, rather gently, 'She's fine. Bella's fine. But she knows, Maggie. She knows about you.'

I shouted, an unplanned cry, and swept his carefully laundered clothes onto the floor. The coat caught on a stool as it fell, its innards splayed, a ghastly paisley.

'Well, that's hardly going to help, is it?' he said, righting his things. 'I'll give you a moment, shall I? I need to make a call anyway. This way to the garden?'

I drank a glass of water straight and listened to the low rolling of his voice. Touching base with Jan, no doubt.

'OK?' he said, when he came back, and the conversation set off down a well-worn path. Chris calm, rational, pedantic; me fearful and butterfly-brained.

'I suppose it was the papers,' I said. 'It wasn't my fault,' which I hated myself for, the second it was out.

I pictured Jan, cross-legged at her breakfast bar, grapefruit untouched, coffee upended. Clutching at that slender neck in shock.

'No, Maggie. It wasn't that. It was your mother,' he said. 'God. You do know that she's passed?'

I did, a solicitor had called six months ago with the fact of it, as she had specified in a letter, an adjunct to her will. But no message, nothing more.

'Your mother told Bella. The two were very close.'

I remembered their affection. In the first months it had brought me comfort.

'It was at the very end. I'm not sure she even knew what she was saying.'

He wore his contemplative face, one of my very least favourites.

'Did you and she ever? Your mother, I mean,' he asked.

'No. She never made contact,' I said.

He passed a hand through his hair, then ran his fingertips the length of his parting, flipping errant strands left and right, into place. The old affectation, dating him so painfully.

'What did you say to Bella? Afterwards?' I asked.

A final shake to settle things. So neat it looked sewn in.

'You know the answer to that. Just as we agreed.'

'But how though?'

His hands were still beautiful; more so now. Less manicured, a bit of heft.

'Does it matter, Maggie? A car accident, if you must. Your mother's idea.'

I knew where she'd got it from. Those tragic old movies she loved. Cast me as a doomed Italian heroine. But also made it clear that I was reckless.

'How ridiculous,' I said.

'Yes. Well. It wouldn't have been my choice.'

'And that. Went OK?'

'She was three years old. She accepted it, if that's your question. It didn't hurt her.'

He adopted a tragic air, fully committed to the falsehood.

'To be honest we rarely spoke of you, and I'm not saying that to be unkind. She just left it alone. Though she talked with your mother, it now appears. Who rather liked the subject, as I understand.'

So she grew up with my mother's edits. Quite the historian, Helen, with her claims to impartiality. 'Don't you worry about what I think. I'll tell you all about it and you can make your own mind up.' Character established by carefully chosen anecdote.

'And Jan? She. They got on?'

'She was wonderful, is wonderful. And extremely grateful to you actually,' he said.

I imagined a thank-you note, perfumed and cloying. I wouldn't put it past her.

'And there's just Bella, is there?' I asked.

'Of course. It was not possible for Jan. You know that,' he said.

'Yes. Oh, well.'

'Bella told us only recently that she knew you were alive. She had been hoping. To bury the knowledge, I think. Out of some sort of respect for our family.'

He was lost now, in contemplation of his magnificent daughter and his own contribution to her. She'd made a fool of him – I saw that straight away – a stupid fawning old man of him.

'I don't think she wanted to betray your mother, or us for that matter. She wanted to keep things as they had always been. She is so. Such a thoughtful girl.'

'And what did you tell her?'

'I told her the truth, Maggie. Nothing but,' he said.

'And what is that exactly?'

His patience broke.

'That you became pregnant with another man's child. That you chose to go and make a new life elsewhere. The truth. At least the way I remember it.'

He gave a short harsh laugh and spoke again.

'Oh, you mean the sordid details? Well, no. I didn't go into all that. What do you expect? Would any child want to hear it?'

I said nothing.

'Maggie, I can see by the look on your face that you're about to go into one of your. Episodes. So I'm going to get to the point here. Bella doesn't want to see you, all right? Not now or ever. If she had her way, none of this would have come out. Jan and I, even, would still be in the dark.'

'So, why, Chris? What the fuck are you doing here? Why tell me at all?' I said; I shouted.

He came towards me, just one step, and I wondered how far he could be provoked.

'Because a woman has been hassling her, Margaret. That's why. Someone claiming to act on your behalf, though it's clear you know nothing about it. Anja Maric, whoever that may be. Not that I give a shit, to be honest. Just call her off. I mean it.

Get her to leave Bella alone, if you have any decency at all. And unless you want me to fill her in on the rest of it.'

He passed me an envelope.

37

Inside, two sheets of A4. Three emails, printed. A one-way exchange.

Hi there,

You don't know me, but I am a friend. This may be a shock to you when I say I am close with your mother, Margaret Benson. She has said nothing of what happened in the past but I can tell you that she is a great woman. Look at this.

http://metro.co.uk/2013/09/03/news/crime/local-woman-saves-trafficked-girl-gatwick-8925880.html

I know you are the right person. You two look just the same. There are photos of her on Facebook, if you would like to see.

I wanted to do something for Maggie. That is why I have contacted you. Please reply!

I sincerely wish you well.

Anja Maric

Hi Bella,

I am sorry not to hear from you.

I don't want to put you under pressure. I realise this is a big thing.

Maybe we could meet and I could tell you a bit more about your mother? Do you know you have a sister? Her name is Rose. She has a child. Your nephew!

Just to know that you are well would be so great for Maggie.
Best wishes,
Anja Maric

Hi Bella,

I am going now and your mother will be alone.

I will have my own child soon. I cannot think why she would leave you but she must have had a reason and it hurt her very much. She grieves for you every day. I know this. SHE IS A GOOD PERSON.

You have the power to make someone happy. Why not use it? Maybe if you do, you will make yourself happy too?

We can change the past. Your mother taught me this.

Good luck and best wishes in your future.

Anja Maric

I read them time and again. Examined them for tone and meaning. For a clue to her, to her intent; something I'd overlooked. But there was nothing beyond the words on the page. Her voice rang out, plain and artless. Her own truth, unvarnished. Bearing no relation to mine.

38

I never got to bed, that last night with my baby.

Bet was given to theatrics and sobbed noisily in the hall for a while after my mother left, pressing my hands between hers. But Helen was waiting outside, terrible and implacable, and soon Bet went to her.

When I came back in, I found Bella sitting on the stairs in a strange in-between state. This was not unusual; she often reappeared long after she'd been sent to bed, silent, on the edge of things, waiting to be noticed.

I knelt to her and asked if she was OK but I knew she wouldn't reply. I took her hand, warm and limp, and told her there was nothing in the whole wide world to worry about. I felt afraid of her like this, hearing but unspeaking, as though the wrong move might trigger something dreadful.

She sat at the kitchen table, feet dangling useless above the floor. I got her milk and jabbered to fill the space. She drank it and laid her glass down gently but when I wiped her top lip clean with my thumb, she gave no sign that she felt my touch.

It was half past five and I led her back upstairs. Her head touched the pillow and she slept. But as I left her room, a floorboard squeaked its long wonky note and she woke again. She sat up instantly, a different child, my usual child.

'Mumma,' she called with a slow Cheshire-cat grin. That last day began.

Chris let himself in about nine and tossed his keys onto a table, noisily, to tell me he still lived there, no mistake.

'Maggie. Are you there?' he called.

I let Bella go to him and heard him swoop and swing her. It was not unusual for Daddy to arrive in the morning, or leave late at night. It was part of his allure.

'Christ. Haven't you slept?' he said, when he saw me. I still wore my dress, spots of duck fat patterning the sleeves.

'Do you want to watch the *Mr Men* video, love? I'll put it on for you. Let's grab a banana,' he said, and did those things while I waited in the kitchen. His manner surprised me. He was not angry, or cold. He was careful and I felt frightened, then, of what he was going to ask of me.

'OK, will you sit?' he said.

He had brushed his hair very recently and I imagined him parked outside, peering up into the thin slot of mirror. Both fastidious and vain. His nails were not clean though and I knew that he would hate that when he noticed.

'This is a mess, OK? You and me both. I don't deny it. But I have a proposal to make and I want you to hear me out.'

I pressed my head against my palm, emptied out by tiredness, but some survival instinct must have triggered, for I felt pings of adrenalin in my temples, and straightened again.

'Maggie, I think you are going to find yourself in a. In an uncertain position.'

He steepled his hands between us, as if he were my lawyer.

'I'm assuming this baby is what's-his-name's, the piano teacher's, Ben's?'

I kept my face steady.

'It doesn't matter. But I'm not an idiot, you know. I could

239

see there was something between you and I chose to let it run. Given my. Given what I had undertaken with Jan.'

I wondered if he had loved me and if so, when he stopped.

'This though? Pregnant? I thought you had more. Well, ambition, to be honest, if nothing else. Anyway, as I'm sure you are aware, he has a wife and two young children. The chances of him leaving them are small, I would have thought, but that's your business. Still even if he does, do you know how much I pay him an hour to teach you? Not enough to keep you in. Hand-made curtains, for instance.'

They hung in the lounge, purple and black stripe – my choice, I admit it – made from a fat book of swatches that a woman (Jan's recommendation) had hauled out of her boot and left with me. She phoned every other day for a week wanting to know if I had decided, until I told her to hold on, flipped it open and chose what I found. The fabric name – 'Ali Baba', written on a sticker – was so stupid that I almost changed my mind, but the density of the pages had already pushed the book shut. And it was Chris who grabbed a thick fistful when they were up, stepped back to take a better look, declared himself thrilled.

'I imagine you'll have to work, after that baby is born, simply to make ends meet. There is the question of your mother. She has nothing, after all, bar her pension. None of them do. And they are all getting older and sicker and more expensive.'

I had never heard him talk like this. The truth, so unvarnished, so impolite.

'You are a family of unprotected women, Maggie. Please don't take offence. You know this to be the case and your mother knows it too. And not just because you have no men, but also no money and no prospects between you. Don't bristle. You could have changed that with your work but you chose to give it up. Your choice. No one else's. I was to provide the ballast, Maggie, and I was happy to do it. For all of you actually. This is what amazes me about the whole thing. That you would simply be so foolhardy. But anyway.'

Bella was in the doorway, looking from me to him.

'Daddy, the Mr Men aren't talking,' she said, and he left to sort it out. I thought about his words. There was nothing to dispute in them.

He came back and shut the door. He looked grim. I think it was the reality of his daughter, the fact of her precariousness.

'You will now have a life exactly like your mother's. Uncertain. Hand to mouth. Vulnerable to the next disaster. But I will not have the same for Bella.'

'Of course,' I said, no inkling of what came next.

'The thing is, I want her with me.'

I think, at first, I merely laughed.

He came over and knelt before me, balanced on his toes. It took everything not to knock him down. It needed just the gentlest push. Finger or foot.

My silence made him angry.

'Put yourself aside, for once, Maggie. Do something for your daughter,' he said.

I told him to get up.

He rubbed his hands, returned to reason.

'Bella will be happy here with Jan and me. I can take time off to get us all settled. If you do what I ask, I'll make sure that you're comfortable. I will. A lump sum. If you don't, I imagine life will be hard for you, Maggie. And this new child. Think of it.'

241

'So you want to buy her, do you, Chris? Been on the phone to your father, have you?' I said, cheap but well aimed.

'I will have her, Maggie. I will not let her go,' he said.

I looked at him, my face drained, but I felt his need and it scared me.

'OK. Well, I didn't want to have to do this, but here's the thing. Bells,' he called, but it sounded rough, a voice meant for me. He adjusted his tone.

'Bella, darling. Could you come through here a minute?' he said.

'What, Daddy?'

Her nightdress was long and flowered, with a pin-tuck front and embroidery at the wrists. The pink of her big toes showed under.

'How's your head, darling? Where you fell over yesterday?' he asked.

'OK, I think,' she said and put her hand to it.

'Let me have a look. Oh yes, there's a nasty bruise, isn't there. Ouchy.'

He lifted her hair and there was a right-angle of cut and a cushiony lump in yellow-purple.

'I think you'll be fine, sweetheart. Now go back to your programme. Good girl.'

He faced me again and said: 'I will put her in the car now. I will take her to A&E and I will tell them that you did that. And they will check the records, and they will find the broken arm and I will tell them that you did that too, and they will believe me. And they will take her from you, and that new baby as well.'

I got up and walked away, laid my forehead against the cold

glass in the back door. It was wet, and screamed softly as I rubbed my skin across it.

'That's how it will work. My mother was a nurse, don't forget. I have talked this through with her and she will get involved if she has to. She will say what needs to be said.'

She would, I knew that, though she might not like it. I moved my head, pressing my cheek against the damp.

'I know this seems hard, Maggie, but it's for the best, don't you see? It is in you, after all, isn't it? Your temper. You can't deny it. I know that it frightens you. Look at your mother.'

I wondered if I would have a black eye. Her hand had caught the bridge of my nose when she hit me the night before.

'Life will be harder for you now. Who knows, under pressure, what you might do? I can't take that chance and nor should you.'

Chris kept talking.

My knees went, and I slid gently to the floor.

One good night's sleep, I believe, and I would never have let her go.

'I will be back for her later. There's no point in prolonging it.'

At the door, he stopped, spoke downwards.

'I am not punishing you, you know,' he said thoughtfully. 'I simply cannot have you in my life. You have humiliated me completely.'

He looked down at his filthy nails as he said it.

'I'll leave you now. Go and speak to. Whoever you need to. But you must know that there will be no going back. To pop up at some later date would be unbearably cruel. Keep away. And I swear to you that I will never be in contact again. Not unless it is essential.'

39

After Chris left, I went to find her. I knew she lived at the Oval end of the Brixton Road, past an Internet place that was also a launderette. It was a start, and I had nothing but time. I shut the dog in the kitchen and hailed a cab.

A long time since I'd travelled in a taxi, beyond my own clutch of streets; less than a minute and the roads were new. He took the A5 and we passed through layer upon layer of London. Skylines bunny-hopped; a cut-and-paste effect. I thought of Alice and her 'Drink Me' potions. And all those places of worship; I had no idea so many people still prayed.

At Marble Arch, we hit Christmas; coloured lights and shops and drunks. It was slow and I was impatient. I listened to a caller on the radio and the noises of the road and watched people mouth and gape outside my window. A glimpse of Victoria Station, which used to take me home, and the river, at last – mud brown and choppy. We got there not long afterwards and I paid him in great handfuls of coins.

Out, and I felt new to the city. I reached for my bag and left my hand there, like a tourist.

The Internet place came along soon on the right, recently updated in sharp bands of yellow and green. There was one old lady inside. I took a place in a cafe close by, and watched. Drank two huge coffees – perhaps an hour passed – and then a caffeine jangle got me up, and I made to leave, with no better idea. Three girls came in as I paid; Anja's age, clothes like hers, accents that were not London. I spent a minute pretending to look in my bag while they chose drinks, and followed them.

Their pace was relaxed. They travelled outwards as much as on, using the full width of pavement. One minute they were close, heads tight, and then they broke apart in laughter, spreading, just far enough, and drew back together in a loose alliance. I was just thinking how confident, how entitled, how comfortable they were in the world, when a girl of a different sort drew my attention.

First a burble of radio. A police car had stopped and an officer climbed out. He walked up to a house, a stack of Georgian features. Wide stone steps to a huge front door with a semicircle of fanlight above it, mirrored in the tops of the sash windows. Half-height shutters pulled to. A grand place of aged yellow stone and black and white paint but also a dump, water-stained and blasted by weather and exhaust.

A girl was crammed into the crack of doorway, talking to another PC. I could see a long thin strip of her, one leg sticking out in a towelling tracksuit, a flip-flop on her foot despite the weather, a sharp pale profile. She looked poised, alert, like Anja had when she first arrived. Expecting some sort of violence. Ready to run, or submit, as the occasion required.

I listened hard but the sounds of the street splintered off into competing elements. The buses won, with their long queeny gasps. I risked a few steps forward.

The girl's eyes swooped but her mouth barely moved. The policeman waited at the edge of the porch, stood back into his heels. The other had paused halfway up the stairs.

The girl looked behind her into the house. A hand gripped

the door from inside, and she ducked beneath it and was gone.

Someone new; older, more in charge.

I stood now, at the foot of the steps, pretending to read my phone. Two men in their sixties slowed on the pavement and yelled: 'Bout time too,' but when the policeman craned to find them, they moved on meekly. His eyes passed over me.

They had rearranged themselves in response to this new person, shoulder to shoulder, their backs a wall. I couldn't see a thing.

I took the first three stairs.

Up closer and the woman was all bluster. She shouted and postured until a radio blasted interference and there was silence, for a stretch, as the policeman listened. A crackle that made me start. The officer unclipped a pad from his belt and spelled a word out clearly.

'M. A. R. I. C. Anja with a J. Over.'

I climbed the next three.

That the police wanted to leave now became clear. The woman made a noise in her throat and was gone. She slammed the door with a flourish and the time between the gesture and the bang seemed too long. It came at last, and the knocker gave a faint answering clack. The glass shivered tinnily in its panes.

I was noticed.

The officer nearest paused. A look laced with confusion.

'Excuse me,' I said. 'I just. I couldn't help but overhear you mention Anja. Anja Maric. It's just. She's my friend.'

'OK, madam. And if you could give me your name?'

I did, and it seemed to ring a bell.

'Well, perhaps you can help. She's missing, I'm afraid. Could you please tell me when you last saw Miss Maric?'

40

I got the Tube home from Oval, a horrible mistake. It took the walk to my house to slow my heart and stay the tremor in my limbs. As I slid the blade of the key into the lock there was a re-acceleration; something, I suppose, to do with being so very nearly there. Then I was in, but the house did not feel mine. The acknowledgement of wrongness was immediate. Quite why took a second or two more.

The dog, first; he should have barked. The sitting-room door was open and there was a lamp on in the far part of the house; I could see the traces of a low orange light reaching out into the kitchen. The hall was cold and dark. I stretched my arm and felt the slick drop of her parka.

I pressed the switch. Her coat was on the peg, hung clumsily from one shoulder. A fat canvas bag I didn't recognise blocked my way. Still she did not call and I didn't hurry. I laid my own things on the sofa and went through, reluctant to break the hush of the house.

She sat out in my spot, facing the garden. Her ponytail dangled over the back of the seat, a few snapped hairs sprouting outwards from the band. I could see one foot bent behind her; a baggy loose-knit sock, worn at the heel and ball, a week away, at most, from holes.

There was a mug of tea on the floor and she ate from a great stack of toast that she had balanced on the chair's arm. Buster sat before her, his paw up to beg, his tail narrowly missing the cup. He looked to me, but wouldn't abandon his efforts. She inclined her head in some acknowledgement, but still I couldn't see her face.

'I came,' she said. 'Like you wanted me to. Is it OK for me to eat this bread? I'm starving.'

I walked round to the front of her.

'Oh, sorry. This is your place, is it? You moved things. Shall we go through to the sitting room?' she said. Her face was expressionless.

'Say please.' She looked back down at the dog and he lifted his foot, which she shook. 'Good boy.'

She put her nose in his ear and gave him half a slice of toast, which he took with gentle teeth.

'Not too much. You'll make him fat,' I said but she didn't respond.

She got up; I took her mug through to the sink, and followed.

I found her on the sofa stroking the dog's eyes shut.

'I've been calling you, Anja. And texting,' I said.

'I know.'

Her rhythm was slow and steady. Buster made his happy noise, a throatier version of a purr.

'Why didn't you reply?' I asked.

'I'm here, aren't I?' she said.

His front legs slid out and he dropped a heavy chin to her knees.

'I know what you want anyway,' she said, after a bit.

'I was calling to say I was sorry. Am sorry. About our fight. And that I wanted us to be friends again.'

I cringed at my own language. It didn't impact her at all.

'But there is something else, right?' she said.

She bent the dog's ear back so she could watch him correct it. It was unkind, but it amused her. Worry was plain on his face; still she did it again. I wanted to tell her to stop.

'Well, yes. There is now. Of course there is.'

'I guess that would be Paul's money,' she said levelly. She moved her hands to her lap but Buster nosed her until she resumed their game. A forgiving beast.

I leant into the wall. Everything ached; the big muscles of my thighs, my shoulders. I needed a shower or they would set this way.

'Why did you take it, Anja?' I said.

'Easy. Because they wanted me to. That's what it was there for.'

I had the idea of lying, of making this simple, but I tend to avoid that path. When it was clear that I would say nothing, she puffed out her contempt.

'Look. You could get into trouble over this,' I said.

'No, I won't. They won't find me. I was thinking of leaving and now my mind is made up.'

'They were friends to you, Anja. You abused that.'

'They are not friends or they would not have done it. That shows what they think of me.'

Her voice was high and bitter.

'And so you went and proved them right,' I said.

'Why not? They are happy now. They think they know how everything is.'

'It was still wrong,' I said, though I heard my own uncertainty.

'We do what we have to. Remember? You told me that once.'

There was a siren a few streets away. We were still while its sound grew and diminished, mournful and animal.

'Have they told the police?' she asked.

'I don't think so.'

'Well, I've left my place anyway. I'm not going back.'

A teenage slump on my furniture; her shoulders low and her legs spread wide. No vanity, Anja, none of what we used to know as feminine charm.

'Is that sensible? They are looking for you, you know. They think you're missing. Someone must have reported it. They're worried something has happened,' I said.

'For five minutes only.'

She pushed up from her chair.

'You think I'm so stupid, Maggie. I know I will not win my case. There is not a good chance. I knew it from the start. Everyone does. It is only you.'

'I do. I do know that now,' I said.

'So I am making my own arrangements, right?'

'I would have given you money. I will give you money,' I said.

'I have some now, thanks. To start me off. And you know that I work hard.'

She put a hand on her back and the bump was clear, a compact ovoid pushing out against her zipped-up top.

'I need to get my things. I've left some stuff,' she said.

She found her slippers and a book. I said she could keep the dressing-gown if she liked but she shook her head. I offered her a sandwich, some more of Rosie's clothes, the cash in my purse, but she would take none of it. I trailed her feebly.

'Anja,' I asked, finally, as she bent down to her bag, 'why did you email my daughter?'

She stopped, low to the carpet, her back long and curved.

'Oh,' she said. 'So you know?' Poised. Interested.

'Yes, I do.'

Her hair was pulled back viciously and I saw her reach round for the sore patch of scalp. She found it and, as she stroked there gently, I saw a dark shade of growth beneath her finger.

'I saw the birth certificate. I thought I could find her for you. There is Facebook and Google. It's not so hard.'

She pressed her palms flat into the floor, as though preparing to sprint.

'Have you met her? You guys look alike, you know. I could show you, if you like.' A note of invitation in her voice.

'What were you doing in my drawers?' I asked.

'Curious. About Rose first. Next this new person. It was not locked.'

No question of apology.

'So she has been in touch?' Anja asked, and I think I heard some hope in her.

'No. She wants nothing to do with me,' I said.

It hurt no more than it always had.

She pushed up in her sudden way and took my hands. Hers were greasy under mine and I smelt my body cream on her, and unwashed hair.

'Oh, I am sorry. I hoped. I did not want you be alone,' she said, in a gentler voice.

'Alone?' I repeated, stupidly.

'Alone, Maggie. After I am gone.'

Her face was smooth thick putty in the pinkish shade she liked. Plasticky and featureless. There was a web of vein in the white of one eye and, as she blinked, I saw a contact lens that I had never known she wore swim gently out of place.

'I am not alone. I have friends. I spend my time with who I choose. That's not the same,' I said.

She held my hands tighter and began a massage at the base of my thumbs; a circling pressure.

'Maggie, you are the loneliest person I ever knew,' she said.

'Well.' I stalled, and tried to pull away but she held me too hard.

'You know, I am a bad choice for you,' she said sadly. 'We could never be anything to each other. That was never possible. I was always going.'

'Anja. If I were you, I'd be more concerned.'

Her fingers were strong and the feel of them deep in the muscle of my hand was unpleasant.

'I just don't understand it. You are not so old, Maggie. Why do you behave this way?'

She flicked out the bottom of my hair.

'You hide yourself. You could be pretty again. If you tried. Go into the world.'

I felt an awful blush spread upwards from my chest.

'Reach out for your daughter. If Bella does not want you, how about Rose? She is not so far. Just the other side of the city. And her beautiful baby boy.'

'What did you say?' I asked, though I had heard her clearly.

'Reach for her. Why do you make things so hard for yourself?' she said, a teasing kind of scold in her voice.

She ran one hand the length of my arm and squeezed at the

top. She worked the loose flesh steadily, between her fingers, like dough.

And I had hit her, a flat-handed slap to the side of her face. A clean pop of sound that split the room open. Somewhere inside it was her inhale, her shock, which is the real power of a slap.

A brief scald on my palm, the memory of the hard ridge of her cheekbone and it was over.

She laid her own hand on the place where I had struck and for a last second I felt her unreadable gaze. She thought to speak, I waited for her words, but she spat out a sound instead that I had never heard, a combination of disdain and revulsion, a perfect insult. She left me.

41

Not a long day, or a hard day. No row with my husband, nor previous sleepless night.

A slow build of frustration, then, that finally came to a head? A pad-footed despair, perhaps, at last, showed its teeth?

None of these.

I have been back and back to look for signs, but there were none. Just an ordinary day in my ordinary life.

Chris and I were neither happy nor unhappy. Nothing's ever enough, my mother used to say, that's the problem with you. And she was right, to an extent. There was an itch sewn into me, though I've long since cut it out. A certain yearning and, yes, it could flare up, but it did not govern me. I existed, still do (tragedy to one side, and I know nothing of ecstasy), within a narrow band of middling emotion. I am not, for the most part, given to extremes.

She would not eat. That was how it started. But she never ate. His mother said don't let her get down. Mine was perplexed; she had not heard of a child who didn't finish the plate. The book called it a question of control. Said that patience and flexibility are key. That seemed fair.

So it was not new to me to watch her spit it out, whatever I'd made; her tongue thick and muscled, expelling my food. Nor see the spoon flung to the floor, or her bowl flipped over in a caricature of disgust. I no longer dreaded the mess, wore sensible clothes and cooked enough that there was always more.

An average Saturday; we were out that night, the cleaner due in an hour to put her down. Chris flew the next day so we wouldn't be late.

Halfway down a glass of wine placed safely out of harm's reach. I hadn't eaten since lunch and it sat alone and happy in my stomach.

Chris in his office doing paperwork and I could have called for him, had I needed. He would have tucked a tea towel into his collar and done his bit; bent in from a distance. But that hadn't been necessary. It was fine.

And the meal had not gone badly; she had eaten something, enough. I held on to her chair and she clambered down, leaving a baked-bean print on her mat.

'Yoghurt, please,' she said, from somewhere below me.

'No, love. Not if you don't eat all your tea.'

'Yoghurt, please,' she repeated, surprised; she had, after all, said please.

'No, Bella. Go and see what Daddy's doing.'

I withdrew my attention. Resumed the tidying. Thought of the evening ahead or whatever played on the radio. I heard the suck of the fridge. She stood in its glow, stretching up. She saw me see her and stepped a foot inside, lunging for her treat in the last seconds before I got there. Her hand shut over a pot.

'Give that here, please, Bella. Now. You are not to eat it.'

She held it behind her and backed away cautiously.

'I mean it. Give it here now, please. I don't want to have to take it off you.'

She wore a curious look; an animal look. All pupils, eyes

locked on mine. I had the idea that if I snatched for her food, she might bite.

She reached the wall and pushed her pelvis forward to make room for the yoghurt she hid. There seemed to be a taunt in it.

'I don't know why you're doing this. It's very silly and very naughty. You're going to be in a lot of trouble soon.'

A sudden flurry of anxiety that didn't reach her. She watched me steadily.

This scene was a new one, she had not done this before, this level-eyed defiance. But isn't each new phase, every new behaviour, good or bad, in your child's life, strange? When they are everything, something different becomes huge, a devastation. And why does a mother, why did I, feel it as an affront? It's not all about you, after all, as they say.

I could have diffused it, I see that now, in any number of ways. The subtlest cue of retreat; a straightening, maybe, for I had bent, poised for what was coming. I would not let her pass.

She bolted and I caught the top of one arm, and was pleased when I did.

She bent her face away from me as far as it would stretch. There was the sideways L of her jawbone, the impossible peach of her cheek. Still I heard her say, 'Get off me, Mummy.'

Her other arm was outstretched. She squeezed the yoghurt and it burst, a great dollop travelling over the edge, on its way down to the floor.

'Give it to me. That's enough.'

'No,' she said.

'What did you say, Bella?'

256

Louder. Emphatic. A little elongating of the N.

'No.'

And then she tried to get away. She was strong, pulling with everything she had. She tugged her arm out of my grip but I snatched for her and caught her wrist, just.

She heaved against me, arm taut, feet scrabbling for purchase as she put all of herself into resistance.

She was making me ridiculous and I wanted it over.

I lunged for the pot, and she saw that she could not win, that I was simply too big. And so she chucked it, not back into the kitchen, even, but out into the hall. We both watched as an arc of artificial pink splattered the carpet and the pot came to rest, crumpled, dripping thickly. She looked back to me and she grinned.

My feeling for her was buried by the anger that shot the length of me and I saw her plainly, as if a stranger's child. She was limp now at the end of my arm, dangling, done with this game and the effort of supporting herself and I saw her open pleasure in her win.

And so I yanked her, pulled myself up to my full, adult height, and brought her upwards too. Did she have the chance to take her weight into her feet; to stand, as surely I had intended? I don't know. But it didn't happen, and I felt it as more refusal.

So I let go, a deliberate action; opened my fingers starfish wide and dropped her, pushed her, even, and she fell, and her outstretched arm hit the floor at its joint with the hand. There was the moment of impact; a static moment when I saw that her arm should have bent, but instead stayed stick straight. Her fingers tweaked towards me and she toppled to one side, her arm laid out elegant across the floor. A ballerina's tension and grace.

I felt confused and distant, my brain overloaded. Chris was there.

'I saw that. For fuck's sake, Maggie, why did you let her go? What were you thinking?'

He spoke the words ahead of him as he rushed to her. I stayed where I was.

I believe that had he not left his office, had he not appeared in that second, the whole thing could have become something else. In the space of that pause, in the second or two before he arrived, my brain had been rearranging events to fit the shape of an accident. Not a lie, as such, not a conscious deceit, but a matter of interpretation; of survival, of sanity. For everybody's good. I think I would have come to believe it myself, over time, had he not shown up.

But it was witnessed, and, in being so, my act named for what it was.

He got to her but she did not cry. Shock had bleached her face. She was perfectly still except for her eyes, pinned wide, which followed me as I paced the edge of the scene. Then she spoke, called my name, 'Mumma', and I knelt to her. Chris phoned for the ambulance.

'What happened?' they asked, when they arrived.

'She fell,' we said.

'From where?' they wanted to know.

'Just standing. I had her hand. She slipped,' I told them.

'That's good,' they said. 'No distance.'

Chris looked at everything but me.

The fracture was in the bottom of the radius, the big forearm bone, where it met the wrist. They X-rayed her in the hospital and showed me the faint white line that was the break. The commonest type.

Later on, a nurse checked Bella for bruises, efficiently and without apology. Chris and I stood at a distance, in terror, both of us; I could feel it pulsing out of him. She worked carefully, running her hands over Bella, limb by limb. My daughter shivered at the touch.

'What happened, sweetie?' the nurse asked, sat on the end of her bed.

'I fell,' Bella said, with a spacey grin that ended on me.

It was her left arm, thanks heavens – not that she wrote, she was just three – but she loved to draw, the same picture always. Gardens full of human-faced flowers. I found a pen in my bag and started a version on her cast as we waited, and another, changing the shapes of the petals and the aspects of each face. When she lifted the load of her bad arm across (it broke my heart, this effort), she gasped.

Someone brought us a mug of felt-tips and we drew for another while, her awkwardly, at an angle, me increasingly fluent. I recall this hour with a pleasure so acute it rips the breath from me.

The lady at reception said, could she try one too? And next a man who sat by, one leg raised in his wheelchair, his ankle huge and waterlogged. His drawing was wild and jungly and Bella asked if he would do her some more. When we were finished, it was beautiful. She cried, a month later, when the cast came off and begged to keep it, an artefact, a discarded limb. She laid it on a shelf by her bed; a constant rebuke.

I wondered what she remembered. I asked her in the following days: 'Tell me, sweet, about the day you slipped.' Always

259

the same. 'I fell, Mumma.' Nothing more. I wanted to push, but didn't dare.

'I'm so sorry, darling,' I said, again and again, and held her face, too hard, in my hands and looked down into her, deeply, desperately, but there was nothing to see, just the quiet smile of a child.

Did she know what I had done? Did she forgive me?

All I know is that I would have forgiven my own mother anything, except the act of abandoning me.

I have a temper. My mother's temper. But that?

Well, yes. There is no denying it. I did a bad thing, the bad thing. I hurt my child. I broke her arm, an accident of course, but for that sliver of second in which I wanted to hurt her. I wanted her to fall – I must have done, that is why I let her go. And when the day was over, and she lay upstairs bandaged and sleeping, this knowledge doused me in terror. And from then it was always there; it lived at the fringes of everything.

I had done it once; how could I know I wouldn't do it again? It had come upon me quickly. No warning. Nothing that I could recognise, should it threaten to strike. No alarm to send me racing to my bedroom, hand trembling at the lock, until the urge – was that what it had been? – had past.

There remained just the moment. My decision, though it was all too fast, perhaps, to name it as such. The impulse, then. Some structural weakness. Not that it matters, my reason or the words I choose to describe it. The act alone is what endures. Or rather the outcome, and I bet her wrist still stiffens in the cold and she twists it, first one way and the other, to ease it, as she began to when the weather cooled that year; an action that, every time I saw it, stopped my heart.

I swore to myself, for there was no one else, that I would never do it again.

And I did not. I never raised a hand to Rose. Or anyone, until that day. Until Anja.

42

I saw her one last time. She came to me four days later, on a Tuesday, at eight o'clock prompt – the time that we had once arranged for her to clean. She knocked instead of using her key.

'Hello, Maggie. Can I come in?' Eyes that wouldn't meet mine.

I am at a disadvantage first thing. I suppose everyone is, but at my age it takes time for sleep to leave my face and a dressing-gown is always an encumbrance. I had drunk too much the night before and when I finally got off, my dreams were fitful. All of this showed; I glanced into a mirror on my way to the door and noticed deep creases lining one cheek.

'Of course,' I said, and stood aside.

She lifted a new bike across the threshold, grimacing at its weight. I followed, watching the wheels spin pointlessly and shed tyre-tread lattices of dry mud onto my floor. She hit a door frame as she passed, and chipped out a deep cleft of wood. I found the piece – jagged, glossy with paint – and toed it against the wall. I refastened my belt. Wrapped myself up a bit tighter.

I put on the kettle and pushed some bread down to toast. I could hear her struggling with the French doors but didn't offer to help.

'Would you like a cup of tea?' I called.

'No, thanks,' she said.

'Do you mind? I was just about to shower.'

I was down in ten minutes, and found her where I had left her.

'Maggie,' she started. 'I didn't mean to bring you trouble.'

Her apology landed on me with a terrible weight.

'No. Anja. You didn't. God, don't think of it that way. If anything it was the other way round. And I am so sorry. Sincerely sorry.'

'It's OK. Really.'

She blinked her relief at me, which was even worse.

Her hair was high and her face blemish-free. My slap had left no mark. She wore heavy mascara, a different look, which had clumped her lashes, and ear-rings in more of her piercings. The uppermost had reddened and I wondered if she had boiled the pin before she opened it. She looked fierce, a touch worn. Younger too. I wondered where she had slept.

'No. It was horribly wrong. What I did. And I'm sorry. It's not OK,' I said. 'Don't ever think it's OK.'

She gave a wry little smile and I felt shame.

'Look, seriously, Anja. I want you to.'

'Please, Maggie. Just don't. Will you please just leave it?' she asked.

I said nothing. It seemed the least I could do.

'Thank you,' she said. 'And by the way, do you have a tissue?'

She pulled a funny face and pointed at herself. Sure enough, two fat black tears had started down the gullies either side of her nose.

I ripped her a square of kitchen roll and she folded it and seesawed under her eyes. She handed it back to me, streaked, and I felt her brief dry touch.

'Anyway. I have come to say goodbye. There is a coach tonight,' she said.

Her voice was calm but I felt the shift between us; her caution, her sense of my volatility, and would have done anything, anything, to go back.

'Oh, right,' I said. 'I'm so glad you did. And do you know yet? Where you'll be going?'

'I have some plans but I don't want you to have to lie if they ask so –'

'OK,' I said. 'I understand.'

I bent across the sink and looked up, trying to find the weather. The sky was a milky blue. Somewhere in Queen's Park the sun was shining but it would be hours until it reached down into my own shaded space.

'It looks all right out there. If you want to, you could spend the day with me? If your coach isn't till later?' I said.

'Yes! Of course!' she said. Her old smile back.

'Good. Brilliant. But first, we eat.'

There was some bacon in the fridge and enough eggs. I had the idea of pancakes. We had eaten them every weekend for a while, after Chris brought back the notion from New York, but I couldn't remember the recipe, so Anja found one on the computer and I cooked off instructions on the screen.

No maple syrup, but the golden type did fine.

They were delicious; Anja loved them. Like me before her, she had imagined the combination strange until she tried it. Simple delight; that's what I saw.

We decided on a final walk and I told her I'd take her somewhere new. We used the car, which hadn't been out for months. My door was stuck and the air inside stale, but we opened the windows and the day rushed in. Buster, on the back seat, head between us, stuck out his tongue to taste it.

We set off in the blinding frozen sun and I asked her to find something on the radio, and she did.

We walked in Richmond Park with takeout coffee and a muffin between us. She marvelled at the deer and tried to tell me a story about a dog she'd seen chasing them on YouTube, but I wasn't paying attention. The day felt suddenly perfect and I had the rarest sense of inhabiting it. She babbled away happily.

We stopped for lunch in a pub and sat outside, to save shutting Buster in the car. They thought us mad, but gave me a tray and I carried out our cutlery and a bunch of red paper napkins. The dog lay patient between her legs. I drank a glass of red and treated Anja to a beer.

I told her I had drunk through both of my pregnancies; that we hadn't known any better in those days.

'Was it ever OK, Maggie? With Rose's father? Can I ask?' she said.

'Of course it was.'

'In the early times?'

'Well, yes.'

'Like when?'

She curled her arms around herself.

Like that dinner dance at the Dorchester.

It could have been the bubbles, or the pep it gives a man to wear white tie. It pulls him up, draws his shoulders back and loosens him, from top to toe. Fred Astaire all over.

But he held my hand as we took the stairs, passed beneath the sign and a fat ledge of close-packed carnations in bands of red and white. People watched as we went, and wondered if we were someone.

Was it my gown, perhaps? His pleasure at the press of my hip through the drop of silver silk, or the cut of clavicle I had emphasised with a mineral sweep under the bathroom bulb?

'You know that hollow there?' his boss asked, later, drunk, with an audible swallow and his finger, smudged with Béarnaise, trembling at my neck.

'I'd like to drink champagne out of that.'

'Shall we dance, sweetheart?' Chris called to me across the table.

'Why not?' I said.

'Are you all right?' he asked, as he took my hand, but I pushed my cheek into his collar and we moved nearer to the band. We danced for hours, telepathic, step perfect, and when Sinatra came on, 'The Way You Look Tonight', and the packed floor pushed us even closer, he broke into a crackled whisper; he sung to me, at the chorus, I'm sure he did.

We were our best selves at a distance. Together, across space. His face high above me and the idea of each other brilliant in our minds.

'My god, what does it take to get a woman like you?' that drunk man called as I went for my wrap.

'Wouldn't you like to know?' Chris said, under his breath, and we dashed for our cab.

'We liked to dance,' I told Anja. 'That was nice.'

'Oh great,' she said. 'What type?'

'All sorts.'

'Cool. So what went wrong?' she asked.

'Hard to say. We were not a good match.'

'How come?'

All surface and activity, Chris. Then huge swathes of silence.

'What is it that you want?' he once cried, in a rare flash of feeling. 'This thing that is so important to you, that I lack?'

'We just miss each other. Every time. We can't seem to meet,' I told him.

'I don't even know what that means. You'll never be happy.' The row ended there.

'Oh, I don't know, Anja. We weren't quite right. That can spread, you know. Grow solid.'

She asked me why I left my daughter.

I tried to explain, but I'm not sure she understood.

'What about your mother?' she said. 'And the aunts?'

'We fell out. We didn't speak again,' I said.

'Not ever? Not even Frannie?'

'Once or twice. She sided with my mum.'

'That's sad,' Anja said. 'That makes me feel sad.'

Anja got cold, her clothes so horribly thin. I lent her my scarf and asked what she'd done with the yellow one.

'Oh, yes!' she said. 'In my bag somewhere?', and I knew that she had lost it. I told her she could keep the one she wore.

We ate two dodgy ploughmans of supermarket cheese and soft pickled onions and went back to the car.

In the footwell I found a luggage tag from the day we first met. I chucked it in the back, my throat all closed.

We got home, held each other briefly, still in coats, and said our goodbyes. She told me not to worry and I said that I would try. I stood at the door as she pushed off on her bike, her strong calf pulling the leg of her old jeans tight, the bag on her back threatening to topple her.

And she was gone, and it was Buster and I once more.

43

A month on. Christmas a week away. It might sound strange but this is my favourite time of year. The backdrop of life changes, or rather assumes an earlier, more familiar shape. I have renewed relevance on the high street and in the adverts; even the music they play is old. I recognise it all.

The boys were to host, though I must stop calling them that. We were fine once more, and hadn't spoken of what went on. I imagine they felt ashamed of their part. They are good men.

Maureen was coming too – she planned to do her stuffing, plus sausage rolls. She'd been surprised to hear that Anja had left, and in such a rush, but hadn't lingered on it. She is a woman who knows when not to ask.

I had offered to bake but they told me to bring Prosecco instead, and bags of oranges to press for Buck's Fizz. And treats for the dogs' stockings.

I could not wait.

Rose had met her sister, whom she didn't know she had. She called me with this news from the street, the first time I'd heard her voice in months.

'I've met Bella, Mum. I've just come from Bella. My sister,' she shouted.

'What?' I said, though I heard her perfectly well. She said it again, but I still couldn't catch her tone above the traffic. I waited for her next sentence to fall, struck with certainty that this final great omission would mean the end of us.

'It's a lot, I know. But can I come round? Tomorrow would work,' and I heard her excitement; elation even.

'Of course,' I said.

'Brilliant. I'll bring Sam. Oh, no, I won't, he's at nursery. Can we do it before lunch? Something like eleven?'

'Of course.'

'I've got about half an hour. See you then.'

I held it all at arm's length, and opened the door to her next morning with no plan, no expectation.

'Hi, Mum,' she said, bright and vague and cooler, now. She came in for a hug, which was easier than looking at me. Brief and bony. She was the one to break it. She hung up her coat without thinking, on the same rack, in the same spot as she'd have found it in the old place.

'Wow,' she said. 'This is very weird. Kind of the same as home, but different.'

'Yes. I suppose.'

'Oh! I recognise this!'

The sofa, I think.

'And who are you? I thought he – oh, that was the old one. Crikey. He's friendly enough.'

Buster had jumped up and she caught his paws to save the front of her clothes. He stood chest high on two legs, panting happily, and I wondered what he saw in her. Still I told him off, to fill the gap.

Then: 'Where's my piano? I would have taken that!'

Her hair was shorter than I'd seen it, and better styled. A bobbed cut, longer at the front. I knew her hair, which had tightened into curls as she grew, and it would have taken a blow-dry to get it into that shape. She wore proper trousers and a decent pair of shoes.

'You look smart,' I said without thinking, and waited for her to prickle. But she didn't. Instead: 'I've got a new job. At an arts centre, raising funds.'

I couldn't see Rose on the phone asking for money, but what do I know?

'Weird, isn't it?' she said. 'But I love it. And it feels worthwhile.'

I was happy for her. She prowled the room, looking out old things.

'I'll make us a hot drink, shall I?' I said.

We stood opposite each other in the kitchen with a tea each, though she no longer took sugar, and it was heaven just to watch her. She had come into herself in looks, a late bloomer, as was I. She seemed strong and well and contented.

She could not match my gaze and talked a lot, but, baby steps.

'I haven't come to start it all again. I just want us to try and. Move on a bit,' she said.

'That's good,' I said. 'Me too.'

'Do you want to know about Bella?' she asked, tentative.

I wasn't sure, and I think that must have shown on my face.

'Because if you don't, Mum, I understand,' she said.

But she was here to talk; that was the levy.

'No, it's all right. If you like,' I said.

She came towards me and we embraced once more. It was better, this time; she smelt the same at the back of her ear.

'You gave up a child?' she said, above my head – I hadn't remembered her so tall, though that would be the heels.

'Christ, Mum. I can't even imagine.'

The terribleness of it seemed to have afforded me some respect.

And so she started to tell me.

'She messaged me first. Quite an emotional message. Explaining who she was and asking if I'd be willing to speak to her.'

She threw me glances to check that I could take it.

'That must have been a shock,' I said.

'A shock? Well, yes. But more of a surprise. A wonderful surprise. Though she asked that we keep it a secret, at first.'

I felt this as an offering, held up to me to recognise; some shared attribute between me and the child I left behind.

'So we emailed for a while. She told me how upset she'd been. By this. Anja person.'

Rose's discomfort was plain.

'Yes. Well. That wasn't my fault. She did it without my knowledge,' I said.

'I realise. And Bella knows that too. But. I. Is everything OK there, Mum?' she asked.

'Fine. She's just. I helped her, that's all. And she went behind my back.'

I heard my betrayal of her, but how to explain it, as it had really been? That I had loved Anja. And I think that she had loved me too.

'Well, anyway. I don't suppose that matters any more. She hasn't been in touch with Bella since. I guess you know that?'

'Anja's gone,' I said.

'Oh, good,' replied Rose.

'So, that woman stopped emailing and the whole thing could

have ended there, but that was when Bella realised she didn't want to let it go.'

I saw Rosie warming; how much she loved this idea.

'She decided to get in touch. Too weird, obviously, with you, so she tracked me down instead. And do you know what she told me, Mum?'

She no longer sought my consent. She was borne along on the magic of her story, this fairy-tale connection she had found.

'She said she was a Benson, deep down. That she had always known it.'

'A Benson?' I said, and felt my own heart stutter. 'What on earth is that when it's at home?'

'Good question! We've been discussing it quite a bit actually!'

I dropped wonkily onto a stool. It tipped, and for a second I thought I would fall, but she had my arm: 'Take it easy, Mum.'

'You know Bella spent a lot of time with. Granny?' The word shy in her mouth. 'Well, apparently she talked about you loads.'

'What do you mean?' I said.

She smiled a huge screwy smile.

'She said you were a real firecracker!'

Rose misread my face.

'I know! Crazy, right? She told Bella this brilliant story. Do you remember some old dear – Marjorie, I think, Granny's friend who used to lord it up over them?'

'Marie, it was,' I said; came for tea the last Friday of every month, gloves whatever the weather and hair she hadn't touched since she was a girl, set twice a week at the place at the end of our road. I used to see her there on my way back from school, bubble-headed and oblivious in the window, looking down into a puzzle book while her hair dried; clicking the end of a long narrow pen as she thought.

'Oh yes. Marie. That's right.'

Frannie would bake; Bettie had flair but Fran's results were more consistent. Mum made sandwiches the night before, all packed together tight and bound in a spritzed tea towel to keep them fresh. China out the drawer.

A family friend from the old days, Mum had told me. Come round for a catch-up, but it was clear she came round out of nosiness and spite. I hated their submission to her.

'Bella told me what you did! How old were you? Ten?' Rose said, bright-eyed at my rebellion.

Eight years old. My first real transgression and Mum's first taste of my dissent.

I had sat myself apart from them, head bent to a book at the table. Not listening as such, but alert to dipped voices, which meant something worth overhearing.

They tried to please her. They offered her tea, but she would only take Earl Grey – 'My latest thing!' – which they didn't have; had never even heard of. She scrunched her face at every name they mentioned: 'Milly Henry? Don't think I recall.' Refused the cake I'd iced with Fran the night before, patting her tummy to show that she was full. Buttercream and lemon piped through the star-shaped nozzle in one unbroken swirl. I hadn't tried it yet. I'd been told to leave off and wait my turn.

Marie stood – 'Do excuse me' – in the middle of Mum's story, and walked past me to the loo. The sisters started up in whispers.

She was quick, I thought, when I heard the lock go. I saw her pause in the corridor, an ear out, and move deeper into the house.

She bent low to some photos on a corner table. Three of them, all my parents' wedding. She rubbed a smudge off the glass with her thumb, which would have killed Mum to witness.

Then she straightened, and I looked down at my page, but she didn't come back. She moved on to the kitchen.

Under the window, raised on its stand, stood the cake. Marie approached and took a long deep smell. She reached for a teaspoon on the draining board and ran it the length of the cake's cut edge. I watched a thick shaving of icing curl into the spoon, and then she sucked it, eyes shut. As she came back through, she made a sudden pattering on my table with her fingertips. I've still no idea what she meant by it.

'Perhaps I will have a slice,' she said, sat down again. 'Just a small one, mind.'

Marie's mistake, I believe, was to overestimate the store my mother set by decorum. It might even have been a test. Either way, Mum was back in an instant, the cake held before her and brought to rest, with a wallop, across my book. Dangerously askew.

'Well?'

'It was her,' I said, straight away. 'I saw her,' and pointed at Marie, just to be clear.

The next part was fast. Marie, who'd never been so insulted in her life, left. The cake, poised above the bin, Mum's eyes on mine, gone too; helped along, when it stuck briefly, with a cuff. Her hand still felt sticky as she yanked me up the staircase to my room. I stayed there through till morning. No tea. I never even tried to plead my case.

'She thought you were so brave,' Rosie said.

'Pardon?'

'Your mum. They laughed and laughed after you went to bed, Granny and her sisters. Fearless. That's what she called you.'

'I was in my room from four in the afternoon. She dragged me up. She left me there.'

I could still feel the injustice of it.

'Well, she thought you were brilliant. That's what she told Bella, anyway,' Rosie said, and I wondered if I could remember laughter, much later, from upstairs in my bed.

'I wish I'd known her – Granny, I mean,' Rose said. 'Oh, Mum, don't look like that. I promised you I wouldn't ask, and I won't. Have you got a biscuit, by the way? I'm starving and I need to be gone in the next five minutes.'

I gave her one, and an apple from the fridge to take on her way.

'So what's she like then?' I said, all in a rush. 'Bella, I mean.'

'Oh, right,' she said. 'OK. So. She's a marketing director, for a big company in town. She did tell me who, but I forget. She's single. I get the idea she's putting her career first. Dark hair, like us, though actually blonde, you know, highlights. Kind of well put together. One of those chunky men's watches – probably thousands. Blue eyes –' She moved her face closer. 'Darker than yours, actually,' and so she ran on, and nothing that she said bore relation to the child that I had known.

'But she was right, you know. After a while I did see a bit of Benson in her,' she said.

Our stubbornness, perhaps; our temper, our spite?

'Our sense of humour, for a start,' said Rose, of all the things.

'Our sense of humour? Whatever do you mean?'

275

'Hmm. How to put it? Not obvious, I suppose', and I had to smile at that.

'I enjoyed this, you know. We should do it again,' she said.

And we did. I popped over, the following week, to see Sam. A dear boy. Still, we agreed to take it slow.

The two girls speak regularly – to make up for lost time, Rose says, and seem in the throes of something close to romance. To say 'my sister' gives Rose a charge and this is a salve to me. What they are building together shrinks my failure of them.

After a while, Chris gave Bella, who in turn gave Rose, the name of her father. In getting it she seemed to forgive me completely.

'Mum, honestly,' Rose said. 'I know you were married and he was married, and younger and your teacher and all, but really, not so very scandalous. Not these days.'

She gave a snort at the silliness of it. My silence, it appeared, had been my power, my significance. Once she thought she knew, I became as any other mother; tolerated, largely disregarded.

They found Ben on the Internet but he was dead, thank god. A piano teacher to the last, Rose told me, survived by a wife and two girls. But she would not be in touch. She would let sleeping dogs lie. This seemed the grown-up decision, she said, straight-faced.

'Don't you see, Mum? How easy it can be? No need for all these secrets!'

An aside as she sat at her laptop while I cooked my grandson tea. She thinks that she has worked out how to live, and wants to show me too.

I chopped and mashed. Said nothing.

And she has kept her promise. She has not asked for my

version. Perhaps because she does not want to be disappointed, or maybe it is no longer important. I wonder what I would tell her if she did.

Would I mention the first time that I knew of Ben's feelings?

That would be the moment of our introduction. He was a naive boy, a child, twenty-two to my twenty-eight and he swallowed too deeply as he took my hand; I saw his Adam's apple bob. Chris saw it too; I think he might have even thought that it would help.

Or would it be when I saw that he would speak? Poor dear, it took him three attempts across the space of an hour, any one of which I could have stopped. But I let it happen, out of boredom, and because we all love to be loved, me more than most, once upon a time.

I let him down gently, implying that though these feelings were shared, I could not possibly act. His eyes filled at the tragedy of it. Maybe mine did too.

I could have told her either of these tales, or others; embellished in whatever way I saw fit. Added period detail for accuracy or upped the heartbreak for a kick. I could, but I would not have been telling the story of her father.

44

That began in, what would it be? 1982.

Bella coming up to her first birthday; early perhaps to embark on this kind of thing, but my figure had snapped back and we didn't breastfeed in those days.

I cannot claim I was depressed; I was not, that had passed. I was empty, bored, underused, but that is the lot of many women.

It began with a crash, a plane crash in Japan. I have googled it to get it right. I found the following on Wikipedia:

February 9 – Japan Airlines Flight 350 crashes in Tokyo Bay due to thrust reversal on approach to Tokyo International Airport, killing 24 among the 174 people on board.

It was the pilot's fault; a deliberate act in a moment of insanity.

There was another accident, too, I found, the month before:

January 13 – Shortly after take off, Air Florida Flight 90 crashes into Washington, D.C.'s 14th Street Bridge and falls into the Potomac River, killing 78.

Two in two months.

I don't remember the American one, though we must have spoken of it, a pilot and his wife. And we knew no one aboard the Tokyo flight; mine was not a disaster on that scale.

The first I heard was from Chris's brother, Michael. He called from Gatwick, waking me up, shouting news of disruption and delay. He was supposed to be flying into Japan that morning. Now he was stuck.

'I couldn't stay, Mags, could I? Just tonight? Catch up with you both. Meet the little one. I'll be off again tomorrow.'

Chris and I had been together five years and I had met Michael as many times, a couple of Christmases, their parents' anniversary, our wedding. He lived abroad, but that they didn't get along was apparent, if unacknowledged.

'Chris's not here, I'm afraid. He's flying.'

'Oh, right. Well, I wouldn't ask but I'm a bit strapped at the moment, what with Claire. I just thought. Two birds and one stone?'

His wife had left him. A shame, I'd liked her. She carried her advantages lightly.

'OK then, he'll be back tonight anyway,' I said.

'Great. I'll bring a bottle.'

He arrived before eight like someone awaited, arms wide on the doorstep, a grin that showed his teeth. I took a step towards him and we hugged – there was no choice, his hands were full and he wasn't moving – and I surprised myself by recognising his smell. Sweat, a lime cologne, and hair cream – warm rubber and coconut. Delicious and alien. I breathed it in on his shoulder and felt the push of his belly against me. His flesh was soft, and eased as we stood there, pressed together; rearranging itself in reaction to me. It was new and intimate and not unpleasant. He pulled back, and moved his hands up to my shoulders.

'And how are you, Maggie?' he asked, as if I were in recovery.

279

'Oh, fine, thanks,' I said.

'Good. You look well. And where is she?'

'Bella?' I said, to help him out. I remembered this now, his comfortable charm. The ex-pat chat.

'She's only one, Michael. You can't expect her to come running, you know.'

He glanced back at me, thin-eyed and amused.

'You're right. I'm hopeless with children, birthdays, obligation of any kind. My mother and brother will have told you that, though, I'm sure,' he said.

'Not at all,' I replied, though he was right. I remembered that I liked him.

'What were you doing in Japan?' I asked.

'Oh, business. Helping a friend find local partners,' he said.

I called up what I knew of him. Lazy, alcoholic, shady in his business dealings – a subsidiary to journalism. And flippantly dressed, in the foreign manner, which enraged his father. But Pa, as they called him, was wrong, I thought, as I followed Michael through to the lounge.

His look was considered and effective. Crumpled cotton with chestnut brogues and a battered document bag; the perfect collision of privilege and insouciance. But the bag was old, a hand-me-down from Pa or a gift, perhaps, from when it had all still been ahead of him. And well looked after; I could see on the strap where the stitching had been mended and the texture of the hide was mellow from wax. He worked at this. And he relied on people underestimating him.

He sat on the sofa and reached out to Bella. She smiled at him and stretched up for his hair; longer, darker and more curly than Chris's.

'Ouch,' he cried, as she pulled it, hard.

'She's gorgeous. Very much a Benson,' he said.

'Do you think? People say that. I can't really see it myself.'

'Too close, I imagine.'

He gave her a teddy picked up at the airport.

'Now you get on with your day, Maggie. Don't let me interrupt. I need to do some work anyway, if that's OK? Is there somewhere I could sit, do you think?'

I put him in the dining room and made a coffee he didn't drink. After a while he asked if he could use the phone – his friend would call straight back – and it rang and I heard him say: 'Oh, hi, Chris. – It's Michael. – Michael, your brother. – Waiting for you, of course, what else? – OK. Hold on. I'll just get her for you. Maggie?'

I took the handset.

'Hello,' I said.

'Please explain to me what he's doing there,' said Chris.

'He got delayed. That crash in Japan.'

The line dropped for a second.

'Hello,' I said again.

'Oh, right. Christ. When did he arrive?'

'First thing.'

'Well, there's a problem here, too. I've been waiting to call. I didn't want to wake you.'

'What? In Hong Kong?'

'A near miss. The runway's a nightmare, remember? I told you. Anyway. I won't make it back tonight.'

'You're kidding me,' I said, my stomach jumping. I could see Michael bending over Bella, bouncing her chair with his foot.

'Maggie, I'm sorry, really. I can't believe you're saddled with my brother.'

'Don't worry. When will you be home?'

He couldn't hear me. I repeated the question, louder.

'I don't know. I'll let you know as soon as I do. I'll make this up to you, I promise.'

'OK, bye,' I said.

I put the phone down, my throat hot.

'No Chris?' he said, still pulling faces at Bella. 'Stuck in Japan?'

'No. No. Something else. But he won't be back tonight, I'm afraid.'

'Oh, well. Next time. Tell you what, shall I cook for us? If you were at mine, it would be Beef Randang but given the shopping restrictions, will lasagne do?'

'Delicious,' I said, relieved.

'OK. I need to finish up here and I'll get on with it.'

It was a hard day to occupy and I realised how used I had become to being alone, the only adult in a still house. I spoke to Bella self-consciously but whispered, too, right in her ear, silly things that made her shriek. We went out in the buggy and I bought a pound of mince.

I listened to him on the phone, and heard his voice change between client and colleague. Michael wielded his accent to get things done. My husband had vanished his and I wondered why. Surely not to fit in, that was not Chris. And I realised it was to negate his advantage, to make things fair, so that he could be certain that his triumphs were his own. Chris's arrogance to Michael's expedience.

He came through at five and mixed us two huge lemony

gin and tonics. This made me want to smoke though I usually waited till Bella was down. I pinched one of his, as if that made it better, but it was far too strong and I stubbed it out halfway. It amused him and I felt like a teenager. I put the radio on, and he turned it up a couple of clicks.

'Do you mind?' he asked, and took off his shoes. He left them in the hall, heels tucked against the wall, and when I went to put Bella to bed, I saw that his surname was written inside. From school, then, the boarding school that Chris had loved and Michael loathed.

I came back in and there was something sweet and sad about him in his socks, sleeves rolled up, cutting onions in my kitchen. He sliced fast and thin on a board next to the oven and I stood the other side, holding my own cigarette, now, to the open window. The night beyond sucked out the smoke. We each drank a second gin.

He told me he used to cook a lot, but now there was no Claire, it didn't seem worth his while.

'Do you still see her?' I asked.

'I do. We are friends. She has a new fellow, very nice, much better suited.'

'What went wrong?' I said.

'I disappointed her. I fell short in some unspecified way.'

He was smiling as he said it. He stirred the onion and garlic but the gas was high and I worried it would catch.

'Do you add a carrot?' he asked.

'I don't myself,' I said.

'Nor me. Now for the mince.'

He held the bag above the pan and pulled the meat out gradually, loosening the kinked strands between his fingers. A pouch of blood had collected in a corner and he raised it carefully, set a narrow stream tumbling into the oil. It hissed and spat and he stirred it through.

'Were you upset?' I asked, 'when she left?'

'I was, but I saw it coming. This happens to me,' he said, with a glance across and raised eyebrows.

'Would you get me a glass of red?' he said. 'I brought some. I think I left it in the dining room.'

I went in and found the wine, wrapped in white tissue. When I lifted it, the bottle nearly slipped from my hand.

There were papers all over and I wanted to look, to find out something more of him; uncover a secret, even, but didn't dare. I picked up his passport and bent it open to the photo. It was an old shot and he was thinner and more handsome, with a bright open look. I felt it then, a kick in the pit of my stomach. I enjoyed the sensation for that second, and went back.

'If you stir, I'll open,' he said.

I stood over the heat and kept things moving, smashing up the lumps; the noise of frying loud and agitated.

'There's some herbs, in that drawer, if you like,' I said.

He chose a jar of oregano and came across to show me the label.

'Enough?' he asked.

'I think so.'

'Glasses?' he said.

'Up there.'

He reached into the cupboard and took two from the back – huge, wedding presents, rarely used – manoeuvring them carefully over the rest. He poured the wine, handed me mine and, stretching in front of me, tipped the bottle into the pan.

A rush of alcoholic steam rose, catching in my eyes and throat and turning to liquid on my skin. I moved away, a hand over my face.

'Mags, I am so sorry. Are you OK? What a stupid thing to do.'

He took my glass from me and I felt his hands on the top of my arms.

'Mags. Speak to me,' he said.

I uncovered my face slowly, feeling stupid and tearful. He was very close.

'I'm fine,' I said.

'Thank goodness. What an idiot.'

He picked up a tea towel, wrapped it round his right hand, and dried my face gently.

'Oh dear,' he said. 'I've smudged your mascara.'

I went off to the loo. I was flushed and fast-eyed and I knew that look.

We drank more while the lasagne cooked, its smell from the oven filling my mouth.

He asked me about my world and it felt tiny in the telling. I told him of the passion of loving a child. I wondered, would he like his own some day? But he didn't know.

I spoke of the frustrations of suburban life, and he said he understood. That some simply don't fit and he himself had felt a cuckoo, always. Unsuited to the steady English life, even as a child.

'And my family hated me for it,' he said.

'Surely not.'

'They did and they do. They see my difference as an attack.'

'Even Chris?' I asked.

'You know your husband, Maggie.'

We talked some more about Claire.

'She says that I'm missing something and I think she might be right, actually,' he said.

'What do you mean? What thing?'

'Something in me. The solid bit.'

'You mean you're frightened of commitment? That's not so uncommon,' I said.

'Not that. She said I don't seem to need the same things others do. But anyway.'

He told me funny tales of growing up; the various ways in which Chris excelled and he stumbled. It was warm and good-natured and in another context might have made me feel proud for choosing my husband.

He brought the lasagne to the table.

'*Voilà!*'

'It's beautiful,' I told him, and it was; baked golden, two neat rows of sliced tomato running its length and meat bubbled up at the edges.

He served me a huge slice, then seconds, and I picked burnt cheese from the dish's rim as we talked. He went to the cabinet and came back with what was needed for Singapore Slings. The drink was red and sweet and he had found a tin of maraschino cherries on the tray. We drank two each.

'God, it's getting late,' I said, at midnight.

'And I'm on a plane first thing tomorrow,' he said.

'Oh. So it's all back to normal, is it, after the crash?'

'I've missed Japan. That meeting went on without me. I'm going straight home to Hong Kong. Has Chris ever told you about the Runway 13 approach? It's famous, and magnificent, but extremely hairy –'

'Hong Kong? That's where Chris is. That's where he's stuck.'

'Really?' Michael said. 'I'm surprised. They sold me a ticket this morning. Kai Tak? Are you sure?'

'Yes. The runway. He mentioned the runway when we spoke,' I said.

'Oh, right. Well, I guess they must have sorted it out.'

He stood up with the dish. I hesitated, aware in some loose way of the reach of my next decision.

'Will you find out for me?' I asked, as he stood there at the sink.

'Find out?' he said and stopped the tap to better hear.

'What happened in Kai Tak. If anything happened,' I said.

'Yes. If you want me to.' A little grim, a little grave.

Michael used the phone in the hall and as I waited alone I felt a speeding inside me.

I thought of a girl, cabin crew, who ran up to Chris and me once, at Gatwick, calling 'Captain! Captain!' like something from an advert. Her mother's car had broken down and seeing as we were neighbours would we mind terribly dropping her home? She trotted and chatted all the way to the car, stowed her bag in the boot before he had time to offer, and watched the back of my head as we drove, in swipes of look that were curious and confident and challenging. When Chris let her out at her modest home I called, 'Bye then. Enjoy your weekend, dear,' and she dropped those eyes and walked the path back to her mum as a scolded child.

'What a silly girl,' I said, as we pulled away.

'Indeed,' Chris replied.

I'd thought that I had won.

Michael listened, mainly, but I understood that there had

been no near miss; that Chris had lied.

'One advantage of being press, I suppose. There is always someone you can call.'

'So there isn't a problem?' I said.

'No.'

'And nothing earlier?' I asked. 'You're sure?'

'Yes. I'm sure.'

'I suppose he must be in Japan,' I said.

Michael shrugged. He made no move to sit.

'Who knows?'

'He flew in three days ago. He must have stayed.'

'For any number of reasons,' Michael said, but he watched me.

'He lied, though. Didn't he?' I said.

'Yes, Maggie. I suppose he did.'

He waited. It was my move.

'Is this news?' he said, in the end.

'Not really.'

'Do you want to talk?'

I didn't. That night I slept with my husband's brother.

We were together maybe twelve times. When Chris was flying, always at my house. He would stay a night or two; once, memorably, three, but it became harder as Bella grew. I locked the bedroom door and dreaded her call, but she never once came.

They were strange abbreviated days. He hid in my room while I rushed her off to nursery; then we had the time together until lunch. He left when I fetched her, but never went far, circling us in the samey streets; aimless, footsore. He came back when she slept, full of stories; even Purley assumed a charm, the way he told it.

We spoke every week though, sometimes more; long wandering calls, and I loved him for all the reasons that Claire let him go, because he was easy and weightless and left no traces, or so I thought. He made my life happier and my marriage easier. I felt no guilt.

Two and a half years from the start, I fell pregnant with his child.

45

Chris took Bella away in her pyjamas, with just a bear.

He made me a cup of tea before he left.

'For god's sake, Maggie, look after yourself, can't you? When did you last eat?'

I tried to drink it but the sensation was invasive, as if a hot drink were a new invention. The liquid pooled in the back of my mouth and I had to force myself to swallow. When it hit my stomach, I felt a disturbance, a contraction.

I had a week to sort myself out while they stayed with his parents in Thurlestone.

I went straight to Michael. Is there shame in this? To do it without a man, if I had any choice at all, seemed, at that point, unthinkable.

Would I have told him about the baby, given a free hand?

I do not know. I'm not sure that I was, am, that brave.

Rose could have grown up as Chris's second daughter, as beloved as his first. Perhaps there are worse things. Who knows? It is unhelpful, I find, to dwell on alternate lives.

Michael called out with surprise when he heard me on the line – we had spoken just the day before. I told him in two sentences that he was to be a father and that Chris and I were done. He asked if he could phone me back.

I waited, and imagined him pacing the city with a smoke, but it was hot and wet out there, so more likely he simply stood in his room and tried to think. I willed him towards the right decision. The phone rang ten minutes later.

'OK, Maggie. The situation is this. I will be a father to our child but I cannot live in England. What little I make, I make here. There will not be much, you must understand. What there would have been from my father will not come now, of course. If you want to be here with me, I will do my best. Or I will send you as much as I'm able. That is what I can offer.'

It felt like something. I told him that Chris had taken Bella, that I had money, a decent sum; that Chris had given me cash. Michael asked no questions. His plans changed.

He found us a flat in a Bayswater block and I was in it by Friday. We were renting month to month; nothing certain beyond that.

I shut my new front door with a wheelie case and a plastic bag containing milk, tea and a bottle. I was struck by the smell of other lives and felt a dizziness and a heat and by the time Michael arrived, I was delirious with flu, in bed under blankets in the clothes I'd arrived in. He took me to St Mary's in the end but I was over the worst.

Two melancholic days as a couple and he told me of his commitment; that was the word he chose. An opportunity he'd been aware of for some time and that now, thank god, thanks to me, he could grab. What did I know of the Hong Kong property market?

'Commitment?' I said.

'I would rather have talked to you first.'

'Commitment?' I said.

'I would have found another way to raise the cash.'

'What is this, Michael?'

'Look, I'm in. I've borrowed the money already. A short-term loan. There was a deadline.'

'And so now you need me to hand over mine?'

'Well, ours, I thought, and when you let me tell you –'

I gave him what he needed, and threw him out. That it was far too much took me very few weeks of paying for myself to see, but I was still rash and haughty then. I fancy though, that was the day I changed. I sat down and did the sums on the ripped-out title page of a novel, and saw how things would be. From then, there were no more stupid mistakes.

He phoned, a lot, but I left Bayswater when the month was up and moved west, began my Queen's Park life – the first of them. Perhaps he could have found me if he tried.

And, at a stroke, I was back to a Benson; an expediency, nothing more. Names mean nothing to us, to women like me; we take them when they're offered, and shrug them off when we're done. What we inherit is written deeper, right into the marrow. It runs all the way through, like a stick of Brighton rock.

I assume he never told his family of his child, of Rose, and got his father's money anyway. No doubt he went on to lose it. I know that he is dead for I found his obit. in *The Times* after I heard on Radio 4 that you could search online.

Michael Hughes Kent died after a long battle with cancer in Kingston Hospital on 9 September 2010, aged 59. Funeral to be held at St Mary's Church, St Mary's Road, Wimbledon at 10 a.m. and cremation at Putney Vale Crematorium at 11.20 a.m. on 13 September. Family flowers only but donations, if desired, to Cancer Research.

Childless, survived by no one. And buried in England, which surprised me at first but perhaps it is not unusual to end up where we start, despite our best efforts.

It struck me that I could visit his grave, leave some supermarket flowers, a note, or some such. Lay my ghost, make my peace, but it didn't seem right.

I haven't thought of him much across the years, but I have a knack for that. It is possible that he felt the whole thing rather badly and yet I feel no sympathy, even now. Our choices demand payment.

46

Something non-dog owners rarely appreciate – the canine's acute sense of time. One minute to five and Ernie, the previous one, was up standing by his bowl and if I didn't come, he'd howl for me, such a sad wolfy sound. Buster is less smart but as I rinsed my breakfast things, he started to whine and nose the drawer where his lead is kept.

Two days into the New Year and the park was still busy with larger than usual family groups. The atmosphere felt cheerful and steady now we had passed the fizz of Christmas and I walked briskly through to the Green beyond. The first time that Mo, Paul and I had been together since our celebrations; a lovely day.

Buster saw Sammy first and began to bark and rear. I let him off and he launched towards her, long and low as he gets. Paul's girls raced in too and they met in a squall of nips and lunges. A parent hurried his children past but we didn't care; this is dogs' fun. We met in a three-way hug and started off.

Mo had been in Chislehurst with her eldest and had a wonderful time. She told us of Marks and Spencer canapés and black plastic sacks full of gifts. The eight-year-old got an electric car that he drives around the garden.

Paul had his parents, did tapas; a great success, he had thought, until his father asked when the main course would be through.

I had Boxing Day at home and ate in a restaurant with Rose and her in-laws the day after that. The first time I had met them; she and Will married quietly. It all went well, I think.

The McKinnocks were down from St Albans for the sales and chose a place that she, Sinead, had read about. Vast, glass-lined and Italian; my own dish lacked a certain grace, but she told me that this is the point – the food is 'real'. Sam sat between his grandmas and I was careful to share nicely. He couldn't keep his socks on so I held his foot under the table to keep it warm and made him giggle by scampering my fingers up his leg.

Conversation was easy and Rosie and Will seemed relaxed. I found that I drank more than I ate, and listened more than I talked. Little was required of me.

A wedding walked through to an extravagant table, and I saw the bride's face, a tight clench of joy. Everyone clapped and Will and Rose shared a look of ennui, which I hope is OK.

When I think of my own wedding, I mainly see myself. I know this is not a trick of memory; I felt it on the day. Distant, stuck inside my own head, and happy to be there. Which is not to say that I remember nothing.

We were married in the big bright room of a bland hotel somewhere just inside the M25. A mute place that suited us perfectly. Gold gilt chairs, white flowers, black waistcoated staff, one arm stuck behind their backs. I read its chill as chic.

I enjoyed the shock on the faces of the guests when I appeared at the top of the stairs and they saw I wore a suit. Chris did too; we shared that when the pianist began to maim our favourite song and he looked backwards to find me.

His father walked me up the aisle. There was no other choice, though none of us acknowledged this. As it was, I would have been better on my own. My hand was butterfly light on his arm. He could have been anyone. I needed no one.

There was the polite separation of our families, all stuck smiles and eyes that missed.

I ate nothing of the meal but remember trying to swallow some cake at one stage, a wedge of marzipan that refused to yield.

We danced, as we had arranged, and were soon joined on the creaking stage by his father and my mum. I sniggered into the stiff weft of his jacket at the spectacle, until I looked at her again and saw that she was buoyant and far away and added a kick to her turns. Then we all rushed back to our seats.

I went to bed calm; content even. Happy with my beginnings and confident of my route, that smooth upwards curve that was to be my life. I don't know what Chris felt that night. Something along similar lines, I would guess.

There was a smash at the long table next door, which brought me back. We all looked over, couldn't help ourselves; me, at least, hoping for drama. Sam lifted an arm to point but Will's mother pushed it down again efficiently.

'It's part of the wedding,' she cried. 'Don't worry! We've been to an Italian wedding! Have you not? It was in Verona! Just like *Romeo and Juliet*. Absolutely wonderful!'

She told us all about it, and as I listened I watched the new couple grind a glass into dust on a white silk square with their perfect shoes.

We had biscotti and Vin Santo; on the house, I think. Sinead's tone became more reckless and I started to like her better. It amused Rose too, but bothered Will, an only child. The husband, was, is, a blank; though looking back, I think he may have had a moustache.

I described all this to Maureen and the boys as we walked the margins of the park. It made them hoot and us feel that we had chosen our own companions well.

What I didn't say was that when Rosie and I made our goodbyes, I felt a complicity between us. We shared something in our hug, some outlook or view. I have tried to pin it down; thought at first it might be an opinion on her mother-in-law, though I have no evidence for this, or a more general appreciation of the occasion, of the pleasures of good food and wine. But it didn't feel like that; it felt like something different. A memory, almost, way past and hazy. Of the way things used to be with us, a long long time ago. I don't know how I know this, but I do, and I am holding it very close.

In the park, the night felt wild; cold and mobile. There was a moon, but brisk clouds interfered with it. We agreed to take the long route home.

We made a plan, for the following week, to be together outside of the dogs. What and where, as yet unconfirmed. I like the idea, though knowing me I'll cancel. I am walking too, next month. Morocco is the suggestion, and Susan in charge; she'll email soon, no doubt.

In my pocket I held a card. A ratty old bear clinging to a pink daisy, a ghastly thing, that read: 'Thanks a million!!!' Inside, lots of hearts and a printed message.

Dear Maggie,
    Just to let you know that I (soon we!) are fine and settled! I am working. Things are good! Will be in touch soon.
    Love to Buster! xoxox

I don't know where she is. The envelope was franked; she will have bought it off a website. But she is well, and that is enough.

Paul turned off first, then Maureen. We parted in the usual way.

I got home, lit the fire I'd laid before I went out, and settled for the night.

The dog breathes moistly at my feet. I have a glass before me, of whisky – a new one – Peter's Christmas gift. An Islay single malt with just a splash. It is peaty, but I am coming to like it. Later, perhaps, I'll pick up a book.

Such are the constituents of my days.

Acknowledgements

I didn't write this novel alone. That it exists is thanks to three people. First, Jill Dawson, my earliest reader and mentor through Gold Dust, her peerless tutoring scheme. She was the person who made it seem possible: she recognised what I was trying to do before I did and she helped me get it down onto the page. I wouldn't be an author without her. Next, Antony Topping, my agent, who took a leap of faith on a novel half-done and a writer who couldn't tell him what happened next. His vision, patience and honesty helped get the manuscript finished. I want to thank him for his time, commitment, and all those annoyingly good ideas. He also found the book a perfect home with Sarah Savitt at Faber. Sarah committed to it instantly, whole-heartedly, and then went on to improve it immeasurably. Her input spanned the biggest questions through to the minutiae. Her talent and rigour got the novel reader-ready. Plus she gave the book its title.

Other thanks go to:

Sophie Portas and Mary Morris and team for their expertise and enthusiasm. Everyone else at Faber who helped realise the book so beautifully.

Hannah Westland, my toe in the door.

Zoe Gardner at Asylum Aid, whose work is so important, for her insight into the complexities of the asylum system.

Tommy Bouchier-Hayes and Adam Luck who offered advice on matters news-related.

Shiraz El Showk, Dorothy Hourston and Francesca Jakobi for their comments, time, and for taking me seriously.

And Neil, Archie and Martha. Thank you for your belief and for your love. I dedicate this book to you.